The Elementals

Also by Francesca Lia Block

The Elementals

Francesca Lia Block

St. Martin's Griffin ⚞ New York

THE ELEMENTALS. Copyright © 2012 by Francesca Lia Block. All rights reserved. Printed in the United States of America. For information, address St. Martin's Press, 175 Fifth Avenue, New York, N.Y. 10010.

www.stmartins.com

Design by Anna Gorovoy

The Library of Congress has cataloged the hardcover edition as follows:

Block, Francesca Lia.
    The elementals / Francesca Lia Block.—1st ed.
        p. cm.
    ISBN 978-1-250-00549-6 (hardcover)
    ISBN 978-1-250-01842-7 (e-book)
1. College students—Fiction. 2. Missing persons—Fiction. 3. FICTION / Contemporary Women. 4. Berkeley (Calif.)—Fiction. I. Title.
    PS3552.L617 E44 2012
    813'.54—dc23

                                                                2012028277

ISBN 978-1-250-03629-2 (trade paperback)

St. Martin's Griffin books may be purchased for educational, business, or promotional use. For information on bulk purchases, please contact Macmillan Corporate and Premium Sales Department at 1-800-221-7945, extension 5442, or write specialmarkets@macmillan.com.

First St. Martin's Griffin Edition: September 2013

10 9 8 7 6 5 4 3 2 1

For Gilda
October 9, 1932–September 24, 2010

The Elementals

Prologue

Did you cry, did you scream, did you try to run? Was it dark, did you stumble, did the leaves skitter and claw, ratlike at your feet? Could you see the moon; it was full, that much I know. And that you were alone, wearing a striped T-shirt and jeans that hung too big on your hips, carrying your Hello Kitty purse when you left the dorm—we saw on the surveillance camera in the lobby. But when it happened, did you speak in your soft voice, with the lisp of the S, trying to persuade? Did whoever took you notice the flash of your lashes, the dimples when you smiled, the way you ducked your head when you laughed? Did you smile, did you laugh, before you knew? Were you with someone you thought you could trust? You were too trusting, always too trusting. Did whoever it was know you were smart, much smarter than me, did better in school, though I used the bigger words, spoke up a bit more? (Not anymore.) Did they know you worked at a dog rescue center on weekends, that lost animals made you cry? Did they know that you had no idea how pretty you were? That you couldn't really see why people were so drawn to you? That you would shrug and duck your head at compliments, even from me, even though you told me not to when I did the same? But when it happened, whatever happened, later, what did you think of? Did you think of your mom and dad? Did you think of the eyeliner-and-music boys you never made love to? Did you think of me? Did you think to yourself, *Ariel won't give up. Ariel will keep looking. Ariel will find me.*

I wanted to; I would have done anything to go and look for you, Jeni. But my parents said no.

"How can we sleep at night with you there?" they said.

I couldn't explain that I would never sleep at night unless I went to the city where my best friend disappeared and did all that I could to try to understand what had happened to her.

But then, and not the way I wanted it to, everything changed.

Part I

Freshman Year

1. Death is one of them

There are certain things you have to accept. Death is one of them. But when you are seventeen and your mother sits you down and says what my mother said it is really hard to accept death. When you are sixteen and your best friend vanishes without a trace it is hard to accept death. You keep thinking there has been some kind of mistake. Or that you can do something to stop this thing that is so much bigger than you are. Or that, at least, you can make it go away by pretending it isn't there, like a child who covers her eyes and thinks she is invisible to everyone else.

But death is stronger than that and when you cover your eyes you are the one who can't see the dark. The dark still sees you.

My parents hadn't agreed to let me go away to Berkeley the day they sat me down on the couch in the living room to tell me my mom was sick. We never really used that couch because we liked to hang out in the kitchen, or sit in the den and watch TV together. The living room couch was overstuffed and pale enough to show stains. We saved it for company and important talks. It is where we sat when my parents told me that Jeni had not come back from the school trip to UC

Berkeley, the trip I should have gone on with her. It is where the detectives showed us her image from the dorm surveillance camera as she went out alone. It is where we sat the day my mom told me she had cancer.

"We have to talk to you about something," my dad said. His eyes looked puffy and he was holding my mom's hand too tightly.

"What's wrong?" My heart beat faster. It's like your body always knows before you do.

"I got back some test results," my mom said. "There is a problem but we're going to do everything we can to take care of it."

When I was little I used to ask them how long they would live and my mom always said, "We plan on being around for many, many years." I realized, then, for the first time, at seventeen, that it was the perfect answer because I could never accuse her of lying to me, just in case. Now she hadn't said, "We're going to take care of it." She had said, "We're going to do everything we can . . ."

My right hand fumbled with the bracelet on my left wrist. Jeni had made it for me with baby block beads, and one for herself that said my name. I never took it off. Besides the postcard that arrived after she disappeared, it was the most important thing of hers I had left. "What's wrong?" I didn't really want to know but I figured that was what I was supposed to say.

"I have a small growth." My mother was looking directly at me and she wasn't crying. She sat up straighter, smoothed back her hair and then leaned forward with her elbows on her knees. I wanted her to hold me and also I didn't. Mostly, I wanted to run.

"A tumor," she said. "It's not benign. They have to do some procedures."

"I think I have to go." I swallowed back the huge lump of sand that was getting bigger every second at the base of my hourglass throat.

"Okay," my dad said. "But if you have any questions, we're here."

Part of me wished they had made me stay. I wanted them to grab me and hold me down and reassure me, but they didn't. They were looking at each other with so much love, sealed up in this bubble where no one could touch them. It was the first time I hadn't been in there, too.

It was hard to move; it felt like there was a mass in my chest, weighing me down, and my arms and legs tingled as if they were expanding to the size of a giant's, but I made myself stand. As I did, I felt the photographs watching me. My mom never put up paintings, just family pictures scattered among the rows of books on the bookcase. There were artsy black-and-whites of me as an infant and huge glossy prints from their wedding. There were all my silly school photos with the swirly blue backgrounds and our professional Christmas shots with the good lighting. There were photos of me in costume for my ballet recitals. A picture of me and Jeni, laughing as she held my waist-length braid under her nose like a moustache. In the pictures before the previous summer I looked hopeful and smiling and even pretty, I guess, as my mom and Jeni always insisted I was, but in the few taken after that, the ones taken after Jeni vanished, I looked pale and lost beneath my too-long hair, wraithlike you might say, fading away. But I realized that the girl in all the pictures—the ones before Jeni and the ones afterward—was different, suddenly, than the girl the pictures were watching.

I walked past all those eyes to the door and stepped outside. It was a hot late spring afternoon. The sky burned blue and the eucalyptus trees gave off a smell like medicine. One black bird strutted across the grass in front of our house. He paused and turned his head so I could see a cold black eye.

That was when I started to run. I ran and ran as fast as I could along the pavement. Sweat poured down my face, mixing with the tears that had started to come. I could run fast. But you just can't run faster than time, not faster than death and, as I'd find out, not faster than love.

2. *Les bienfaits de la lune*

People didn't talk about it much when Jeni disappeared. You'd think it would be all they talked about. But maybe it would have made them all insane—mothers and fathers chaining children to their beds even though it had happened in another city, girls clutching at each other wherever they went, waking at night thinking they saw strangers standing over them. Instead they went on as if things could somehow be normal again. They went over to the Benson home with casseroles and flowers. They greeted Jeni's parents politely but nervously on the streets, as if to get too close would endanger them, as if Joanne and Mike were tainted in some way. That was the worst thing we did (I include myself in this)— not go up and hug them every time we saw them, not ask them to talk to us about her. If we did that, the whole thing would have been too real. We would have had to acknowledge that one day there was this girl making name bracelets or ones out of strands of colored thread for you to wish on, working the table at the pet giveaway where her voice went up a notch every time she spoke to the dogs, hugging you like you were her childhood teddy bear, and the next day—

not. Some people helped put up missing-person posters but most figured the ones on milk cartons and flyers were more effective. At first we refused to believe she had been stolen away, kidnapped, or possibly worse. We wanted to believe she had run off, somewhere, or, if taken, that it was by someone who did not harm her, not really, someone who would one day leave the chain off the door so she could escape. At our worst moments we wished to hear that she had died, that her bones had been found, so that we could stop hearing her crying in the night, so that we could stand at a grave and put her to rest. And, slowly, everyone seemed to be giving up, except for her parents. And, most of the time, but not enough, me.

Now I had a chance to prove that I had not forgotten her.

After my mom found the lump she changed her mind about letting me go away to Berkeley, to the school where Jeni and I would have gone together. My parents told me they thought it would be good for me to be away while my mom recovered.

Maybe they were willing to let me have this one thing I wanted so much, after so many sad things had happened. Maybe they were too preoccupied with the illness to worry anymore. After arguing with them for months for this chance to get away, I had, with one word, been cast out of their protective circle. And that word hadn't even been said aloud.

They drove me up north one late August morning, our Prius packed with my belongings. No one said much the whole way. We didn't take the scenic route because we wanted to get there fast, so instead of blue-misted coastline we moved through the dry, barren landscape of I-5; the air stunk of manure and exhaust. It changed as we neared the Berkeley area. The sky was a clear summer cerulean and the hills were covered with green. The little town looked appealing with the Claremont Hotel, grand and white on the hill overlooking the grid of tree-lined streets, the athletic, tanned young men and women riding their bikes and the smell of good coffee in the air. You could see the campanile rising above everything, a white clock tower like a place where a princess would be imprisoned in a fairy tale, and as we drove into town we heard the heavy bells tolling three. One. Two. Three. I tried not to think of it as a sign. The loneliest number. The number in which bad things come.

"The charm," I whispered, instead.

When we got to the dorm I unsuccessfully attempted to swallow the latest lump of sand in my throat. It was just a tall, bleak-looking building with high windows that would have delighted any suicidal freshman but the thing that made my throat close was this: it looked exactly like the one in which Jeni had stayed. In fact, they faced each other. The camera in the lobby was no comfort, more of a threat, a reminder. I paused in front of it, remembering the staticky image the detective showed me of the girl in the striped T-shirt slipping away.

My room was a cubicle with twin beds, two desks, two closets and two chests of drawers. My roommate hadn't arrived yet. I'd never shared a room with anyone in my whole life; it was hard to imagine spending every night for the next nine months with a complete stranger.

"Let's eat, ladies," said my dad when we were through unpacking. He was trying to sound cheerful but I could tell he was distracted. He kept shooting glances at my mom when she wasn't looking, like he was checking to make sure she was still there. She was busy, moving even more quickly than usual, fussing over the bed corners and making sure the Degas and Arthur Rackham posters were evenly hung.

"It's important," she said when my dad told her I could do that later. "It'll make you feel more at home, baby."

We went to dinner at a famous restaurant on the north side of campus, a little wooden two-story house with candlelit tables and nasturtiums in vases. My father ordered gazpacho, salad, goat cheese pizza, figs and prosciutto, grilled salmon and a bottle of pinot but I couldn't stomach much. It was supposed to be festive but no one felt that way. I was secretly wishing that my parents would stay the night. We'd get a hotel room and I'd sleep on a cot at the foot of their bed.

When I was a baby, my mom found me convulsing in my crib from fever. Meningitis. She stayed with me in the hospital the whole night, nursing me in the narrow bed among a tangle of I.V.s. The doctors had told her she couldn't stay but she insisted. She lay on her side all night, my dad told me, with her breast in my mouth.

Her breast where something now grew.

I felt some wine burn back up in my throat.

As we drove to the dorm under a fat white moon wallowing low, we passed the homeless; so many more than we saw in the San Fernando Valley. They drifted like ghosts through air smelling sharply of burnt cheese and rotting fruit. There was a large woman with pale eyes, dancing in circles wearing a pair of children's torn gauze and glitter fairy wings. A small person of unidentifiable gender held the train of her long dress. One man with dreadlocks stood on a corner, prophesying to himself. I tried to make out the words.

They were something like this: "The daimons exist everywhere. If you deny them they will appear in your head! Arise!"

We were stopped at a light and he seemed to be looking right through the dirt-streaked car window at me. I turned my head away to look out the other window and saw another man, a huge man—he must have been close to seven feet tall, even hunched over. He limped along the other side of the street, swaddled in rags, then slowly turned his head so that I saw his eyes watching from under his protruding brow. When he raised his hands up I could see; each one was the size of my head.

I glanced over at my mother; she looked pale and exhausted, small vertical lines showing around her lips. My parents might have allowed me to go, now, but they were still afraid; I could see the night in their eyes.

When we got back to the dorm my roommate was there. Lauren Barnes. A very blond, tan girl in a low-cut T-shirt, tight jeans and diamond studs. I was suddenly conscious of my pale skin, my frayed, mousy hair, shabby vintage sundress and beat-up cowboy boots. The baby bracelet on my wrist that spelled my missing best friend's name.

Lauren took one look at me and my posters. "How did they manage to match us up?"

I didn't know what to say but she laughed and hugged me, a little too hard. "J.K. Just kidding. I think it will be great to expand my horizons." Then she went back to putting away her cashmere sweaters.

My mom fussed around the room some more, straightening the sheets and plumping pillows until my dad made her stop, and then we said good-bye. They were going to get a hotel somewhere along the way back home, they said. I was the one to pull away first when they hugged me. I watched them walk to the parking lot from the ninth-story window of my room. They looked tiny and scared, holding onto each other.

I went down the hall to the coed bathroom, hoping no boys were there yet. I washed my face and brushed my teeth as fast as I could. It seemed unnecessarily cruel not to have separate men's and women's restrooms but my parents had chosen the cheapest option, plus I think they reasoned that I'd be safer with nice young men around. I went back to the room and put on my pajamas while Lauren sat on her bed reading a *Cosmo* magazine. I couldn't imagine getting used to changing in front of her but it was better than trying to do it in the bathroom stalls with boys shuffling by. I got into bed, flicked on the reading light my mom had bought me and stared at my book of Baudelaire's poetry without actually registering a single word. It didn't matter; I knew them by heart anyway—and this was my favorite poem, the one about the capricious moon overtaking the pale green-eyed child in her bed, "tenderly crushing" her throat so that she always longed to cry.

Finally my eyelids got too heavy and I marked the book with Jeni's postcard, rested my head on the pillow and turned off the light.

As I was drifting off, I thought of how, when I was a little sleepless girl, my mom would come in my bed with me and curl up at the bottom.

"I love you," I'd say. "You're the best mommy in the world." And she'd say, "I love you more." We went on like that back and forth. One night she added, "Someday I hope you meet a man who loves you as much as I do. Because every girl deserves that much love." I reached out and took her hand and that was how I had been able to sleep.

There were no nightmares then, not real ones, no malignancies, no missing girls.

3. The residue of lonely

I almost went on that school trip with Jeni, and the other students and the chaperone Mr. Kragen, but I got the flu at the last minute. I wonder if I'd gone, would she still be here? She would never have wandered off alone. I'd have been by her side the whole time. After what happened I wanted to go to Berkeley even more. I wanted to be where she had been—to find something, to find myself. Since she'd been gone, I'd gone missing, too.

I woke early to avoid the boys. For the first few days I managed it but at the end of the week I came out of the shower stall and saw three massive males shaving at the sinks. They were all completely naked. One of them winked at me in the mirror and I felt my face redden as I ran out. They grunted with laughter. My embarrassment wasn't just that I'd seen them; it was that it had excited me as much as it made me feel sick to my stomach. Not that I wanted them, but I was curious, my body was curious. I was seventeen but I couldn't remember ever seeing a penis before. Jeni and I looked at pictures on the Internet (the nude Nureyev by Avedon was our favorite) but that was it and I'd lost interest, even in the most beautiful ballet dancer in the world, after she wasn't there. The three naked bodies were meaty and hairy, bodies of men who could do harm if they wanted.

They were all football players—Todd Hamlin, Jake Glendorf and Will Merrell. Lauren knew everyone's name and talked constantly—that's how I found out. I started getting up even earlier after that.

I went down to breakfast in the cafeteria, where I always ate alone; no one asked to sit with me and I was too shy to introduce myself. People seemed to divide up into the usual groups right away, just like in high school—preppy kids, jocks, tech nerds, artsy and Lauren Barnes and her friends Kelly Wentworth and Jodi Bale who looked like sorority girls with their shiny hair and perfect clothes. I didn't fit in with any of the groups and I guess I didn't really try. In high school it didn't matter that much because I had my mom and dad and Jeni. If she were with me everything would be different, I told myself. We'd have been roommates and eaten every meal together and taken the train to San Francisco on the weekends to see all the places we dreamed about. We would have shared iPod speakers listening to our favorite band, Halloween Hotel, and talked about indie boys and music, antique books and vintage clothes, late into the night until one of us crashed out. The other girl would have smiled to herself in the darkness as her last question went unanswered; she would be eager for morning.

I didn't mind school; it wasn't obvious, in class, that I was alone, that parts of me were gone. I could get lost in the books and the lectures and I could forget, if only for a little while, about my mom and Jeni and the way it felt to walk around that big campus by myself, like some kind of ghost.

There were times it would have been good to really be a ghost, though. Like when I had to face the naked football players in the bathroom or run into one of them on campus where they would wink at me and wolf whistle and then laugh. My face would always flame up, reminding me, and not in a good way, that I wasn't a bloodless ghost at all.

After school I went on runs through Strawberry Canyon or the amphitheater-shaped Berkeley rose garden, now barren of blooms. Then I got an early dinner at the dorms, where the food was always terrible—overcooked vegetables and "mystery meat" in brown sauce. I missed my mom's lasagnas, paellas and enchiladas so much it made me want to cry into the plate of iceberg lettuce with cold tofu that was all I could stomach. I grabbed an energy bar from the care package my mom sent, got a coffee on the way and went to Doe Library to study.

On the weekends everything was basically the same—reading, writing and running. My big treat was dinner on Saturday night—a colossal frozen yogurt that made my stomach hurt and my hands feel like ice sculptures. If there was a party in the dorm I went just to get the free alcohol and then left.

I talked to my parents then, too, but not usually during the week, which was strange since I had basically at least spoken to, if not seen, my mom every day for my entire life.

I did all of these things, the things every freshman does, but there was something else I did, too, those first two months in the city of her disappearance. I searched for clues.

Dressed in baggy jeans, striped T-shirts and sneakers, my hair in a ponytail, just like her. Hoping to lure anyone who might have wanted Jeni. But I didn't have those dimples or those lashes, half the magic.

The dorm across from mine could have been the same building. Every day after school I wandered those halls. I even went to the room where she had stayed and knocked on the door and asked if I could look around. Two girls wrinkled their noses at me. They were identical in stature (slight), hairstyle (bangs), even outfits, and for a moment my chest squeezed with longing for a companion, not a phantom twin. They let me look inside but it could have been any freshman dorm room, though I wanted to get on my knees and press my face into the mattress. I left and walked down the stairs, out the front door, imagining I was Jeni. Where would she have gone?

Everywhere I went I imagined she was walking with me. I tried to see things through her eyes; it wasn't hard. I knew how she thought. The faces she would find beautiful or interesting, the scruffy and disabled dogs she would stop to pet, the jewelry she would lift from black velvet on the street vendor's table, examining to see how it was made, the buildings she would want to live in. I recorded anything that seemed important in the notebook I always carried. Sometimes I wrote stories trying to understand more about a world that made no sense to me.

Once I took BART into the city, to the Conservatory of Flowers in Golden Gate Park because that was the photo on the postcard she had sent me. *Miss you. See you soon.* The postcard had been sent from a Berkeley post office the day she disappeared and it arrived after we already knew she was gone. She hadn't chosen a Berkeley image but a San Francisco one. *We should live here someday.* I wasn't sure if she meant the city or the actual building of the conservatory; the lacy white wood-and-glass Victorian greenhouse looked like a fairy palace. I wandered around under the dome, among the orchids and across the lawn outside and even handed out a few flyers but I felt helpless and lost in the fog so I went back to Berkeley where at least there was evidence she had once been.

Sometimes when I saw the campus police or passed the station I wondered to myself what I would say to them.

"I want her back," I would say. "Can you help me find her?"

So instead of making a fool of myself with the police, I did it with everyone else; wherever I went, that late summer and early fall, I carried a stack of flyers in my backpack. I tried to hand them out, asking if anyone had seen her face. Most people looked at me strangely and wouldn't even talk to me.

In Berkeley you learn to build a wall around yourself, to protect yourself from the onslaught of flyers and petitions and upturned palms and catcalls and insults. I did it, too. So I understood why I was being ignored but I didn't give up. Maybe I seemed insane—paranoid, schizoid, obsessive-compulsive—padding after people, holding up the photo of the girl with the dimples and huge, dark eyes. Maybe I was.

It didn't matter.

"Excuse me," I said. "Excuse me, have you seen her?"

There was one person in my dorm—a classic goth girl with powder skin and bottle-black hair—who seemed interested in the picture.

"Who is this?" she asked, taking a flyer and tapping it with bitten black nails.

"My best friend."

"What happened?" Her pale face seemed to grow smaller behind her cat-eye glasses. "She looks familiar."

A tremor of dumb hope and shrewd fear traveled along my spine. "She was visiting here summer before last."

"It was in the papers," the girl said. "I remember. I collect that stuff."

"Have you seen her, though?"

She shook her head. "Sorry." Before I could say anything else, she was gone, gripping Jeni's picture in her hand.

After that it seemed that whenever I looked up she was watching me from across the dining room. I heard Lauren say she was a sophomore named Coraline Grimm, or at least that was what she called herself. (Anyone who had heard of Neil Gaiman or those brothers who wrote the fairy tales was a bit skeptical.) Once when I got up to go sit with her—she looked so lonely—she swallowed her last sip of orange juice and scurried away.

My English teacher, a grad student named Melinda Story,

took the flyer graciously. Her blue eyes seemed to darken with concern and she stroked her long blond braid.

"I heard about this," she said, with her soft lisp that reminded me of Jeni's.

I stood frozen, waiting for her to go on.

"If you need to talk, I'm here," she said.

So all she could offer me was sympathy and the concerned looks that she shot my way while lecturing about *Beowulf* and *The Canterbury Tales*; I needed much more than that.

"If you have any leads for me, let me know," I said.

There was one other person who stopped with interest to take my flyer—the giant I'd seen the first night we'd arrived. Up close he smelled like nicotine and mold and I saw that the dark shade of his skin was from dirt. He was much younger than I'd thought, only a little older than I was. But being on the streets and perhaps whatever had brought him there had made him look like an aged man.

When I held out Jeni's picture, he grabbed at it, his hand almost black with grime, darker than the rest of him; he wore a sock that had been cut open to free his shaking fingers. Before I could say anything he was limping away. I ran after him.

"Have you seen her?" I asked. "Do you remember her face?"

He shook his head and made a moaning sound, lifting his hands to either side of his face, as if to ward off a blow. The look in his eyes is nothing I can describe, nor can I forget. It was the way I felt. It was despair.

And after that I did what I had been avoiding—I went to see the police.

Jeni's missing-persons report had been filed by the San Fernando Valley Police Department even though she had disappeared here. I was interviewed by Detectives Ryan and Rodriguez then.

Was she the type of girl that would have gone out all by herself or do you think she was meeting someone?

This I did not know. She went everywhere only with me and I wasn't there.

Was she at all sad or depressed when she went on this trip?

I knew this one: no and no. She was giddy, giggly with excitement, saddened only when I called to say I couldn't go.

Was there anyone she didn't get along with?

Not that I knew of.

Would she have dressed differently if she was going to a party or to meet a boy she liked?

No, she didn't dress up. (I almost said *we* and added *except in our dreams of tulle and faded satin.*)

Did she have a boyfriend that you knew of?

No. And I would have been the one to know.

When was the last time you saw her?

This question made me pause to catch my breath as if the pleasant detectives had punched me in the stomach. They waited patiently and told me to take my time.

It was a sunny afternoon. We'd been talking about boys in my room, filling my scrapbook with cutouts of indie film stars and musicians, planning for the trip up north.

"What did the boys look like?" they detectives had asked when I'd calmed down and I showed them. Spiky hair, eyeliner, piercings, tats.

"Why?" I asked. "Is this relevant?"

"Everything is relevant," they said.

But that was over a year ago and I wasn't sure the Berkeley campus police would feel the same way, at least not anymore. I knew there was an officer assigned to the case in Berkeley; Ryan and Rodriguez had given me his card.

I wondered at the time I spoke to them how you keep your

compassion at a job like that, how you keep from turning as hard as a bulletproof vest. The losses again and again.

Officer Liu met me a few days later at a coffee shop on Shattuck. He looked so young it was disconcerting. I found myself wishing for the broad builds and lined faces of Rodriguez and Ryan.

"So it's been over a year now," Liu said, scowling at some paperwork he'd brought.

I nodded and removed my tea bag from the cup. It made a puddle in my saucer.

"And you're coming to me now because?"

"I'm at school here," I said.

He nodded. "It's been a year," he repeated.

Those were the words I'd been dreading. Why hadn't I come here sooner? I thought of myself at home—going to school, running, eating, sleeping—how could I have done anything except look for her?

"We've done everything we could. Search parties, investigations. The case is still open, though. We're always open to new information."

I nodded and looked at the ovoid of his face, not knowing what to say. My cup rattled in the wet saucer when I set it down and some liquid spilled onto the table. I tried to wipe it up with my napkin.

"Is there anything you can tell me about it?" I asked.

He shook his head. "I'm sorry, Miss Silverman. Since you're not immediate family there's nothing more we can disclose. But rest assured this is being handled by experts. We'll continue to do all we can."

He paid for my tea and suggested grief counseling. That was the worst part, somehow; I took it as a sign that he had given up.

———

So I continued to carry the flyers with me, stapling them to the ragged, splintering wood of telephone poles and plastering them on construction-site walls. As if they would help, as if it wasn't too late.

When my eighteenth birthday came in October I could literally taste the despair on my tongue like the residue of the pistachio frozen yogurt I had for dinner that night. I'd received a card and a bunch of red and white roses from my parents. They were always giving me flowers; every birthday and holiday I got an oversized bouquet. I loved flowers but a part of me wished my parents would stop, because it made me aware of how no one else had ever even given me a single wildflower (except for Jeni—which made it even worse) but I couldn't tell them about my ambivalence. Besides, at least I could pretend the flowers were from a boy.

"What are you doing tonight?" my mom asked.

"I'm kind of tired."

"Do you have a friend to celebrate with? Maybe your roommate?"

Yeah right. "I might go to this dorm party." I just wanted to get her to stop asking.

But when we got off the phone I decided I really would go to the party in the lounge in case she asked. Even if it was just to try to wash away the taste in my mouth with some free, cheap gin, and to hand out flyers.

Tommy Leeds was there. I'd overheard Lauren say he played bass in a punk band—not that it was hard to guess. Skinny jeans and old-school platform suede creepers that made him appear taller than he was. His almost metallic hair stood straight up in an electric shock and his eyes were always a little red. The plugs stretching out his earlobes gave me a wincing feeling but I also found myself fascinated by them.

Tommy was in my psych class, where I was sure he would recognize me throughout the pages of the *DSM* (paranoid, schizoid, schizotypal, antisocial, histrionic, avoidant, dependent and obsessive-compulsive) if he even knew I existed. This thought confirmed the paranoia at least.

That night he was with a group of guys dressed just like him. They all looked bored.

"Hey," I said. "I heard you're in a band."

He blinked his red eyes at me. "Yeah."

"What's your name? The name?" Lame.

"Intrepid."

"Cool." I paused, not intrepid at all. "You're in my psych class."

"Aw, yeah. Cool. I hate that class. I keep thinking I have all those disorder thingies."

I felt better then. "Yeah, me, too! I'm totally paranoid, obsessive-compulsive and dependent."

"Wow," he said. "For real?"

I realized I'd blown it. "No. I mean it's just funny how so much of it kind of feels relevant like Ludkin says."

"Yeah. Whatever. Everyone's kind of fucked up. Especially in No Cal, man."

I wondered what it would be like to kiss him. He smelled like gin, clove cigarettes and hairspray—we were close enough, it was hot enough, for me to tell. Maybe I hadn't blown it. He'd said everyone was fucked up, especially here. I wanted someone fucked up to kiss me on my birthday, to sting my mouth with alcohol and nicotine. It would make things better; they couldn't get worse.

"Is it less fucked up where you're from?" I asked him.

"Yeah. Hollywood all the way, man."

A bang of blood at my temples reminded me of what I was supposed to be doing here at Berkeley, why I had come. It wasn't about boys, at least not in that way. Kids from Holly-wood High had been on the trip with Jeni.

"You weren't on a class trip here after junior year, were you?"

He squinted at me with his eyeliner. "Yeah. It sucked. You?"

"No. I had a friend who was."

An Asian girl with long pigtails, a checkered dress and cartoon-sized platform Mary Janes came up to him from behind and kissed his cheek. He flung his body around, grabbed her.

It was no longer about a kiss. I tapped his shoulder.

"Hey," I said. "Could I talk to you sometime?"

He frowned. "Dude, kind of busy now."

"It's kind of important. Dude."

The girl made a face as if she'd eaten something rotten and dragged him away.

In my notebook I wrote, *Tommy Leeds, Hollywood High. Berkeley school trip. With Jeni.* As if it meant something. As if it were a sign.

After I left the dorm that night, I went roaming the streets like a little lost cat. I almost wanted to mewl and howl in the cold.

That was when I saw three people walking together, holding hands. They were in costumes and carnival masks—the men in ratty old tuxedos and the woman in a corseted dress made from bits and pieces of lace and velvets. They paused when I passed and I saw their eyes watching me through the masks that looked as if they had been made from tree bark; I felt a chill run through my body, then a wave of heat. It was the most alive I'd felt in a long time, almost as if they had kissed me as they passed, put their hands beneath my clothes. The kiss, the touch that I'd always wanted and hadn't even known how much I did. I thought of the Baudelaire poem marked by Jeni's postcard in my book; it evoked the same kind of indescribable enchantment these three people made me feel.

I didn't want to think about Tommy Leeds anymore and how he had been on the trip with Jeni, maybe seen her, maybe spoken to her. I wanted the world where these three lived. I wanted some kind of escape.

But by this time they were already gone, down the street. I turned back to look at them and one of them, the tallest boy, was looking back, too. Sliding ice lovingly down my shirt with his gaze.

Someone else was watching me, too; I saw that when I turned back around. The giant I'd seen on the first night with my parents. He swung his head back and forth slowly, like a pendulum, his eyes flickering at me from among the rags that swaddled his head.

I went to my room and pushed a chair up in front of the door. As I undressed I caught sight of myself in the mirror. The red and white roses my parents had sent watched me uneasily from a vase on the dresser.

I'd always kind of liked my breasts, since they'd arrived, a little late but with certainty—more than any other part of my body. But my breasts, though smallish, were very round and tilted up nicely, with large areolas. I lifted one arm and pressed two fingers against the soft tissue, feeling for lumps like I'd learned from the pamphlet my mom sent me with a note that read, *My doctor thought you should have this—it is only a precaution.*

I heard a key in the lock and the rattling sound of the chair by the door. I dropped my arms to my side and grabbed my shirt, held it to my chest.

"Don't let me interrupt you," Lauren said, sweet as pie.

Embarrassed as I was, part of me was relieved I'd been interrupted from my search for tumors; I didn't want to know.

4. House of Eidolon

I was eighteen and I'd never had sex with anyone; I'd never even kissed a boy yet. I'd kissed one person, though. When we were fifteen, I kissed Jeni.

We were in my room, braiding each other's hair, filling scrapbooks with photographs, 3-D stickers, pressed flowers and birthday party invitations, listening to Tori Amos, "Bells for Her." We were discussing boys, what our first kiss would be like. We both had a crush on Brandon James. We liked them dark and brooding—indie, emo types—which was one reason we hadn't found boyfriends yet; our taste was a little too "champagne" for our school, as Jeni said. But, that night we were talking about Brandon and how we were scared we wouldn't know how to kiss right if we had the chance. We'd stolen wine from my parents' liquor cabinet and I took a sip from the bottle and handed it to her and said, "Want to practice?"

It wasn't the kind of thing I usually did but the music and the wine had gotten to me. And I loved Jeni. There were so many reasons to love her. Her baby dimples, the way she rolled her eyes when I put myself down, slapped my hand, and said, "Oh my god, you shut your face, beautiful!"

That night in my room she giggled, leaned over and tilted her head to the side. She smelled like bubblegum and wine.

I pressed my lips to hers. They were so soft, it was like kissing a peony.

If I thought of it, even almost three years later, my lips still buzzed gently with memory.

Now, in the dorm lounge, I took a plastic cup and filled it with punch. Sick, and not the good kind, as in, *awesome-sick*. The cheap liquor under the sugary taste burned my throat but I downed the whole thing anyway. Then I had another. It seemed like everyone had found their group by this time but I stood alone by the large window, looking out at the town below. The streets formed neat rows, a quiet grid of trees and low buildings. I squinted, trying to imagine a girl walking out of the opposite dorm and into those streets. I filled my cup a third time. I hadn't eaten much dinner and the alcohol raced through my blood but it didn't make me any braver. And still no one spoke to me. The dormies were dressed up like vampires, clowns, football players, cheerleaders and ghosts. It was Halloween. I didn't wear a costume. Only jeans, a hoodie and a T-shirt with the name of Jeni's and my favorite band—Halloween Hotel.

Todd Hamlin came over to me in his football jersey with a bloody wound painted on his neck. For one second I was happy to have someone to talk to; then I noticed Jake Glendorf and Will Merrell watching us.

Todd held out his hand.

"I don't think we've been properly introduced all this time. Todd."

"Ariel," I said warily.

"Not dressed up, Ariel?"

I shrugged.

"Know what I am?"

"A football player? Like in real life!" The sarcasm came out in spite of my mom's lessons in politeness under almost all circumstances.

"A dead football player. A vampire bit me." He showed me the sloppy red marks on his neck, probably scrawled with his girlfriend's lipstick. Vanessa Carlisle stood with Jake and Will, watching us. She wore fangs and a black cape over a black corset and fishnets.

"Hey, Ariel," he said. "Jake, Will and I were wondering if you could help us out with something."

I saw his friends snickering over their drinks, no longer able to contain themselves.

I turned away.

Todd put his hand on my arm. "Because we were wondering if you happened to notice which one of us is the best endowed. Since we like, uh, noticed you checking out our cocks the other day and we figured you were probably kind of an expert on cocks."

Only on dicks lately, I thought.

I saw the neon EXIT sign over the stairwell door flicker. Its message was clear.

I passed Coraline Grimm on the way down the stairwell. She was dressed like the Corpse Bride. I nodded at her—she looked like an ally after the people at the party—but she only froze on the stairs and watched me descend.

The night was spinning when I stepped outside into the cold.

I had to avoid the party and I didn't want to go back to my dorm room. By this time Lauren had a boyfriend—Dallas Tate—and they were usually there making out—in between classes and all night long. After I'd gone to sleep I'd wake to hear them moaning just a few feet away in the next bed. It made me feel the same way that seeing the naked football players did—nauseous with disgust and a perverse, desperate excitement—and sometimes I slept in the lounge when it was really bad, but I hadn't gotten up the nerve to say anything about it.

I walked toward Telegraph with my head down and my hands jammed into the pockets of my sweatshirt. There was a purposefulness to my stride, in spite of how drunk I was, like I knew what I wanted. It was the same thing I always wanted.

I walked past groups of laughing frat boys in monster masks and sorority girls dressed as sexy cats, sexy witches or sexy fairies in accessorized leotards and tights. The homeless were out in full force as well but the Greek kids were ignoring them in the usual way, as if they were invisible, phantoms. But I saw. The woman with the wings held a skeleton mask over her face and her small companion was dressed head to toe in clothes that looked as if they had been dipped in blood. The man with dreadlocks had twisted them into horns. He approached me, mumbling and waving his hands. I froze. As he got closer he shouted, "The end is near and the parallel universe is not near complete!" He kept walking past me and I resumed breathing. The air smelled of coffee and chocolate. I stopped at the corner and looked around. People were sitting in the cafe. It seemed so warm and cozy in there. Through the low window I saw a couple dressed as a two-headed monster huddling over one huge mug, their faces close together, warmed by the steam.

When I turned around again there was a movement in the shadows.

Loneliness can do weird things. Loneliness and fear together—a sinister concoction.

It was hard to breathe or even see for a second. It was hard to speak but . . .

"Jeni?" I said.

The man came out from behind the bushes. The giant from the street. He held something out to me and at first I thought it was the flyer I had given to him before. I took it (after all, he had accepted mine), bracing myself to see her smiling face.

It was a flyer for a party. A picture of a beautiful woman draped across a marble headstone. HALLOWEEN AT HOUSE OF EIDOLON, it said.

When I looked back up the giant was gone.

I left the din of the main avenue and crossed more streets, walking through town to the north side, then up into the hills. Families and groups of students lived in these old wooden houses with gardens and broad-pillared porches. There were jack-o'-lanterns on the front steps.

The house on the flyer was one of the older ones, a three-story wooden Craftsman structure hidden behind tall oak trees and rosebushes. I could hear music coming from inside and warm light pulsed behind the windows.

On the porch were four of the biggest, most intricately carved pumpkins I had ever seen. The door was open. The wooden floor of the front room was strewn with a mixture of what looked like dried flower petals, feathers and glitter that sparkled in the candlelight. Fresh white paint made the walls glow. Candles were everywhere, dripping thick tears of wax and scenting the place with honey. Silver cobwebs that looked uncannily real draped the doorways and banister. Old, leather-bound books lined the built-in shelves that stretched from floor to ceiling. There was almost no furniture, besides a worn red velvet couch with lion's feet, but people in carnival masks were reclining on large cushions or standing by the speakers, shuffling their feet and moving their arms above their heads in some kind of drunken trance, while an old

Smashing Pumpkins song played. I didn't recognize anyone and they seemed too high to notice me. A large steaming vat of dark liquid sat in one corner. I pushed my way over, found a cup and filled it.

I went through the main room into the kitchen, a fairly large one with hand-painted floral tiles, an old-fashioned stove and a long, scarred wooden table. I leaned against a tiled counter and swallowed my drink. It had a viscous texture and a spicy taste and it made my skin tingle. But suddenly everyone seemed to be pressing in too close; the heat intensified. I couldn't breathe properly. The masked faces of the party guests gave me a strange, anxious feeling in my solar plexus.

There was a glassed-in porch that ran along the outside wall of the house, overlooking a garden. I angled through the crowd and onto the porch, then opened the door and stepped outside.

Trees grew close together, twinkling lights strung through their branches. The air smelled of roses and I wondered how they could grow like that this time of year.

I wrapped my arms around my torso to keep warm; my hands felt like I was holding cubes of ice but it was a relief to be away from the party.

There was a thick hedge and the garden seemed to dip away into complete darkness. Part of me wanted to explore but I was drawn back to the house. A Death Cab song was playing—"I Will Possess Your Heart." The voices of the party seemed to have gotten louder but the warmth felt good now. My hands prickled slowly and painfully to life. I walked through the kitchen and back to the front room, then down a short hallway. The other rooms off the hall were closed and when I tried the doors they were locked. I went upstairs.

All the rooms up there were locked also, except for the bathroom. It had a large claw-foot bathtub and shiny black-and-lavender tile. I looked out the window at the garden and thought I saw a small shadow dart across the lawn.

Why did I imagine it was Jeni? I had freshmania, that temporary first year away from home insanity. Of course I did, especially under the circumstances.

When I looked at my reflection in the mirror I saw someone who seemed too young to be away from home, too young to be wandering around in the night alone, chasing a friend from her past who was most likely dead and buried. I shivered again, as cold as I'd been in the garden. *Mommy. Daddy. Jeni.* There was no one.

Maybe it was the drinking and staring so hard at myself that called up the monster. My face turned red and my eyes bulged out of my head with tears. I dug my fingers into the sockets around my eyes and sobbed into my hands. My whole body was shaking; I felt skeletal, as if there weren't any muscle tissue or skin holding me together. *Stop it, you freak!* I told myself. *Stop it and go home!*

Home was far, though, too far.

There was a tapping on the door and I tried to catch my breath. I splashed cold water on the ghoul-face in the mirror and waited, gulping down the last shudders of my sobs.

The knocking continued. A man's voice said, "You okay?"

I paused, trying to compose myself, listening: scuffling outside and then silence. I opened the door. No one was there.

But the door across the hall was softly closing as if someone had just entered.

I went up to the door and knocked. Inside was the sound of voices, rustling, and then someone spoke: "Yes?"

"I wanted to ask you something," I said.

At first there was an unsettling silence as if a room full of people were holding their breath and then the door opened a crack.

I only saw a slice of his face and chest. His hand held the door open and where his white shirt was rolled up I could see tattooed letters on his wrist but not what they read. He had a lot of silver rings on his fingers.

"What's that?" he asked. His voice was deep. His slanted green eyes were watching me behind a small pair of wire-rim glasses.

I reached into my pocket and pulled out a rumpled piece of paper and handed it to him. He glanced down at Jeni's face.

"Have you seen her?" I asked.

He shook his head. "No. Who is she?"

"I'm looking for her." It was all I could manage. My voice lodged in my throat like a chicken bone.

"I'm sorry," he said.

He turned to the room behind him and I saw a man and a woman sprawled on a large bed, both wearing masks over their eyes. I smelled smoke and something else—an intoxicating floral, as if I had jammed my nose inside a rose, or maybe a gardenia?

"What does she want?" asked a woman's voice with a light accent I didn't recognize.

The man turned back to me and moved to block my view of the bed. I saw his face in full now. He was in his early twenties, with sleek black hair and very fine, high cheekbones. There was an indentation in his chin, exactly as if someone had touched him with a fingertip and left an impression. I couldn't tell what race he was. He wore the white shirt with faded jeans, torn at the knees, and his feet were bare.

"She's looking for someone," he said to the woman behind

him. But while he spoke his eyes were studying my face so closely I wanted to back away.

"They're not in here," the woman's voice said.

The man shrugged—"Sorry"—and closed the door. I stumbled back down the staircase into the party crowd. Screamin' Jay Hawkins was screaming, "I Put a Spell on You," his voice writhing like a snake.

As I went outside I saw someone watching me from the shadows of the trees. Someone tall, very tall, perhaps seven feet, even stooped.

I ran all the way back to the dorms as fast as I could, an anvil named fear hammering my chest.

5. That her bones had been found

It was evening when I went to see Tommy Leeds in his dorm room. Music thumped through the halls and the air smelled of stale coffee and burned toast. Tommy's roommate, Ian Larsen, a science geek who must have been matched up with him by the same person who'd matched me with Lauren, said Tommy was in the lounge.

He was sitting with a group of guys, playing acoustic guitars. At least the girlfriend wasn't there.

"Hey," I said from the doorway. They kept playing.

I walked in. "Hey. Can I talk to you?"

Tommy smirked at his friends. "Practicing, man."

"I know. Sorry. Can I speak to you about something? It's important." I held the picture of Jeni out in front of me. They all looked at it glassily.

"Whatever." Tommy shrugged at his friends, got up and came toward me.

"What's up?"

"You were on that trip, right?"

"Yeah. What's the deal with that?" He patted his jeans for cigarettes and wrestled a box out of the tight space, tapped the box with his finger.

"I had a friend on that trip. Jennifer Benson. The one who disappeared." I held out the flyer again.

Tommy took a cigarette and jiggled it nervously between his fingers. "Yeah. That was fucked up. You knew her?"

I nodded. "She was my best friend."

"Sucks. Sorry. What do you want from me, though?"

"Did you see her that night?"

He frowned. "I didn't see shit. And I got to practice. Sorry." He popped his head back into the lounge. "Going for a smoke."

"Wait," I said. "Do you know anyone else who was on that trip?"

He held up his hands. "Nothing more to say."

I wanted to shout, *To the cops you will,* but of course that was bullshit. As usual, I had nothing.

The rest of the guys shouldered me aside as they went toward the elevator.

I took the stairwell. Outside it was getting dark already and the cold bit. My head was pounding. It occurred to me that the combination of so many words, and too much caffeine, and alcohol, could do strange things to a person, especially a young, impressionable one with a sick mother. I thought about the drink I'd had at the party the night before— ever since then I'd felt weird, jittery, too awake, and I'd wanted more, the thick darkness of it, the strange, subtle fragrance, the indescribable taste. Maybe that had affected me, too. Add in the way college isolated you, left you feeling as if the rest of the world, including your past and your family, was just a dream compared to what you read in your books and on the faces of the other students, and anything could happen.

It had. Way before freshman year had begun. And it continued to happen—anything—because as I turned the corner there was the guy from the Halloween party. He was standing with his hands in his coat pockets, his back bent under the weight of his pack. His brow was furrowed and his mouth was slightly pursed with the same kind of worried concentration as he spoke to a blonde woman in a long red velvet coat seated at a small table with tarot cards spread out before her.

I wanted to call out to him but it was impossible to speak. A cold wind swirled up, trying to get inside my coat like a ghost, reminding me why I was here at all.

I turned my head to the side, imagining Jeni standing there wearing a knit Hello Kitty cap, smiling at me so the dimples showed. *He's cute, right?* When I turned again the man had disappeared into the crowd.

The woman at the table was watching me with pale green eyes and I found myself going over to her, instead of after him as I really wanted. Her hair was cropped short, dyed platinum with a few streaks of red and orange like flames, and her delicate nose was slightly rounded at the tip, with visible, sensitive-looking nostrils. When she spoke it was with a strange accent that sounded vaguely familiar, and a slightly petulant pout of her lips. "Tarot reading?"

I nodded, thinking of the dark-haired man's hands on the same deck, and sat across from her. "How much?"

"Twenty."

I gave her a crumpled bill from my pocket. She looked into my face and held out the cards.

I shuffled and picked three and she laid them out in front of her, flipped them over, examined them. I recognized the images; my mom had bought me this deck from a New Age bookstore and Jeni and I spent hours with the disconcertingly bright pictures of often brutal scenarios. The Nine of Swords, in which a woman sits up in bed covering her face, the weapons hanging ominously on the wall behind her. The black-haired Magician in his rose arbor. The Six of Cups— two village children with gold cups full of white flowers. I couldn't remember what any of them meant.

"You come from sorrow," the woman said. "You have lost someone dear to you. And you fear you will lose more. But there's beauty in your future." She looked up at me, her skin so smooth and golden it almost glittered. "Great joy and celebration in this city built on sacred burial ground. A child."

Why did her voice sound familiar?

"What can you tell me about the loss?" I asked. Every time I walked by a neon sign reading PSYCHIC I was tempted to ask about Jeni but I was afraid it would only terrify me and confuse me more. Now, sitting so close to this woman, I couldn't help myself.

"Someone you love. Someone who loves you."

"Where," I asked, "is she?"

The woman bit her lip. "I don't know. I'm sorry." She took the twenty out of her pocket and handed it back to me but I shook my head. Taking it would have been an admission of some kind of defeat.

At that moment something fluttered in my peripheral vision and I turned to see the homeless woman wearing the wings. The smaller person was holding the train of her dress.

"You think you're fine now," the winged woman said. "But just wait. It gets harder. Then you'll be just like us."

Suddenly I longed for walls around me, even the confines of a room shared with Lauren. I got up to leave. "Thanks."

The tarot woman smiled. "Blessings," she said.

6. When it hurts the most

When I spoke to my parents on the phone they always had the same detached, calm tone, as if they were talking about a TV show or baseball game rather than an illness that harvested and killed a large percentage of the population. I didn't ask many questions, either. I really didn't want to know. Mostly we talked about my classes and how many more days there were until I came home for Thanksgiving vacation. The weather, dorm food, if I needed more warm clothes. So they wouldn't worry, I told them that I had a friend. The name that came to my mind was from a Tori Amos song. "Bean is in my English class. She's really nice. She's from Marin County. Her parents have this beautiful house there." I could tell this made them happy. I didn't mention how much I was drinking, of course, or the flyers I tried to hand out, or that I roamed the streets alone at night. They didn't ask me much, either. This was unlike them; they always used to want to know every detail.

I took BART by myself, but it seemed safe—so clean and well-lit and there were other girls traveling alone. It struck me, seeing them, how I would never have done this before. If Jeni had been too trusting, I had always been cautious. Now I was reckless. Intrepid. But I put my hair in a ponytail tucked into my coat and wore my low-heeled black cowboy boots in case I might need to run.

When I got to the Tenderloin I was even happier with my decision to dress down—not that I had much to dress up in. Girls in short coats and high heels stood shivering on the corners and cars cruised slowly past. Even the neon had a lurid glow.

The theater was in a historic building where every famous band had performed. The marquee read HALLOWEEN HOTEL. Inside, the place was decorated in rose and gold with a huge chandelier that looked as if it were made of shattered stars. People filled the lobby and I felt smothered by the warmth of the bodies around me and the music vibrating through the speakers.

I wandered around by myself for a while—in and out of the restroom, through the lobby as if I were looking for someone; I was always looking for someone.

But the one I found was not her. I looked across to the bar and saw the man from the party.

He was alone, too, it seemed, one elbow propped on the bar as he downed his drink. He adjusted his glasses with his middle finger and stared myopically across the room in my direction.

Mine, I thought reflexively, as if I had thought it many times before. *Mine.* I wanted him to be.

What were the chances that I would find him here? What did it mean?

I went over to the bar as near to him as I could get and ordered a 7UP. When I turned my head he was watching me. I felt some kind of pang in my chest, a cold, hard sensation as if I'd been struck from the inside. If only I'd been able to order a real drink, I thought, anything to take the edge off so I could speak to him.

You're going to anyway.

He turned sideways and took a long swig of his beer. I was

afraid to look but it seemed as if his head was inclined in my direction, that he was going to come over to me . . .

But then he was sliding some dollar bills down for the bartender. I held my breath as he moved away and I lowered my head and stared at the shiny wood surface of the bar. My cheeks were burning with embarrassment for having imagined his interest. But I needed to speak to him, no matter what.

Then, a hand on my arm.

"Greetings."

His fingers were long and tapered, but not especially thin, covered with those silver rings. I couldn't look at his face.

"Jonathan Graves. John."

"Ariel."

"Like in *The Tempest*." He paused. "You were at our house the other night," he said.

"Yeah. Cool party." Trying to act casual. Twirling the thin red straw in my 7UP, poking at the poisonously red maraschino that floated there. Were those things even real fruit?

"You had a picture of someone."

He'd called my bluff. Nothing was casual. Everything mattered too much. "My friend, Jeni. She disappeared from the dorms on a school trip last year. They don't know what happened." My hand felt for the flyer in my pocket. I hadn't had the heart to pass out any more lately.

"I'm sorry," he said. "I think I heard about that. It's terrible."

I lowered my eyes but the silence was so palpable I had to look at him. His irises behind his glasses were soft. They had gold rings around the green and I felt mildly dizzy, as if I'd been staring too long into a kaleidoscope.

His eyes were focused on my face so fully that it made the

nape of my neck tingle. My stomach ached; I wished I'd put something besides coffee in it before I'd left. Ever since Halloween my appetite had been waning.

"You go to Cal, then?"

"Yes. I just started. Do you?"

"Do. Still. It never seems to end."

"Don't you like it?"

"Sometimes I just want to forget about my dissertation and get as far away as possible."

"What's it on?"

"My thesis? The soul in literature. How it manifests and if there is some secret hidden in words that enables the soul to continue on."

"Sounds like something you shouldn't run away from," I said.

He loosened the green scarf that was looped around his neck, intensifying the color of his eyes. His lips had a brooding quality as he fiddled with the rings on his fingers.

The lights dimmed, signaling that the show was starting.

"Are you by yourself?" he asked. When I nodded he motioned for me to follow him.

The crowd closed in and he took my hand. His palm was cool, with light calluses. I tried not to cling too tightly or not tightly enough. Someone's pulse nestled between us. It must have been mine; my heart was pounding along with the music. I realized how long it had been since someone had touched me.

As we wound our way through the pack of bodies I thought I saw Coraline Grimm standing by herself. Yes, it was her. She gave me an odd look, tilting her head, staring from me to my companion and back again—so odd that it kept me from saying hello—and then we'd moved past her.

We took our places in front of the stage and he removed his wool coat—a fitted, turn-of-the century style. The crowd jostled me against him. I shrugged off my jacket and wiped sweat from my temples with my thermal sleeve. I wished I had worn something pretty and light. We waited like this, not looking at each other, for the band to start. Halloween Hotel was a post-post-punk band that sounded a little like early Joy Division, with a girl singer who looked like PJ Harvey. There were hundreds of Web sites devoted to decoding their weirdly beautiful lyrics. They were something else Jeni and I had shared.

At one point my companion leaned over to me so that I could smell the light, warm fragrance of his hair and he spoke into my ear.

"Some music," he said, "knows how to open your heart. You know? But that's when it hurts the most."

The stage was draped in red velvet. As the curtain lifted I felt my knees grow weak. A small woman stood in the center of the stage. She was barefoot and wore a long white dress like a nightgown and she seemed to be looking right at me.

"The dead children are risen. The bones are singing. You can't forget us. You can't forget us. We are the messengers."

In the crowded darkness someone stood behind me, placing his hands on my hips, his fingers grazing my skin between my shirt and jeans, his fingertips pressing ever so lightly into my flesh.

John Graves gave me a ride home after the concert, in a finned white 1960s Cadillac, asked me for my cell phone number and drove away into the fog, leaving me standing on the sidewalk wondering who I had just spent the evening with.

7. The gloaming

I slept almost the whole day. That night my parents called. It was Sunday, a twilight worthy of the word gloaming, and the town had a melancholy feeling, even in the way the light fell morosely across the streets below my window. I sat on my bed and listened to my mom and dad talk about the weather and a movie they'd seen and I answered their questions about school but when they asked what I had done that weekend I felt tears coming. I bit my lip, fanning my face and putting my other hand over the receiver so they wouldn't hear.

"Sweetie?" my mom said. I had been able to keep myself from crying in front of them until then. I hadn't wanted to worry her but it was too much.

My dad got on the other line and they kept asking me what was wrong and what they could do. I couldn't talk about the cancer. It was as if we'd all made a pact not to mention it. I couldn't talk about the concert and how a strange boy brought me home. I couldn't talk about her but I did anyway.

"I've been looking for Jeni."

"Ariel, sweetie, we're talking about your friend, Jennifer?" my mom asked gently.

She started calling Jeni by her full name a few months after she'd disappeared. I knew my mom wasn't aware she was doing that but it made me sad, as if she had given up. Jeni might come back but Jennifer Benson was already a reference from the past.

"Jeni, not Jennifer. What other one is there?" I hadn't meant to snap out like that. "Sorry," I said.

"It's okay. We know you're under a lot of pressure and stress," said my dad.

"But that's not what this is about!" I yanked the ponytail out of my hair and tugged on a handful of roots. "I'm looking for her. What's wrong with that? The cops didn't do shit."

"Do you want us to come there?" my mom asked, and I heard my dad say quietly, "Natalie . . ." which I knew meant, *You aren't up to traveling anywhere right now, even if your daughter is having a nervous breakdown.*

"Forget it," I told them. "Just forget it. Why do I even bother trying to talk to you about anything except my classes and the stupid weather? You don't ever listen!"

My mom's voice sounded very small when I finally stopped. "I know I haven't been there for you as much as usual. I'm really sorry."

"I have to go," I said.

"Please tell us more," said my mom, but I couldn't.

"I really have to go." And I hung up.

That night as I was changing for bed I saw Lauren staring at me.

When I glanced down at my abdomen I saw what she was looking at. There were five small dark marks there, bruises, like the imprint of fingertips.

What the hell? I thought suddenly of John Graves, his long fingers with the silver rings. He had held my hips from behind—it must have been him—but only lightly.

I was glad for the marks; it meant he was real.

8. The way you are suddenly somewhere in a dream

Fear echoed inside of me like footsteps on the marble floor of Doe as I walked back to the dorms in the dark. We were told the campus was safe at night, watched over by guards, stationed with surveillance cameras and call boxes, but I didn't feel that way, not after what I knew.

Now every tree hid a serial killer and every shadow was one.

I was afraid but not so afraid to stay in at night; I had to be vigilant, I had to keep looking. And part of me was out there for another reason. Part of me wanted someone to come out of the darkness and grab me by the throat and make me forget everything about my life, but not just anyone—John Graves.

"Ariel," he would whisper into my ear as he tugged on my ponytail. "Ariel, like *The Tempest*."

Ever since that night at the concert I thought about him constantly, almost as much as I thought about Jeni. I thought about the smell of his hair and the feel of his hand holding mine and the frown line that formed between his eyes. I thought about the angular shape of his cheekbone and chin and throat contrasting with the softness of his mouth and eyelashes. All I had to remember him by were those marks on my abdomen—they looked like fingertips. The marks were real—I could see them—but I wondered if I had imagined the man. It seemed as if something was wrong in my head now, as if all the stress and drinking and the two events that changed my life had started to do things to my mind. My parents had sent me to a school counselor, Ronnie Wang, a cheerful young woman who let me ramble on about the pressure I put on myself to get good grades, the weirdness of living in a dorm after being an only child and the general loneliness of being away from home. Once I broke into tears about global warming and the smile left her face as she leaned forward to look me in the eye.

"Is there anything important going on that you're not telling me, Ariel?" she asked.

"The planet is in danger. I don't think much else is significant."

"Anything with your family?"

I stood and hefted my backpack onto my shoulder. "I'm just kind of emotional about it," I said.

That Saturday night I got back to the dorm safely—no apocalypse, no serial killers, no John—and went to sleep early. But I didn't really rest; it was like I was running in place in my bed the whole time.

I woke sharply from the head-pounding, half-sleep haze to hear Lauren's moans and Dallas's whispers.

"Go get a fucking room," I said as I jumped from the bed, pulled a jacket over my pajamas and grabbed my shoes.

"This is a room," Dallas mumbled.

"This is my room."

"What a coincidence, it's mine, too!" Lauren said and they laughed.

I put my sneakers on in the lounge and then I sprinted down the eight flights of stairs to the lobby. It was past midnight and the air felt silent and chill. I just started to run.

I didn't know I was going toward the house where John Graves lived—not that I hadn't wanted to before, but I didn't think I'd be going there that night. Not without brushing my teeth and hair and putting on lipstick, not without thinking what I'd do when I got there. But I kept running north up into the hills.

I was standing in front of the house the way you are suddenly somewhere in a dream—without really realizing how you got there. The oak trees surrounded me, leaves like giant hands holding the darkness. Candlelight shone through the windows like wine bottles shine in a dark bar and I could hear music and soft laughter but there wasn't a big party going on this time. I crept up to the window and looked inside.

Three people were dancing in the room where a fire burned in the grate. The woman had short blonde hair and wore a black velvet gown. I recognized her from the table on the street—the tarot reader. Of course, that was how I knew her voice. The woman behind the door. She was moving gracefully in the arms of two men wearing satin smoking jackets, and sharing a bottle of wine with them. One of the men had curly brown hair and the other had black hair, slicked back from his face. I recognized John Graves.

They looked like the perfect friends I dreamed of having, I had dreamed of having since I lost the only real friend I had ever had. But I was not part of this world, I told myself. Why even try? John held the blonde as if she were his lover. They had no need for me. It was worse than the world of the dorms. At least I didn't care if I was rejected there. So I turned away from the house where part of me still remained.

When I got back to my dorm room, Lauren and Dallas were gone—they must have decided to sleep in his room instead. I sat down on my bed, still out of breath from my run. There was something on my bedspread. I pulled back, my stomach turning. It couldn't be that . . .

There was a note that said, *Watch how you dispose of your rag. It made us want to vomit. Love, Your Secret Admirers.*

And, yes, it was a tampon there. Apparently a used one. I

picked it up with a paper towel and almost put it on Lauren's pillow . . . but threw it in the trash instead.

I'd been wrong.

It was worse here. Treacherous beauty, even morbid beauty, was better than real-life shit.

9. What you first fall in love with

Before Thanksgiving my parents asked me what Bean was doing for the holiday and I knew something bad was coming by the tension in their voices.

"Oh," I said, trying to sound cheerful. "She's going to be with her family. She has this huge family in Marin. I told you she's from Marin, right? She invited me to join her if I wanted. Why?"

My dad cleared his throat. "It's just that, your mother isn't feeling great. She has to go through some treatments."

Didn't they want me there? I chewed at my lower lip; my mouth tasted like metal.

"It's really up to you," my mother said. "We want you to know that. But I didn't want you to see me like this, baby. I want to be stronger for you."

"I want to be strong for you," I said, but I knew I wasn't.

"I know," said my mom. "I know you do."

My dad went on. "Your mother and I do want you with us, Ariel. But when things are a little calmer so it's easier for everyone."

I tried, unsuccessfully, to swallow the tinny taste away.

"We were wondering if we could put the celebration off a little," he said. "If you could maybe go with your friends for the holiday? Just this time."

I wanted to tell them I didn't have friends, that I'd be spending the holiday looking for *Jennifer Benson,* but instead: "Sure," I said. "I can see you at Christmas." It wasn't just a taste now; I could hear the metallic edge in my voice.

"We'll make it up to you, baby," said my mom. "I promise. I'll get well and make it up to you."

I wasn't sure if this was true and even though she was still very much alive, I felt the change; a death had taken place.

The day was gray and bleak. The dorms were so quiet; almost everyone had left. I sat in my room reading and every now and then looking out over the empty streets. The tarot reader had said that Berkeley was built on sacred burial ground, some kind of power spot, but that day it just looked like a grim, deserted college town and when I finally went downstairs in the evening the lounge smelled like last night's spilled beer and urine.

I couldn't face the pressed turkey and jellied cranberry they were serving in the dorm to the scattered few who remained. Maybe I'd take a walk outside.

I noticed I had a text and checked the message. It was from a number I didn't recognize.

do u have plans 4 late txgiving dinner john graves

My heart had never felt so full of blood. He had invited me to come to him.

As I ran down the stairs I saw Coraline Grimm through an open door, standing on the bed in her dorm room tacking flyers on her wall.

"I saw you at Halloween Hotel," she said. "I'm all, that's the girl from the dorms."

I made myself stop even though my body was still running downstairs. "Oh. Yeah."

"I've been meaning to talk to you about that." She turned the rest of her body so she was facing me. Her shoulders stooped forward in her black vintage dress. "That guy you were with? I don't think that's such a good idea."

"Why not?"

"He's a heartbreaker. Literally. They all are. You should be careful."

"Careful how?"

"There's some weird shit in that drink they serve."

I was going to ask more but she turned back to the wall behind her and I saw what was there: missing-person flyers, including the one I had given her.

"What's all that?" I asked.

"Oh. It's a project I'm working on. It's called Missing. Do you want to come see?"

Fucking weird. "No thanks," I said, more sure than ever where I wanted to go now, in spite of Coraline's interdiction.

I went among the trees, up the steps, onto the porch, to the door of the house, and knocked.

My heart beat in my mouth like a piece of hot fruit as I waited. And then the door opened.

It wasn't John but another young man.

"Sorry to bother you. I'm looking for John Graves," I said.

He grinned so the gap between his front teeth showed. I remembered reading somewhere that a gap between the teeth signified sensuality. He was wiry and shorter than John, with curly brown hair and brown skin, light eyes. He wore a formal if slightly tattered black suit and a white dress shirt.

"Johnny's not back yet. Who should I say stopped by?"

"Never mind." I started to back away. I could hear the wispy sound of Coraline's voice in my ear. She was probably crazy, "heartbreaker" wasn't exactly a sinister term and I wanted whatever "weird shit" was in their wine, but Coraline seemed to know something about John Graves that I didn't.

"No, wait. Why don't you come in? He'll probably be home soon."

He was still grinning at me and I could smell the house behind him—that intoxicating scent from the party. Beeswax and pollen and the brew they'd served—spicy, herbal and sweet. There was also something new—the smell of food cooking—a complex blend of flavors that made my stomach cramp with hunger for the first time in weeks; food had more and more been losing its taste.

At that moment I didn't care that I was walking into the lair of perfect strangers. I had been here once and I wanted to return. I stepped through the door.

It is hard to remember what you first fall in love with. Usually it is an expression in the eyes, an exchange, or a gesture or the sound of a voice, a word spoken. Those things can get blended with the atmosphere around you at the time—a fragrance in the air, a play of light, even music—so that they become almost one with each other and when you see or smell or hear the memories of a place you feel the love again, but as a pang of loss. Sometimes the feelings get connected so deeply to your body that even your own skin, your own eyes in the mirror remind you of what you no longer have. Sometimes it only takes a few things for someone to attach the way I did—enough hunger, enough loneliness, enough loss, someone who will feed you and touch you and listen. Sometimes attachment—call it love—is more complex than that. When you are in the state I was in, love can be tied up with other things, like excitement and danger and the desire to know what really happened, what actually took place.

I walked into their house as I had walked one time before, but this time, no party. Candles were lit, as I had seen through the window, and they burned on every surface, dripping scented wax. I thought for a moment of fire hazards and then forgot. There were vases of roses everywhere—not the store-bought kind but wild garden roses, blousy and very sweet—I remembered stepping out into the garden behind the house: that smell. Music was playing but this time I didn't recognize it. It was mysterious and soft with a beautiful female voice singing words I didn't understand. *Mellifluous,* I thought, glad to be able to apply the word Melinda Story had used in class about Spenser's *Epithalamion.* I followed the man into a large formal dining room with a long table covered in worn damask—shiny blossoms against a matte background of the same creamy color—more roses and candles and green vines. A delicately branched chandelier of white iron vines and flowers, and missing a few large crystals, hung from the ceiling. I smelled the food more strongly now and my stomach cramped again; all I'd eaten that day was a bowl of cornflakes and half a peanut butter and jelly sandwich.

The woman stepped into the room through the kitchen door. She was taller than I'd realized, with broad, perfectly sculpted shoulders, long thin arms and legs and full breasts, all shown off by the red vintage Chinese silk dress she wore. She was the girl on the flyer the giant had given me. She was the girl on the bed. The tarot reader. The dancing girl.

She looked me up and down. "We've met before."

"On Telegraph. I'm Ariel."

"Like *The Tempest.*" It gave me a queer feeling when she

said that; I didn't understand until I realized that it was exactly what John Graves had said. She took my hand. Her skin was hot.

"I'm Tania."

"Hi."

"De la Torre." She looked over at the man in the suit. "She just appeared at the door?"

"She came looking for John."

"He invited me," I said, wanting to check the text to make sure I hadn't imagined it.

Tania nodded. "So you met Perry?"

I waved lamely at both of them and tried to smile. I steadied myself by holding onto one of the dining room chairs. It had a wooden back carved with flowers and vines and was upholstered in faded green velvet.

"You can join us for dinner," Tania said softly. Her voice was almost as compelling as the smell of the food. "But you have to dress for it." She scowled at my clothes. "Come on."

She gestured for me to follow her up the stairs. Perry came behind us.

The bedroom was lushly, if a bit shabbily, decorated with a large bed draped in red silk velvet and threadbare Persian rugs on the floor. There was a dressing table and Tania motioned for me to sit. She handed me a cup full of the thick, dark liquid I'd had at the party. I took it, trying not to seem too eager. I'd thought about that drink a lot since Halloween.

"Makeover!" Perry said. I looked at myself in the mirror. My hair was limp and scraggly and my skin so pale you could see a vein running blue under the surface of my cheek. I looked like any exhausted freshman but in contrast to the two people in the room with me I was ridiculous.

"What will we do with this?" Tania took my hair out of

the ponytail I always wore and ran her fingers through it. The touch soothed me and I closed my eyes for a second, remembering how John had taken my hand at the concert. I surrendered as she expertly trimmed the split ends, feeling suddenly like a little girl, curious and trusting, not reckless, not suspicious anymore.

I hadn't had a haircut since the summer. My mom used to cut my hair at home, in the bathroom with a towel over my shoulders and the smell of her so close to my face. But I didn't want to think about her now. I reached up and flicked a tear away. If they noticed they didn't say anything. My hair fluttered around me; it was down to my waist, even trimmed.

"Beautiful," said Tania. "Now makeup!"

She wiped my face off with a cleansing pad and then applied a serum, lotion, an eye cream. After that I felt Perry's hands, both thumbnails painted with grass-green polish, flicker over my face, so light it almost didn't seem like he was touching me with anything at all. While he worked he commented on my eyes ("So big and green!"), my eyelashes ("Are they real?") and my facial structure ("Nice bones."). It wasn't that I hadn't been told I was pretty before but being pretty made me feel vulnerable, like Jeni, like someone who could be hurt. I usually wanted to seem as plain as possible, but not that night. They had turned me away from the mirror. Tania came toward me holding a dress.

"Perfect, baby!" Perry clapped his hands. "Exactly right!"

It was a long pale blue satin dress, cut on the bias, as Tania pointed out. It looked like the slip that went under a vintage gown. I was glad I'd shaved my legs that morning. Tania put her hands on my waist and gently pulled my T-shirt over my head. I let her. It was weird in contrast to how I usually felt; I wasn't embarrassed at all. Part of me wanted her to see my breasts. She unhooked my bra, removed it and tossed it on the ground, then slipped the dress over my head.

"Shoes." Perry was holding a pair of silver high-heeled sandals with an expression on his face somewhere between fetishist and shoe salesman. I stepped into them and he knelt and fastened the straps.

Then Tania opened a blue velvet jewelry box and took out a necklace of pale blue and white gemstones and freshwater pearls. It shone in the soft light, iridescent. She put it on me and it lay there, cool against my collarbone. She sprayed some perfume onto my neck. It smelled like the jasmine that grew in my mother's garden, and like something else, like smoke and wind and what jewels would smell like ground up, pulverized into scent. Tania sprayed my right wrist, then paused at my left, fingering the beads that spelled Jeni's name but not asking. After a moment she sprayed the perfume there as well.

"Now you're ready," she said.

I looked at myself in the mirror. I smiled shyly at the girl there.

"Sylph," said Tania. "That's your new name."

"I'm starved!" said Perry. "And you are, too, I bet, Miss." He gently circled my left wrist with his thumb and forefinger just below the bracelet. "Look at the size of that! We must fatten you."

There was butternut squash soup in a silver tureen—the best I'd ever tasted. There was a wild rice dish made with almonds and cranberries, a green salad with beets and goat cheese, homemade bread and butter and more of the warm red brew that they'd served at the party. For dessert there was a caramel apple *tartin* with homemade vanilla-bean ice cream. I ate in a kind of stupor, consuming the food as if I'd never had taste buds before. While we ate they asked me questions about my life and I answered in between mouthfuls. I told them that I was from L.A., that both my parents were English teachers—that was why I was named after a character in a Shakespearean play—that my dad taught at the university, my mom at the high school where I used to go. I had grown up doing ballet, reading. I said that I was an English major, that I wanted to write someday, that I read the way other people ate chocolate. There wasn't that much to tell about myself, I realized; I hadn't had enough life experience to say anything interesting. That is, if I left out Jeni and my mom's cancer, which I did. I had spent three months showing everyone Jeni's picture, waiting for opportunities to talk about her. Now, even with the opportunity the bracelet provided and the fact that Tania had read or guessed about a loss from my past, I didn't want to.

But it was a relief to talk about other things, to have people listen attentively, especially such glamorous, gorgeous ones, the kind who, in my real life, had never paid attention to me before. I forgot that I had ever felt any suspicion about John. They laughed and refilled my glass and they watched me—Perry and Tania—as if I were the most important person in the world.

"What sign are you, Sylph?" she asked. "Wait, don't tell me."

"She always gets it right," Perry warned.

"I have to eliminate first." She hardly paused. "You're not a Taurus, Capricorn or Virgo."

I nodded. "How'd you—"

She held up her hand. "Not Aries, Leo or Sagittarius. And you're not Pisces." She and Perry rolled their eyes at each other. "Or Scorpio or Cancer, although you're in your shell a little, like a Cancer."

I tensed reflexively at the word.

Tania went on. "I'd say, either Libra, Gemini or Aquarius. Am I right?"

I nodded again and took another sip of my drink. "Libra," said Tania.

"How'd you know?"

"Air, you're all air."

"And what about you guys?"

"We're easy as pie to read." Perry grinned. His features were modelesque but also the definition of impish. "I'm Capricorn, goat boy. I always know what's right for you. Tania's the big mean lioness Leo. And John's a . . ."

"Pisces, that bastard," they said together and laughed.

"Pisces is the oldest sign," Tania explained. Sort of explained. I didn't know much about astrology except for the horoscopes Jeni and I read in magazines; she was a Sagittarius who loved animals and travel. "With a Scorpio moon!" Tania added. "Thinks he knows everything."

"As opposed to me, who actually does." Perry winked.

"You're perfect for us," Tania said.

"What about you?" I said, finally, flushed and a little breathless. "Besides the astrology. Who are you all anyway?" Then we all started to laugh.

It seemed funny at the time but I can't understand it now except to say I was drunk, but we laughed and kept laughing, doubled over and clutching our abdomens.

"I have no idea," said Perry with a last snort. He blotted his tearing eyes with his linen napkin.

"Seriously."

"Like what about us? Our racial background? Our jobs?"

"All of the above?"

"We're racial mutts. Between the three of us I think we cover all of Europe, most of Asia and part of South America and Africa."

"Smart, rather useless mutts," Tania said. "Johnny's an English major like you. Almost has his PhD except for that pesky dissertation."

I pointed at Perry and he lifted his palm and lowered his head in mock reverence. "Classics. I like any culture that worships creatures with furry haunches and girls that change into trees."

Tania leaned forward on her elbows so that her bare arms shone in the light. "I'm in psych, actually." Her voice was soft, confiding. "After the dysfunctional shit I went through as a kid I have a lot of experience. Now I like to use my roommates as subjects."

I had a vision of her sitting across from me in a leather therapist's chair, looking like she had on Telegraph, at the tarot table, except wearing a button-down silk blouse and glasses.

The front door opened, I heard footsteps, and followed Tania's gaze to the man standing at the threshold of the room. "Speak of the devil," she said.

"Sorry." John was wearing a suit like Perry's, elegant but old-looking. "I got caught up with some work." My face heated up as he looked at me. "Hi, Ariel."

I nodded. I couldn't get a single word out. My throat had shut.

"Like *The Tempest*," Tania said, staring at him, but his eyes were still on me. "Let's get more comfortable," she went on. "Johnny, bring your food."

We went into the dimly lit front room, the "parlor" they called it. There was a fire burning in the grate and the air smelled of wood smoke and eucalyptus. In spite of the cold night, the room was very hot.

Perry lit a joint and handed it to me.

"This is what you need. It'll help dissolve all that tension."

I'd never smoked before so I tried not to inhale too vigorously but it went in smoothly. My whole body relaxed into the shimmer of the atmosphere.

"Time for some magics!" Tania said. She stood and went to the front of the room. A silk cord I hadn't noticed before hung from the ceiling and she reached up and pulled it. Two pale blue silk curtains seemed to appear out of nowhere, hiding her from view. After a moment she pulled them apart. She was now wearing a black top hat and standing behind a small table covered with a cloth and a tall candle. Then Tania closed her eyes.

"Fire!" she said and the word filled the whole room as if it were filling the world.

She began to rub her left thumb and forefinger together, harder and harder. For some reason I couldn't take my eyes off of her hand, even then. As she rubbed, thin wisps of smoke emanated from the tips of her fingers. My breath caught in a gasp of wonderment.

She picked up a silver lighter and flicked a flame to life, then put it out by stroking it slowly, much too slowly, with her fingers.

She folded up a piece of paper, lit it on fire and then opened her palm. The flame went out; there was only a small coin there.

She lit a string, which burned up to the top and then extinguished into a shower of sparks, turning to a scarf of ruby silk.

I was still staring, huddled up like a child only half-wanting to be awakened from a dream, when the curtain closed. When it opened again Tania was beside me, smiling. I rubbed my eyes. John and Perry applauded but I was too stunned to move.

"How'd you read my cards the other night?" I asked.

She looked suddenly sober. "I've been studying tarot divination as part of my thesis. Parapsychology. I suppose it's part chance and part intuition. You look so sad. But also there is something hopeful when I look at you."

"And the fire?"

Her smile returned. "I can't divulge all my secrets, can I?"

Perry changed the music to something with an intense beat that woke my shocked-to-stillness limbs. The song was in a language I didn't recognize and the sound was thrilling; my body didn't want to keep still, the way I'd felt when I was a kid. But even high, I told myself, I didn't dance anymore. Ever.

Tania started, her arms in the air, her hands like birds, her head back and her throat exposed. She shook her hips and undulated her spine. Once again, as if her fingers were still on fire, I couldn't take my eyes off her.

Perry joined in, moving his pelvis close to hers. His hands reached out and slid down her bare back. The music thumped louder.

"New friend?" Perry scolded. "What are you doing, girl?"

I sat by the fire, watching them. Sweat was trickling down the back of my neck.

"Come on, princess, don't be shy."

I took another sip of the drink I'd brought with me, scared Perry would pull me up.

But he didn't; he was too busy dancing with Tania. John Graves did. He took off his glasses and then his dinner jacket, rolled up his sleeves. I noticed the strange black letters and the thick veins at his wrists. His skin was pale and the veins looked very blue in contrast. Perry handed him the joint.

"You're not going to let us make fools of ourselves alone, are you?" He had a hit of smoke, then reached out and took my hand. I flashed back to the night at the concert, how he had led me through the crowd. I had never been touched by someone like him before that. I was afraid I'd faint.

But he supported me, his hand on my back as we started to dance to the pulse of the song. I could feel the fluidity of muscles through his thin shirt. I could smell him—a musky dampness that I wanted to bury my face in. We danced for a long time, moving around the room, sometimes touching, sometimes not, intersecting with Perry and Tania. John was so graceful, spinning effortlessly, spine and shoulders rippling, hands carving out images in the air. My feet hurt but I kept dancing. I had a flash of memory of a fairy tale I'd been told as a child, where the woman danced until her toes were gone. Jeni and I took ballet lessons when we were little girls. We loved to dance together, for hours at a time, all around the living room, taking turns choosing the songs. Since she was gone I hadn't danced at all.

Then the music slowed and John drew me nearer. The smell of him grew stronger and the muscles of his back tensed under my fingers. I parted my lips and tipped my head back. This would be the moment, I thought. Finally.

And then I felt more hands on me and they were all surrounding me, dancing with me, swaying. I was caught in the middle of them, burning up with heat. I smelled Tania's warm gold skin like smoke and roses, the smoke of roses. I saw, through my fluttering eyelids—it was hard to keep my eyes open, suddenly—Perry's grin with the gap between his front teeth. And I heard John's voice softly saying my name.

I let my eyes close altogether now, waiting.

But then I heard John's voice again. "It's late. I think maybe you should leave now? Ariel?" I opened my eyes to see the strange, tense silence. "I can drive you."

They all released me with their arms but their eyes stayed

fastened like jewels to my forehead and throat and my skin suddenly bumped with cold. Then John handed me the bag with my clothes and shoes.

"I'll give you back the dress." I was already fumbling with the clasp of the necklace. The weight of it in my hand felt almost sexual. I put it on the fireplace mantel.

"Keep the dress," said Tania. "We have more than enough. It's good on you."

"Let me drive you home," John said again but I said no.

I took off the sandals and jammed my bare feet into the sneakers, my head lowered in shame. Why had I believed they would want someone like me at all? Had I done something to make them dismiss me so suddenly?

"Be safe," he said.

As I sprinted home with tears I wasn't sure how to explain pouring down my face, I thought of something. If Jeni had not vanished, we would be spending this night together. But she had disappeared and I had not found out what happened to her. Instead of searching I was dining with beauties. I had failed.

10. And blood was blood

I stayed up watching TV in the dorm lounge until dawn, then slept the rest of the weekend, hardly leaving my room except to go the bathroom. My forehead pounded with heat and I shivered under the comforter while my empty stomach churned.

As I was going through my bag I found a joint in there; a present from my friends? I tucked it in my drawer where I couldn't see it. And the blue silk dress was balled up at the bottom of my hamper so it might seem as if that night had never taken place at all.

When school started again I dragged myself out of bed and went, but I was only half-there. I daydreamed about John, Tania and Perry and at night I hid under my blankets and tentatively touched myself. I hadn't allowed myself to do this for a long time. But now I did it like a starving person taking her first small bite, thinking of the three people in the house, thinking about what would have happened if I'd stayed that night.

After Jeni was gone I stopped wanting to kiss anyone. I didn't even want to touch my own body because when I did I saw her face and then I just went cold.

But now, in bed, I touched the tender marks on my abdomen. They were still there, too, proof, like the dress and the joint, that I had been somewhere other than my room, the campus, Telegraph Avenue.

I had meant to ask John Graves about the marks. Why were they still there? I had taken off my clothes in front of Tania and she hadn't seen them, or pretended not to. I had not spoken. It was like I was a girl from one of the Greek myths. But no one had cut out my tongue except for me; if I spoke I'd be the one to lose.

And what would I have said? *Why did your touch leave a permanent mark?* Would that have upset him, pushed him away? What I wanted from him was something bigger and more final than just his gentle, bruising touch. It was escape from a life of pain into one I didn't understand but wanted. Theirs.

One day I walked up to the front of my English class to turn in the assignment and I heard some stirring behind me. There was a cramping in the pit of my stomach and I reached back to touch the seat of my jeans. Something sticky on my hands.

Someone snickered. The window was open and a cool breeze raised goose bumps on my arms even though my face was flaming. Melinda Story said softly, "Ariel, would you like to leave early today?"

I went to the ladies' room and put in a tampon but there was nothing else I could do except walk all the way back to the dorms with my sweatshirt tied around my waist. It was just menstrual blood, something my mom had always told me to be proud of, never ashamed, but it seemed like a revelation of everything that was wrong with me. And blood was blood; it made me think of something frightening that I wanted to keep out of my mind at all costs.

Melinda Story stopped me two days later as I was leaving class.

"How are you doing?"

"Fine," I said. "Thanks for asking."

"If you want to talk . . ."

I shook my head. "I'm okay, thanks."

She leaned her face closer to mine. "There's a fairly good counseling center here. If you'd like I can help you find someone."

"Oh, I'm already going, thanks, though."

Actually, I'd stopped seeing Ronnie Wang. I wasn't good at hiding my secrets from her. Every time world hunger or environmental disasters made me weep she got more and more suspicious.

In my psych class, before the final, I was going over the mental disorders and reread the definition of schizotypal.

"Odd beliefs or magical thinking, as well as an inability to maintain close relationships outside of the family." Hadn't that been me since Jeni disappeared? I thought about John, Tania and Perry. I wondered if I really was ill—not just an impressionable Psych 101 student; that would have explained everything. I wondered again if the people in the house were real at all. The marks were still there on my abdomen but I'd read about people who thought they were abducted by aliens. They found scars on their shins and arms, on the webbing between their thumbs and first fingers. The marks were real to them but who was to say what was real and how those marks had gotten there? And maybe I'd bought the dress at the used-clothing store on Telegraph. It looked more like a rag now than I had remembered it from that night.

I began to read fairy stories ravenously, as if hidden in their pages I would find some clue as to who these people were. I checked *A Field Guide to the Little People* out of the library and stared at drawings of brownies, elves, fae and shapeshifters as if they were real, as if I might recognize in them some reminder of Tania's neck, Perry's smile, John's eyes. Even though the dark stories made me queasy and gave me shivers, I thought they were better than reality, especially when reality was goblins replicating in my mother's body and stealing my best friend away without a trace.

Whatever or whomever my new friends were I was better for what had happened. I hardly noticed Lauren anymore; nothing she said bothered me. Light looked more beautiful to me than it ever had. Touching the water in the fountain on Sproul Plaza. Shifting through the leaves of Strawberry Canyon when I ran the trails there. Glittering in a metallic haze. I could smell the seasons changing in the air. The breeze from the bay brought salt and minerals. The homeless people were like trees that had come alive to walk the avenue. Everything sounded more intense, too. Drummers on the street sent their beats through my skin. The bells of the campanile made me see streaks of color in the sky. The poetry Melinda Story read to us in class with her soft voice—John Donne, John Milton, John, John, John (did it mean something that they all shared this name?)—sent chills along my spine and made the finer hairs stand up on the nape of my neck. I wept but even that had a heightened air, in spite of what Ronnie Wang believed, as if my tears were for the sky and earth and sea and stars as much as for myself. The only sense that seemed weaker was taste—the only food I wanted was theirs; theirs the only drink that could slake my thirst. I was changing. I was falling apart. Or maybe I was just discovering who I really was.

11. Things that are there that you can't see

Christmas was coming and I'd be going home for a few weeks. I wasn't relieved the way I would have thought I'd be. I wished, for the first time then, that Bean was real, that I could have gone home with her to her imaginary house full of imaginary brothers and dogs and good food that no one would force me to eat but that I could enjoy watching them gorge on. No one would be sick and no one would be too beautiful or too desirable and no one would be missing.

During finals week I shambled around in a daze. The light wasn't numinous anymore by then; it hurt my eyes. The loud sounds made my ears ring. Every muscle in my body was tight, my jaw clenched like a vise and when I had to take tests I broke out in ice-sweats. The sight or sound of Lauren caused the same reaction. On the streets, I startled easily, thinking someone was watching me. The huge homeless man, especially. I saw him more than I would have liked, lumbering by or rocking back and forth on street corners, head cocked to the side, always looking. At night I lay awake, a vision of him looming above me, flexing his hands. What did it mean?

In my notebook I wrote, *The giant is watching.* Then, when that didn't help me sleep any better, I called Officer Liu.

"There's this guy," I said, when I finally got him on the phone. "This homeless guy. Really tall?"

"Burr Linden." I could almost see the annoyance on Liu's face, the way his fingers tapped impatiently on his desk.

"Can you tell me anything about him?"

"Is there a problem?"

"Every time I turn around he's watching me. On Halloween I think he was following me. He gave me this flyer for a party. And now I see him all the time."

"Burr's been on the streets for a few years now. Was a student. Then institutionalized. But he walked and no prior record of anything but vagrancy."

"Was he ever questioned in connection with . . ."

Officer Liu cleared his throat. "Miss Silverman, I've told you, we're on top of things. Now, if you have a specific incident to report I'd be happy to assist you, otherwise I think this is a waste of both of our time, frankly."

No help there. So in order to sleep at night I smoked one hit of the joint I'd hidden in my drawer. I didn't want to use it up—my only proof of the people in the house besides the marks that were still on my stomach—but it was the only way I could rest. When it was almost gone I put the rim of ragged, burned paper back in my dresser. Their mouths had touched it. Their mouths that could provide me with both pleasure and oblivion.

———

As soon as the last final was over I got on a plane and flew into the Valley and my parents were there at the airport waiting for me.

My mom looked different; right away I knew why they hadn't wanted me to come home. She was wearing a scarf tied around her head and she'd lost a lot of weight. Her face looked drawn under the makeup she had on; it was rare to see her made up at all. I tried to smile in spite of how hard it was with the lump clogging my throat.

We hugged and I had to struggle not to pull away first. It hurt too much. If I let myself I'd dissolve in her arms and she was the one who needed comforting now. I couldn't let her see my tears. I also wished that I wasn't so thin, that I had some cushioning for her, a soft place.

My dad hardly seemed to register that I was there. I'd never felt that from him in my life. If anything, he'd always been too attentive. We joked that they should have named me Miranda, also from *The Tempest,* Prospero's daughter, not his sprite. The overprotective, bookish Prospero was a lot like my father. He hugged me stiffly and, picking up my luggage, hurried toward the car. The smog was so thick that the sky just looked like a solid wall of pale gray and if you didn't know there were hills in the distance you would never have believed it.

It made me wonder about other things that are there, things you can't see.

My parents did their best. They didn't bring up anything that might be disturbing to any of us, which meant we didn't talk much at all about anything of depth. If the conversation got tense, my dad asked how things were going with my therapist and left it at that. But I knew they were trying to make the stay nice for me. We pretended to be happy, pretended that everything was fine. We went to movies, out to eat. My mom even took me shopping at the mall on the day of Christmas Eve.

She wasn't a shopper; that was what Jeni and I did. We spent hours at that mall, seeking clues on how to look cute from the mannequins in the windows and the girls parading around. We sprayed each other with expensive perfume at the makeup counter and ate ice cream and saw movies. We loved being in that enclosed, magical world where it was always daylight, mirrors flashing, it was always sweet-smelling, like sugar and candy and the musks and ambers and roses, jasmines, gardenias of the perfumes. We joked about hiding away in a department store one night and playing there until morning like newlyweds in an enchanted mansion.

When my dad dropped me and my mom off I remembered one reason I preferred going to the mall with Jeni: my mother wasn't the most discriminating shopping partner. She just told me everything looked great; she loved me too much to really see. Jeni loved me that much as well but she would have gently made suggestions about the most flattering colors and styles.

Tania would have also told me the truth about how I looked, though not as kindly, but she was far away in Berkeley, with Perry Manners and John Graves. More and more, I wanted to be back there. I wanted a taste of that drink again and to feel the way I had when I danced in their parlor with the night swirling around us outside. In my fantasy we were dancing and drinking their brew. They led me outside into the garden and we took off our clothing and rolled in the soft earth, then splashed each other with water from a fountain. We shivered under the moon, still dancing, still drinking. The moon shone through the branches of the trees, patterning the uncut grass with a lattice of shadows. Back inside the house the fire was burning in the fireplace. It heated our chilled, delighted bodies as we lay tangled in front of it and finally slept.

"Ariel?"

A touch on my shoulder pulled me out of my reverie. Anxious eyes watched me from a freckled face. Katie Leiman?

Katie was one of the girls who had gone on the class trip to Berkeley. In fact, she had been Jeni's roommate on the trip. She had gone to sleep next to Jeni and when she woke in the morning, Jeni and her Hello Kitty purse were gone.

I had gone to see Katie right after we found out. She hadn't wanted to talk to me. She sat huddled on the edge of her bed with her arms crossed on her chest.

"There's nothing to tell anymore," she said gruffly. "I already talked to the cops."

I realized, then, with a sick feeling in my stomach, that I was actually jealous of her for being the last known person to have seen my Jeni that night. Jeni, who would never have snuck out without me.

Katie had wanted me to stop asking questions and leave and in a way I was glad. I couldn't look at her.

She never spoke to me at school after that, only eyed me warily like a frightened animal. I thought of a little possum that my dad ran over once. I saw its little snout turned up in fear, its eyes aglitter, before I screamed and the car passed over and it was too late.

Katie went to USC instead of Berkeley. As far as I knew, every kid who had gone on that trip had decided to go to a different school after all.

"How are you?" I asked.

She shrugged. "Okay. You?"

I forced a nod.

"Hey," she said, glancing nervously back at her friends, who stood chatting obliviously in line at the food court, armed with shiny shopping bags. "I've been thinking about things. I wanted to talk to you. Can we talk?"

We exchanged numbers and before I could ask her any more, her friends called to her, leaving me wondering what Katie Leiman had to tell me after all this time. The three girls threw their arms around each other's shoulders and wandered away.

Katie had reminded me why I needed to go back to Berkeley. It wasn't for the dream of John, Tania and Perry. It was for Jeni.

I couldn't eat the tamales my dad brought home for dinner. The lights on the tree hurt my eyes. I left the table as soon as I could and called Katie. My heart felt as if it had stopped, replaced by the incessant rings of her phone. It was Christmas Eve. What if she didn't pick up?

But she was there. "I wanted to tell you something," she said.

I waited, biting at a cuticle, my legs jiggling up and down. "Is it about Jeni?" I finally asked when she didn't say anything.

"Sort of."

"Sort of? Is it or not?" I was pissed. A year and a half had gone by and Katie hadn't even called me; she'd waited until she ran into me at a mall.

"I didn't like the teacher who took us on that trip," she said. "I think he's a creep."

"Did he do something?" I tensed my thighs to keep my legs from shaking; the repetitive movement was making me nauseous.

"No. And the police checked him out. There wasn't anything. But he just gave me the creeps. I thought you should know."

"Why didn't you tell me before?" I asked.

"I didn't really think about it. But I keep having these nightmares. About her."

I gulped down air. "Like what?"

"He was just looking at her in this way."

"How did he look at her, Katie?"

"You know, leering or whatever. There was something slightly messed up about it."

"In the dream or really?"

"Both, sort of. But like I said, I told the cops. They told me he had an alibi."

There was a pause in which I tried unsuccessfully to straighten out the tangled threads of my thoughts. "I came to you a year ago," I said.

"I know. It hadn't really sunk in yet. I was in shock I think. My mom says it's post-traumatic stress. But when I ran into you like that I thought it was a sign, that I should at least try."

I didn't blame her for reading our meeting in the mall as a sign; that was all I seemed to do lately.

I went over to my bookshelf and found the last yearbook Jeni was in. I hadn't opened it in a long time but now I turned to her picture—the big eyes, the sweet, sweet smile. Tears blurred the image and I batted them away. No use crying now. I had to see clearly. Then I looked up all the kids that had gone on the trip with her: Katie Leiman and also Lex Salverson, Michael Chan, Isabella Franco, Jessica Landers, J.T. Lemus. Everyone smiling, no missing girls yet. They had all come home to Los Angeles and she hadn't. They had all been questioned, nothing found.

I turned to the faculty page and looked up Mr. Kragen, who had chaperoned them. He wore too-large glasses and his face was pudgy and pale. As Katie said, Mr. Kragen had been questioned and nothing had tied him to Jeni's disappearance.

I thought, *But he has never talked to me. In all this time he has never talked to me.*

Mr. Kragen lived on a nice, tree-lined street not far from my house. I'd seen him out in front before, wearing polyester slacks, watering down his cement driveway.

I knocked on the door and waited. A Ford Taurus was parked in the driveway and I could hear the television talking inside. After a while I heard the key turn in the lock and Mr. Kragen opened the door.

He looked just like his yearbook photo except that he was smiling.

"Hello?" he said dully.

"Hi, Mr. Kragen. My name is Ariel Silverman."

He peered out into the dark. "Yes?"

"I went to Reed."

"I have a lot of students," he said. "Were you a student?"

"I was friends with Jeni Benson?"

He coughed and started to close the door. "I'm sorry, I can't help you."

"I was just wondering if you would let me talk to you about Jeni," I said.

The hairs were standing up all over my body like antennae. Why had I waited so long to come? I must be stronger now, I told myself. I must stay strong.

Mr. Kragen stared at me and I thought I saw something change almost imperceptibly in his myopic eyes.

"Why don't you come in, then. Have a cup of tea. Get warm."

I watched him lock the door behind me.

The house was immaculately clean and orderly. It smelled

of disinfectant. There wasn't a live thing anywhere but that wasn't why I felt a chill on the back of my neck as if the night had followed me inside. There weren't any books, I noticed that, because I am always interested in people's books. But maybe he kept his books in another room. There weren't any photographs but that wasn't necessarily strange, either. It wasn't even that cold inside.

I could feel him watching me and I turned around. His face was curiously babylike around the nose and mouth.

"Make yourself at home," he said. "I'll get tea."

He padded into the kitchen and I sat gingerly on the sofa and waited. My pulse was racing and I was starting to sweat in the cold air, so that the perspiration evaporated icily on my neck, but I made myself stay still.

Kragen settled himself in an armchair across from me and poured my tea, though he left his cup empty.

"So you and Jennifer were close?" he said. There was a phlegmatic sound to his voice that I remembered as if I had been in his class yesterday.

I twirled the beads on my bracelet. "We were best friends."

"I'm sorry," he said. "It was an awful thing that happened."

"I'm talking to everyone who knew her. I'm doing this sort of project to remember her."

He pressed his lips together and shook his head from side to side. "Just an awful, awful thing.".

"What do you remember about Jeni Benson?" I asked. "From the trip."

"She was a nice girl," he said stiffly. "Charming laugh, I remember that. But I didn't know her well."

I held out the flyer I'd brought with me and watched his expression closely. His eyelids fluttered as he looked at Jeni's radiant little face smiling back at him. I saw, for just a fraction of a second, his tongue poke out between his lips and then retract again.

"So sad." He looked away from the picture.

"Did you see anything strange that night? I think you were one of the last people to see her." My voice got harder than I'd intended it to.

He cleared his throat. "I've spoken to the police already. It's been quite some time."

"Oh, I know. I just wanted some personal details. For my project."

Mr. Kragen stood up, wiping his palms on the front of his synthetic trousers.

"Maybe you should leave now," he said.

"Just a few more questions. Please."

He shook his head. "I'm sorry. This isn't a good time."

Without meaning to, I grabbed at his arm. His skin was soft and cold. "This is important!"

He shook me off and his eyes flashed behind his glasses. "I'm sorry, Miss . . . What was your name? Silverman? I can't speak to you any more now. You'll have to go or I'll have to call someone."

"Fine!" I said. "Call someone. What are you going to say?"

"That you're disturbing me in my home."

My voice went up a notch. "What did you do to her?"

"The officers have already been here. I'm sure they'll be interested in the fact that you're trespassing."

"I'm sure they're very interested in anything that has to do with you," I said.

But then I saw Kragen pick up the phone and I turned and left.

I called Rodriguez the next day. "This is Ariel. I was a friend of Jennifer Benson's. Am. I spoke with you last year."

He cleared his throat and I heard papers being shuffled. "Yeah, sure. Miss Silverman, right? You doing okay?"

"I found something that might be of interest to you." I hesitated, knowing how weak it would sound.

"Do you want to tell me what that is?"

"I went over to see that teacher who chaperoned the trip? Kragen?"

"Uh huh."

"Something wasn't right."

I could picture Rodriguez's big, handsome face, the way he pursed his lips and rubbed his chin. "Kragen. The teacher. We checked him out, Ariel. He's clean. The guy he roomed with gave him a perfect alibi. I'm sorry. There just aren't any new leads."

I wanted to tell the detective that the hairs on my arm stood up in Kragen's presence. Like most things it would only have made things worse.

12. The secret places I'd show you

As far as Kragen went, there was nothing I could do except to keep an eye on him when I returned to L.A., write about what had happened in my notebook and look for more evidence in the city where Jeni had disappeared. The experience in L.A. had set me more on edge. I was afraid that Kragen had been involved in Jeni's disappearance, afraid that he hadn't because that meant I wasn't any closer to discovering what had happened to her. I was afraid of the homeless man who I believed was watching me, even when I couldn't see him.

There was no one to remind me to avoid John, Tania and

Perry, though; Coraline Grimm was nowhere to be seen and there were rumors about a breakdown of some kind. I wondered, as I rode the shuttle in from the Oakland airport, back down through the little town full of students and three people I couldn't stop thinking about, why—especially considering that my mother had lost all of her hair and one breast and that I was not there to comfort her after her treatments and that she was not in Berkeley to comfort me—I had waited so long to go back to the house where John lived. And not just to slake my desire. Their beauty, their glamour, just their attention, would give me strength.

One day I saw them on campus, near the English building, walking together arm in arm. I moved behind a tree to watch them more closely. All of them dressed in their usual finery, leaning together, laughing at some secret joke. They didn't see me but my body heated up as if they were all holding me in their arms, as if it were theirs.

I decided to take this spotting of them as another sign.

The blue silk dress was still crumpled in the hamper—I hadn't wanted to look at it before. I took it out, hand washed it in the bathroom sink and hung it to dry. I even ironed it with the iron my mom had insisted I take but I never used. On the first Saturday after school started, I put the dress on with my cowboy boots.

I sat at my desk applying the perfume, mascara and lip gloss I'd bought at the mall. As I was brushing my hair out, loose to my waist, I caught Lauren staring at me. "You look all dolled up. Where are you going?"

"Lauren," I said, still brushing. "What's your problem?"

"What?" She tossed her hair back and forth over the side of the bed, eyeing herself in the mirror above her nightstand. "Random! I just commented on the fact that you look *nice*?"

"You know what I mean." I turned away from my own

reflection to look at her. "The tampon last semester? That was fucked up. Come on."

She rolled her eyes. "God! Paranoid much? What are you even talking about? Tampon? I mean, I've heard guys in the bathroom talk about how you don't dispose of them properly if that's what you mean."

"My blood is preferable to your shit," I said, too quietly for her to hear.

"What did you say?"

I put on my coat, went to the door; then I stopped. "And if you're going to have sex tonight, could you please do it before I get back or go to your boyfriend's room?"

Her voice followed me out the door. "If you have a problem with me and Dallas you might want to try getting laid yourself. It does wonders for tension."

I flipped her off but only through the wall.

In the stairwell I practically slammed into Tommy Leeds, who was on his way up. He took a step back and stared at me.

"Hey," he said.

"Hey." I kept walking down the steps.

"Ariel? Right?"

I didn't remember ever telling him my name. All the searching for Jeni had probably given me more of a reputation than I was aware of. I stopped and looked up at him, poised on the landing above. His eyes looked electric, plugged into a hidden socket, and I remembered hearing Lauren say recently that he was a bit of a speed freak.

"Looking good."

I knew he wouldn't have even said hello if my hair was back, if I was wearing a baggy sweatshirt and jeans. "Ready to talk to me about Jeni Benson?"

"I get that was a big fucking trauma but you need to let it

go." I guess I wasn't cute enough to keep from pissing him off about that. He kept walking.

I spun and ran up after him, grabbed his sleeve. "Yes, it was a big fucking trauma and you can speak respectfully about it or go fuck yourself."

He pushed me off of him. "Valium, anyone? Fuck!"

I was sprinting by the time I hit the pavement outside the dorms. I couldn't get to the house fast enough. My heart throbbed in my throat as I ran up into the hills.

They were there. They were there. They had to be.

I knocked on the door, knowing it—I could feel them. Or did I just want them to be there so much that I thought I could feel them? Or was I so terrified that they *would* answer that it had distorted my senses?

There was no response and my hand shook as I held it near the door, ready to knock again. They had to be . . .

If I left, where would I go? Back to the dorm room where Lauren was fucking her boyfriend and decorating with my tampons? To Telegraph where the homeless people wandered? Maybe I could find the dreadlock man and ask him what he had meant when he said, "The daimons exist everywhere. If you deny them they will appear in your head! Arise." I could go to the library and find a book of poetry and disappear inside it. But it was hard to imagine ever wanting to come out again.

The thought of that made my throat close up and I raised my fist to knock again but just as I did the door opened and warm air hit my skin.

"It's the sylph!" she said. "Johnny, it's the sylph!"

It was as if I'd never left Thanksgiving night. I slipped so easily back into their world. They fed me again—a simpler meal this time. Steamy broth with nutty-tasting soba noodles and crisp lotus root and burdock and seaweed and tofu. I recognized everything from the Japanese restaurants my parents took me to but nothing compared to these tastes.

"Eat your lotus," Perry instructed.

"It'll make you live forever," Tania added, in her mysterious purr.

John was quiet, watching me from the other side of the table. I couldn't really look directly at him.

For dessert we had mounds of green tea mochi ice cream in pale pink bowls. It had a rich, sweet, almost chalky texture and a powdery softness. I felt like I'd been starving for months, which was sort of true.

My companions and I ate and drank and smoked and talked. The candles burned, dripping wax onto the tablecloth, illuminating their faces, making shadows in the hollows of their cheekbones. They were even more beautiful than I remembered them. Tania's hair had grown out a little and she had dyed it a soft pink color. She wore a gold mesh dress and gold sandals. The dress showed off the roses tattooed on her shoulders. They were so lifelike; it seemed as if they had blossomed out of her flesh.

"Tell us about your classes," Tania said, licking the ice cream off her spoon.

"I can't really tell yet. English lit, classics, creative writing and I got into an upper division class on modernist poetry." Melinda Story had recommended me to the teacher who was her advisor.

Perry grinned. "Oh the joys of freshman year. How are your grades, Sylph?"

"Good. I got all As last semester."

"Keep it up," Tania said. "Don't let anything slide. That's how we got where we are today."

Where they were. "Yeah, not bad." I looked around at the

white garlands of leaves and flowers embossed on the ceiling and walls. "Do you mind if I ask how three starving grad students afford this?"

Perry lowered his eyes and raised his glass. "To Marisa Manners, boho artist extraordinaire. Who has made up in death"—he gestured around the room—"for her negligence in life."

And Tania clinked and continued. "His mom. She left him this house and a small fortune so we're just biding our time, preparing to be discovered." She threw up her arms.

"Although who gets discovered in Berkeley? I keep telling them we should move to L.A. Or New York," Perry said.

"We'd be miserable there." It was the first thing John had contributed besides a brief greeting when I'd arrived.

I finished my drink; the warmth in my veins made me feel bold. "You never know. You should come visit sometime. I'd show you the secret places."

"Really? There are secret places in Los Angeles?" He was staring at me so intently and I wanted to avoid it but I forced myself to look back at him.

"You should come. You should all come."

"Want to see *our* secret places?" Tania asked.

She and Perry and I went outside. The night was misty and chill—we could see our breath, and the earth under my toes—I'd left my boots inside the house—was soft with wetness. The fairy lights were on, twinkling in the trees. It was like the fantasy I'd had in L.A. except that John didn't come; he said he was going to read a bit. I wanted to run back in and take his hand.

Tania led the way through the trees to a hedge. Where it parted stone steps descended into a dark garden. Roses grew everywhere—I couldn't see them that well in the darkness, except as soft, slightly glowing shapes, but I smelled them and I wondered again how they could grow like that this time of year. In the dim I saw what looked like a small, vine-covered gazebo with a tree growing up through the middle and bits of broken statuary scattered around. I heard the splash of water but I still couldn't make out the source. The whole thing reminded me of the secret garden I had dreamed of finding throughout my childhood. Jeni and I even had a game where we pretended we had found it. We would describe it to each other as we wandered through my neatly groomed backyard—the imagined overgrowth of vines and flowers, the hidden fantasy grottos.

Perry flopped onto the mossy ground in spite of the cold and damp. Tania danced in the moonlight, her dress swaying around her legs. I could see the outline of her body underneath the fabric.

"If you want to be our friend, really our friend," Tania said. She stopped dancing and looked at me. "Do you?"

"Yes, of course," I answered.

"Then there are some things you have to do for us."

I'd seen my mom without her hair.

I had never been kissed by a boy.

Jeni was gone.

I felt in that moment that I would do anything they asked, as long as I could be part of this world.

"Take off your clothes," Tania said.

I laughed. "You already saw me naked."

"Not naked. Only topless in your panties." There was a slight taunting tone in her voice, like the mean, popular girls at my high school, like Lauren, but there was a softness, too, a seductive note, something breathless.

My heart beat faster. They would see everything—the cleft and hair between my legs.

"Why just me?"

"It's our house," Tania teased, just a hint of smile in her voice. "It's our rules. You want us."

"That's only half of it," Perry added breathily.

What did that mean? That *they* wanted me? That's what it felt like. They wanted *me*?

I was barefoot already. It was just my coat, the blue silk dress, my bra and panties. The underwear was cream and light blue lace, a Christmas present from my mom.

I took off the coat and dropped it on the ground. Goose bumps rose on my arms. Perry gathered my coat in his arms, almost tenderly, the way you would pick up after a child you cared about.

I wasn't ready to take the dress off yet so I removed my underpants and clutched them in my hand, not sure what to do with them. Finally I set them on the ground, too, but Perry didn't touch them; I was relieved. It was easy to slip the bra off. The silk of the dress felt good against my bare skin. My nipples were stiff from cold, pushing up the fabric.

"Dress. Now," said Tania.

I hesitated, hoping she meant it as a verb. She didn't.

"It's my dress anyway, remember? I gave it to you."

I turned away from them and pulled the dress off over my head, held it in front of me as I turned back around, covering John's marks, as I'd come to think of them. I felt conscious of how thin I was, how wide and lethal my hip bones looked.

Tania snapped her fingers and held her hand out. "My dress."

"Tania, be nice," Perry said.

"It's just a game." The sweet Tania voice. "Ariel knows it's just a game."

Just a game? This reassured me somewhat. I gave her the dress and stood shivering in front of them.

"Now we are going to ask you some questions," Tania said.

I waited. My whole body was trembling with cold, even my hair and nails.

Perry's voice was softer than usual. "She's freezing."

"This won't take long." Tania stood and came to me. "And it's refreshing for the skin." She took my hair gently and brought it back over my shoulders so it no longer covered my chest. Her hands grazed the tops of my breasts and I felt the skin there instantly warm.

She went and sat down again.

"Answer quickly and without thinking. Have you ever been kissed?"

I took a second. "Yes."

"By a boy?"

My cheeks got hot even in the cold. "No."

"By a girl?"

"Yes."

"Who?"

I stopped. This one I didn't want to answer.

"Who?" she demanded.

"Jeni," I said, my head lowered.

"Jeni who?"

I crossed my arms over my chest to keep myself from shaking. "My friend. The one on the flyer."

It was quiet for a moment. Tania's eyes downcast. "I'm sorry," she said.

I didn't want to stop and think about Jeni. "Go on."

And Tania did. "French kissed?"

"No."

"Been licked?"

"No."

"Fingered?"

"No."

"So you've never been fucked?"

"No."

"Have you ever come?"

Oh God. "I don't think so. I'm not sure."

"Then the answer is no," Perry said.

I felt like a brutalized contestant on a reality TV show. And I was thinking this: if Jeni had not disappeared I would not be standing naked in a garden with these strangers staring at me, humiliating me. No part of me would have wanted it. Now I wanted it.

"Were you ever abused? Sexually?" Tania asked.

"No!"

"I have been," Tania said quietly. "Stepfather." This caught me off guard and I forgot about myself for a second. I didn't know how to respond but I didn't have to. She was already on to the next question.

"Do you know any poetry?"

I nodded.

"Recite something."

I only knew one whole piece by heart. It was the Baudelaire. I saw Jeni's postcard in my mind, the way the photo of the Conservatory of Flowers stuck out of the top of my book, as I said the words.

"Bravo." Perry was clapping before I even finished.

"Very nice," Tania said. "And a Frenchy. Too bad you don't know it in the original." She cleared her throat.

"*La Lune, qui est le caprice même, regarda par la fenêtre pendant que tu dormais dans ton berceau, et se dit: 'Cette enfant me plaît.'*"

"Are you finished?" I asked. "Can I get dressed?"

"No. No. Not finished. Perry has questions, too." She stroked Perry's curls. "Go for it, love lamb."

"Tell me how you define the prevalence of addiction in our current society."

I thought for a moment. I thought of myself drinking, thinking about drinking, thinking about these people in this house, desiring them. I had wondered why the feelings were so strong, what they symbolized. There was so much missing from my life—love, connection, comfort. But my desire was for more than just that. It was for the fleeting feeling I got when I looked at the full moon in the trees or when I watched the play of light on shallow water or for the feeling certain music gave me until the song ended.

"An absence of devotion?" I said.

Perry grinned. "Very, very good." He looked straight into my eyes. Even in the darkness I could see an eerie flicker of light that seemed to be coming from inside of him. "Do you believe in the continuation of the soul?" he asked.

"And why or why not?" Tania added.

I had not been raised religiously. My dad was Jewish and my mom was Catholic but they had both given it up for what they called the religion of poetry. Beautiful language was the way to feel close to spirit. But what happened when the person died and there was no more language left? My parents had never taught me anything about what they believed happened after death. It just wasn't discussed. Now I had to think about it because there was a chance my mom would be gone soon.

Would die soon.

I hadn't let myself fully accept it yet, not until that moment, standing naked in the misty garden before them. And they were asking me about the soul. I didn't even know what that meant.

But I felt something. I just couldn't articulate it. It was connected to those responses stirred by moonlight and water and poetry and music, those resonances that I couldn't explain. It was what I felt when I thought of my parents, especially my mom, and when I thought of Jeni and now, somehow, in a twisted way, when I looked at these two people I didn't know, viewing my naked body and my more naked soul in the green tangle of their garden.

What was soul? And did it continue?

"I don't know," I said. "I wish I did."

"Well, that's not going to help Johnny with his dissertation, is it?" Tania pouted.

"What?"

"He's writing about it." Tania walked toward me, looking me up and down. "I see you can get naked, you can recite Baudelaire and you can answer the addiction question correctly but you don't know if the soul goes on." She came closer. I flinched and she laughed. "You look like you think I'm going to whip you. Come here." She reached out and hugged me. Her body heat relieved the chill that had iced my bones. I couldn't help clinging onto her for an extra moment before she pushed me away—not hard, but firmly.

"There are only two more things you have to do. Since you couldn't answer the question."

I met her eyes and pushed my shoulders back. "Okay. Go."

Tania was pointing to the ground. It sloped downward, toward the hidden center of the garden, growing muddier as it went.

"What?" I asked.

"I want you to roll in it."

"Oh my god, this *is* reality TV."

Perry laughed. "You got that right. I told you, T."

"Reality is bullshit," Tania said. "Kids these days. Come on. It's fun."

"Don't freak. I'll show you how it's done." Perry pulled off his T-shirt but kept on his brown velvet jeans—I couldn't help worrying that they'd be ruined. His torso was perfectly cut—I could see every muscle in his abdomen and that aroused me in spite of myself. He reached out his brown, sinewy arm to me and I took his hand. He brought me down to the ground with him. The mud squished up between my toes and thighs. It had a rich, mineral scent and clung to my skin.

"Not just sit. Roll," Tania said.

I lowered myself down onto my belly and rolled over onto my back, then onto my belly again. Why was I doing this?

I rolled down the slope after Perry—the mud tangling in my hair, getting into my nose and mouth—and stopped by a small pool full of rushes and water lilies. A waterfall spilled from a small outcropping of rocks along the side; that was the sound I'd heard.

"And now water," Tania said. She had followed me. She watched as Perry pulled me up. He was covered in mud also and he pushed me gently toward the pool. I stumbled forward into the water. It was deeper than it appeared and colder. I shuddered.

"Don't stop now," she said.

I forced myself to go in, up to my neck. My whole body was convulsing with cold. I thought of John, back in the warm house. Why was I—

"Okay," Tania said. "Good enough."

I staggered out of the water, shaking so hard I wasn't sure I could stay upright.

"Let's get you inside," Perry said softly, draping my coat around my shoulders. "Are you all right, sweetie? It wasn't too much, was it?" The tenderness in his voice after the rush of coldness made my womb ache. I understood something perfectly in that moment—the eroticism of the soft glove after the whip.

The fire had been lit and the warmth hit me hard as I walked inside. The coat itched my skin.

"May I please have my dress?" I asked. Tania's eyebrows went up. "*Your* dress?"

She laughed but handed it to me and I slipped it on. "There you go. That wasn't so bad, was it? You passed the test, Sylph." I was sweating but they didn't seem to mind the heat themselves.

We went into the parlor, where John lay on the ground with his long legs spread out in front of him, firelight making the watery fabric of his green shirt gleam. Tania and Perry sat on the couch. It was hard to imagine that they had been staring at my naked body a short time earlier.

I sat a bit farther off. I didn't know what I was supposed to do now. The fire crackled in the grate but no one spoke.

"Remember when you told me about your thesis?" I asked John.

He turned his head and there was a brightness in his eyes, probably from the firelight, that I wanted to imagine had to do with me. "Yes."

"You believe in the continuation of the soul?"

"I believe the daimon goes on in some form. In a form we recognize if that's the way we perceive the world."

"The daimon?"

John flipped onto his stomach so his face was closer to mine. "Daimons are the spirits in things."

"Is it like demon?"

"Demons are considered evil. Daimons don't have to be. Daimons are everywhere, every rock and tree and body of water, everything. Every culture has some form of them. But people stopped believing in them so they had to find different ways to be recognized."

"If you deny them they will reappear in your head."

"Exactly."

"There's a homeless man on the street. And the first time I passed him he said that. I thought he meant demon."

"They appear in psychology, in dreams, anywhere they can be accepted. They don't just come for their own purposes. Without them people are nothing, zombies. Daimons are souls and I don't think they ever just vanish into some void."

"Because my friend . . ." I began.

Tania reached out for me. "Come here," she said. "Come, baby, come closer to the fire."

"I'm too hot."

"Come closer."

I found myself moving toward them. The heat was so intense, especially after the cold of the garden. My head was a-throb and it was hard to breathe. Moisture trickled into my eyes like tears.

"It's purifying," Tania said. "It will help you understand."

"Understand what?"

"Who we are. Who you are."

"Who are you?" But maybe I didn't want to understand. Suddenly a black shade of anxiety was dropping down over my mind. I needed air. I was gasping for it.

"Are you okay?" John asked. He got up and came to sit beside me, handed me a glass of water and I took a small sip. He brushed some hair from my cheek. "You sure you're okay?"

"I feel a little light-headed."

John turned to Tania and Perry. "I'll take her home," he said.

Just like the last time he put me in the finned car with the torn upholstery and drove me to the dorms. We didn't talk the whole way; I was too exhausted from the night. I sat breathing that warm, heady flower-smoke scent that seemed to follow them everywhere and staring at a crystal pendant that looked like a piece from a chandelier hanging from the rearview mirror. I wondered if it might hypnotize me if I stared at it long enough.

"We're going away for a little while," John said. "To visit some friends. Can I see you when we get back?"

I nodded, still staring at the piece of crystal. I wanted to ask if I had passed the test, if I was an initiate into their world now, but if he was saying he wanted to see me when they returned, I assumed I was. The question really was, how long could I stand to be away from them?

When we got to the dorm, John walked me to the door of the lobby and opened it for me but he didn't come inside.

13. Nor can the circles of the stars tire out their dancing feet

I went to classics Monday morning and sat in the back of the huge lecture hall as Professor Gordon, a small man with a neat, pointed beard, told us about the origin of tragedy.

"*Tragos*," he said, in a gruff voice, "which means goat dance. The first tragedies were enactments, songs and dances to praise the god Dionysus. Now we are not only robbed of our rituals. Even the gods and goddesses we have left—the actors and actresses we worship in films whom we can identify with all the traits of the traditional deities—are forced to enact mostly comedy, works with no tragic element or with potentially tragic elements that are resolved in Hollywood's so-called happy endings. Without the performance to contain it, the tragic seeps into our daily lives with acts of real violence."

And as I sat there, looking down the steep sides of the

dark auditorium to the small circle of light where the goat-like professor stood, I thought of Jeni again. And I thought of John's question about the soul. Had Jeni vanished because someone had lost their soul? Could someone who killed children have a soul? Did Jeni's soul continue on? In what form? I put my burning forehead down on the cool wood of the desk, wondering if I could set it on fire this way, and tried to stop the questions from forming again and again in my brain.

I was sitting on the steps by myself, forcing myself to eat some lunch, when Melinda Story walked by. Stopped.

"Hi, Ariel. How's it going?"

"Fine," I said. "You?"

"I wondered how you like Professor French's class," Melinda said. She was scrutinizing my face.

"Well, I only had one so far but it seems great. Thank you for recommending me."

I was shielding my eyes from the sun to look at her so she sat down next to me in the shade.

"May I ask you a personal question?"

I knew what she was going to ask and I didn't want her to.

"I'm concerned. Are you getting some support?"

"Oh, I'm really fine," I said as brightly as I could. "I got all As last semester and I like my classes."

"I just want to make sure you're not pushing yourself too much. I did the same thing my first year and I had to drop out. I almost never made it back."

"No, really, everything's okay," I told her.

"Do you have friends to talk to?" There were worry lines in her brow. She was so sweet. Why did I want her to leave?

"Oh, I have friends, yeah. They're great. They've been really supportive."

"Good, that's what I want to hear." Melinda patted my

shoulder. "But if you need another friend, you're welcome to come have dinner with me sometime."

I hadn't lied to her, really. I'd gotten straight As and I did like my classes so far. And I had friends. Well, not really friends, but people. I had shared two meals with them, worn their clothes; we had laughed and talked and danced and touched. I just wasn't sure why they had let me into their lives and if I would be allowed to stay. I wasn't sure if they would even call me again when they returned from wherever they had gone.

Eleanor French was a slim woman in her forties who wore beautiful silk blouses, tailored tweed skirts and designer heels. She rhapsodized about the modernist poets in a smoky voice and it made me feel drunk when I listened to her. She started with Yeats, reading aloud from *The Celtic Twilight* about the Sidhe:

"*'Love with them never grows weary, nor can the circles of the stars tire out their dancing feet.'*"

"What did these beings symbolize for Yeats?" she asked. "What was his fascination at a time when God was being questioned?"

I had wondered about the Sidhe before; my parents were always reading me folk and fairy tales when I was little. But somehow rediscovering them in this book, which seemed, especially when read by Professor French, to be written as factual evidence of mystical experience, startled me, even more so in the state I found myself.

I thought again of the defining characteristics of the schizoid personality, of Tania's long arms as she waved them above her head like wisps of smoke, of the roses tattooed on her shoulders and the strangeness of her voice, of Perry's puckish features and green polished nails and of John, always of John—the glister of his eyes, the black, black hair and the thoughts you could almost see spinning in his head, thoughts I wanted to see and understand.

The Sidhe were tall and thin and beautiful with silvery voices and strange, capricious ways. They dealt in magic, in dance and poetry, and also in punishments for misdoings and in the business of stealing souls. I didn't fully know yet why Yeats was fascinated with them but I knew why I was. My own personal Sidhe were gone and I longed for Perry, Tania and John as if they had taken away with them my soul.

Maybe I'd spoken too soon about liking all my classes because by the second week it was clear that my creative writing workshop teacher, Hamilton Portman, had chosen his favorites, and wasn't going to make things easy for the ones he was less impressed with. I was one of the latter.

Out the tall, thin windows of the English building I watched the sun play on the leaves, turning them brighter green. Portman was discussing the writing of a blonde girl named Jessica Steinholtz. He couldn't seem to contain his enthusiasm; he was practically salivating.

"This is exactly what I'm looking for," he exclaimed. "The restraint, the visual imagery, the rhythmic quality of the language."

Jessica Steinholtz was trying to control a smile that kept threatening to break out on her face. It wasn't her fault that the professor wanted to fuck her, I thought. She was beautiful and her writing was good enough. But it all made me uncomfortable.

We went around in a circle discussing Jessica's piece, which was about a young man obsessed with his sister's beautiful best friend. There was something weird about Jessica's descriptions of the gorgeous blonde, obviously based on herself. I kept thinking she would have been wise to at least change the girl's hair color, since the endless praising of the flaxen locks got a little embarrassing. The boys in the class were almost as enthusiastic as the professor and the girls mumbled praise, afraid to appear disagreeable.

When it was my turn I said, "It's really clean but I'm not convinced about the voice. It seems very feminine. I'm not sure a guy would describe her that way. 'The Jimmy Choo stilettos,' 'the perfectly applied shade of her lip gloss.' They seem a little forced, maybe? Plus, the girl's young. Would she have designer shoes like that?"

Professor Portman glared at me across the table. I could feel sweat trickle down the sides of my rib cage and tried to remember if I'd put on deodorant that morning. I was distracted all the time.

"And you are an expert on how young men describe women?" he asked me. There was a slight smirk on his mouth and I suddenly understood the expression about wanting to wipe a look off someone's face, and not gently.

"Not always, no. But it just sounds awkward compared to other places in the story that work."

"And what about designer shoes? It's true, as a very masculine man"—he winked—"I'm not aware if young women wear Jimmy Choos or not. Jessica?"

She grinned and held out her tanned leg, on the end of which a delicate foot dangled a black high-heeled pump.

The class laughed and I hung my head and stared at my silver Converse from Target. I should have known; how stupid.

"Okay." I could swear the teacher rolled his eyes. "Moving on." He shuffled his papers and pulled mine out. "Ariel?"

I felt the panic rise. I wanted to get out of there, clenched my thighs together, trying to relieve the pressure building between them.

My piece was about Halloween at the house. I wondered why I had submitted it. It suddenly felt as if I was standing naked before the class, blood pouring down my legs. This was private and I shouldn't have exposed it here. Also, it made me miss them more.

Professor Portman made me read a short section in my shaking voice. Then he dug in.

"Firstly, I'm wondering if this is fiction at all. There seems to be no distance between the writer and the narrator. The amount of adjectives clutter the piece and make it hard to extrapolate imagery from it. Sometimes the more you describe something, the more obscure it becomes. Show us, don't tell us what you see. For example, the Jimmy Choo shoe in Jessica's piece is more evocative than all these detailed descriptions of the house. Also, what exactly is happening here?" He snapped the page he held with his thumb and first finger. "You mention the dead girl on the flyer but then just kind of drop it."

It wasn't just me that stood naked and bleeding before everyone; it was Jeni. "The dead girl." *I'm sorry,* I told her.

The students critiqued my piece, mimicking pretty much everything Portman had said. By the time they were done I had sweat stains under my armpits. As we walked out, Kyle Langley, a tall guy in a pink Lacoste shirt and glasses, leaned over me and whispered, "You smell *great,* Ariel! Is that your natural *odor*?"

I *hadn't* remembered my deodorant and the smell coming from my body was the toxin fear.

But I couldn't write my classes off; I needed to do well. It was something I could control, unlike my mother's health, Jeni, John, Tania or Perry. And Tania had told me not to let anything slide, as if she were warning me that I had to get good grades. It had always been easy to do this in high school and I couldn't stop now when so much more was at stake. Maybe what I believed to be my only shot at joy was at stake. Maybe my only chance to see John again.

So I continued to study, I continued to run. I spoke to my parents regularly but I didn't tell them much; I didn't want to be disappointed by their vague, distracted response.

The closest I got to another world was People's Park where the homeless gathered. Sometimes I'd stand at the periphery at night, peering through the trees at the small area of grass, looking for something I couldn't define. A few shadowy shapes moved there, and I wished for John's arms around my chilled shoulders.

At night when Lauren was in Dallas's room I locked the door, put on my headphones and blasted the sound. Metric and Moby and Massive Attack and Miike Snow. Sigur Rós and PJ and Halloween Hotel. And I flung myself like a fool around the room with my phantom brown-eyed best girl friend until I was shaking like a *danse macabre* skeleton.

I wondered, then, if it were really possible to dance, under some bitter and alluring enchantment, until your toes were gone.

14. The cold reminder of the dead

"'I took one look at her head and knew she was the one.'"

In my creative writing class Kyle Langley read a piece about a serial killer.

He took the killer's POV and wrote in first person, present tense about how the guy stalked this woman and killed her and then decapitated her, but for the first two-thirds it read like a love story.

In every scene I saw a girl with Jeni's face.

I couldn't breathe, had to get out of there. My legs jiggled manically under the table as Kyle continued to read. When he was through, Professor Portman nodded sagely. He was graying at the temples and his hairline was receding a little but his features were classically handsome, like an actor playing a professor in a movie. Jessica Steinholtz gazed at him with a half-smile on her glossy lips.

"Good work, Kyle. It's very effective. Creepy as hell. You get us right inside his head and then when we realize where we are, *bam,* it's too late. I think some people may be offended by this piece." He panned the table with his cool blue eyes and I looked down quickly. "But that can be the beauty of something. When you know you got 'em."

My stomach cramped with hunger and with fear. All I wanted was to hear the clock tower chime.

When class was finally over I watched Jessica gather her things slowly and come over to Portman, who stood at the back of his room by his desk. There was something so intimate about the way they leaned in to speak to each other, about the way his gaze dripped over her body, that I looked away quickly. She laughed and tossed back her golden hair.

I thought, *Am I just a prude, jealous bitch? Who needs to get laid? (Where is John? Why hasn't he called?) Or is there something fucked up about having to see your forty-something teacher fall in love with an eighteen-year-old student in public?*

I really wasn't sure which was true. Maybe both. I walked out of the classroom, down the dim hall, down the steps and into the day. I had my iPod on, listening to Björk—her otherworld voice making me feel more vulnerable, lost, in the wrong place. The sun hurt my eyes and I wished I had sunglasses.

I felt a hand on my arm and jumped, thinking it was Kyle Langley, maybe. But it wasn't.

It was John Graves.

I had never been this close to him in the daylight before. It was hard to believe he was really there. His skin looked very pale and he wore sunglasses; I couldn't see his eyes at all.

I reflexively kept walking, fueled by a blast of adrenaline. It seemed dangerous, somehow, to be speaking to him here. I couldn't let the worlds blend; I might lose the one I cared about more.

"May I speak to you?"

"Not here," I said as I kept walking.

He reached out suddenly and grabbed my hand, a bit roughly, and we walked along toward the edge of campus this way. I followed behind him, stumbling a little. My legs were still shaking. I needed to eat something.

As if he'd read my mind he said, "We'll get lunch."

We made our way down Telegraph and then he turned and pulled me through a bamboo gate to a small Japanese garden. The restaurant was quiet, cool and dark and we sat at a booth where the waitress brought us steaming green tea the color of murky jade.

"How are you?" he asked. He had taken off his sunglasses and his eyes looked tired. "We just got back."

"How'd you know where I was?" As I said it, a queasiness stirred in my solar plexus, a mixture of pleasure and mistrust.

"You told us your classes. I know the English department pretty well. I've been here for years."

"Then why don't I see you more?"

"I mostly work at night."

I tugged reflexively on my ponytail holder and let my hair down around my shoulders.

"Why are you so suspicious?" He sighed. "I really missed you."

I didn't answer, couldn't tell him how much I'd missed him, too.

The waitress came to take our order and he asked her for rice, miso soup, edamame and vegetable tempura. He turned to me. "Is that good?"

I nodded. My mouth was already watering.

When she left he said, "I was worried about you the other night. I thought about you the whole time we were away but I wanted to give you a little space. I know it was intense."

"It's okay," I said. I looked into the liquid jade in my cup and lowered my voice. I was afraid that if I expressed any frustration with him for not contacting me, he'd leave.

"How's it going?" he asked. "In school and everything?"

I shook my head. "I don't get it. I don't get why you guys care." I really meant, *Why didn't you contact me while you were gone? Where were you?*

He reached across the table and took my hand. I startled but let him hold it for a few seconds before I drew it away.

"You're important to us, Ariel."

"Why? You don't even know me. I'm nothing. I'm like any other girl you could find on campus except probably less interesting."

"Don't say that."

"Then why?"

"Listen, Ariel. You don't have to question me so much. Or yourself. Tania and Perry and I are just freaks who happen to have the resources to indulge ourselves more than most people. We don't want to scare you. But I'm drawn to you. I wanted to know you better. You seem important to me, almost familiar, and I want to understand that connection better, okay?"

The moment was too intense; I was relieved when the waitress brought our soup. We ate in silence for a while. I didn't really want to talk, I didn't want answers; I just wanted the sensation of warm food in my belly. When we'd finished the meal he said, "There's something I'd like to show you."

I squinted at him. "What?"

"Angels."

We took BART into Oakland and got to the graveyard in the late afternoon. The winter sun was hazy gold through pale clouds. Gray tombstones and crypts stretched out across the hillside among the oaks, pine trees and ginkgos. The silence of the dead hung over everything, even in the exposing light of day. As John had promised, the angels were all there with their eyes raised to the faded blue sky.

"I love this place." He walked beside me, trailing his long fingers, grazing the stones. "I never understood why people don't."

I moved closer to him so that our arms almost touched. My knees weakened and I lost breath; it was hard to continue up the hill. The air smelled pungent with pine needles.

"I like them," he said, and I couldn't look at him. I had to focus on my feet on the ground. "People used to come and dance. They weren't always just austere."

I imagined what it would be like to dance with John in the graveyard, to dance on the graves. Did he want to dance on the graves?

"They're comforting, too," he went on. "In a weird way. They remind me of being part of nature. Like what the Romantics believed. That we go back when we're ready. No heaven or hell."

We walked in silence for a while; the only sound was my

breath and heartbeat and our feet scuffing through the dirt and leaves.

"I can accept my death, better than other people's," I said. "But the part that's hard is not getting to be with who you love. That's what I can't . . ." My voice trailed off into the rapidly cooling air.

"Maybe you'll be with them, just in a different form. Maybe you already were together with the people you love before this."

"Sometimes I feel like that." I wanted to make him stop walking and put my arms on his shoulders, feel the place where his deltoid curved in, the heat through his clothes. I wanted to feel his lips brush against mine like he was turning on a switch that would send the floodlights burning through the darkness inside of me. But maybe he was the darkness.

And he kept walking like he had a destination. "What do you mean?"

"I do feel like I knew my mom, before. And Jeni."

"Ariel?" He stopped walking. "Talk to me."

I shook my head and a harsh little laugh escaped my mouth. "She never came home. I can't let it go. I keep thinking I have some kind of lead and it's nothing. Nothing is anything."

"I'm sorry."

Tears clogged my throat. "I believe there are people who are missing parts of us. But what happens when they're gone?"

He was standing in front of a small tombstone at the crest of the hill. The leaves of the oak tree shadowed his face with shifting patterns.

"You find other missing parts?" He had taken off his sunglasses and his eyes met mine then with the full impact of their green and gold. It was like looking into water or a thicket of trees in a forest. I was afraid of getting lost there like in the eyes of the stone angels, and, at the same time, I wanted to get lost.

I turned away. "Maybe." Across the hills lay the large crypts of millionaires. Why would they need such a palace? I thought of the bones under our feet. I thought of Jeni. How I wished for her to be found unharmed, how I wished for her to be found, and finally, secretly, shamefully, now, when it had become too much, for her bones to be found. Just so we would know.

"Maybe it's us," he said.

Us? He hadn't said "me." Did he mean Tania and Perry, too? John Graves. With me in a graveyard. I hadn't even thought of the irony. Suddenly my back stiffened and I shivered as a breeze moved through the pines and oak trees. The cold reminder of the dead.

He knelt down by the tombstone and ran his fingers over the words engraved there. It was a very small stone. I couldn't see what it said. But John was staring at it like he was trying to crack it with his gaze. He sat cross-legged in the dirt and put his head in his hands. His hair fell across his face.

I came around and stood beside him. I could see the front of the tombstone now. It said, LUCY ELIZABETH WALCOTT 1910–1918. There was a small statue of a sleeping lamb.

A child's tomb. Jeni didn't have a grave. Her parents kept waiting for her to come back.

"I never understood the importance of marking a grave. I believed in fire, ashes, throwing them into the water, whatever. Not this. But something happens to you when you sit here this way." There was a note of deep sadness in his voice I hadn't heard before.

I sat next to him. "What? What's wrong?"

He opened his mouth as if to speak, then shook his head—not a *no* but as if to push something away. "Tell me something about you, please."

"I've been looking for some sign of Jeni. I keep this notebook but there's nothing that means anything. Just all my fears."

"Maybe we can help you look," he said.

I hardly heard him over the onslaught of feelings pounding blood to my head. "And my mom's sick." I hadn't planned on telling him but it was a relief; there had been no one to tell.

His eyes glimmered in the sunlight, so deep like water where you can't find the bottom. "I'm so sorry."

"The C word."

He nodded. "What do they say about it?"

"I don't know. I don't want to know anything."

"Maybe it would help you to know?"

I shook my head, thinking, *Maybe it would help me to know more about you, too. But I don't really know if I want that, either.* "I shouldn't have told you."

"Yes, you should have." He reached his hand out and brushed my arm with the tips of his fingers. I wanted to grab onto him but it felt like if I did he'd have to pry me loose.

I didn't want to be there anymore. I knew the spirits of the dead were already clamoring, disturbed by our voices.

"Can we go now?" I said. I should have just told John how much I missed him when he was gone, how glad I was that he was back, that they were all back, but I kept as silent as the stone angels and their charges.

15. The moon, the goddess, the dark world

After John said good-bye to me at the Berkeley BART station, I went back into my trance. Every morning before class I pounded my feet along the pavement, as hard as I could, running up into the hills and along the trails of Strawberry Canyon, around the stadium and the pool, among the oak trees by the creek bed, over the piles of fallen stones. Around Indian Rock. Morning fog burned away and hawks circled over my head. My mother loved hawks, maybe because my father looked a little like one with his slightly hooked nose and fierce, dark eyes. She was his opposite. A dove. I didn't want to think about it, about them. I wanted to pound all thoughts out of my body.

Melinda Story found me one day as I was leaving Professor French's class. We had moved on from Yeats to Ezra Pound and that day I was still under the spell of *The Cantos* inside my thick, orange book. The mysterious words and symbols sometimes felt like incantations and sometimes like the ramblings of a fascistic madman. Professor French had been discussing Pound's descent into madness. I wondered how connected the poet and the madman were. You could only love the moon, the goddess, the dark world so much without waking before they made you forget that day existed.

"I've been wondering how you are." Melinda had that worried look on her face again.

"Oh, good," I said as matter-of-factly as possible. "You?"

"I was going to ask if you wanted to come to my apartment for dinner. You look like you could use a home-cooked meal."

I thought immediately, guiltily, of the food I'd eaten at John's house. The only food I wanted now. How could anything compare?

"And there's something else I wanted to talk to you about," she said.

There was an element of intensity with which she said it that made me nod.

"So this weekend then?"

Melinda lived near the Oakland border. I took a bus along Martin Luther King, past the police station, and found her place, a small upper-floor apartment in an old building. Inside, the wooden floors were covered with rugs and colorful pillows were stacked on the futon and the floor. Chopin was playing, my mom's favorite composer. And Melinda was into orchids, like my mom. They were grouped by the large picture window—which let the early evening in—observing me like shy little stick puppets. It wasn't easy to stop thinking about my mother. I wondered how it would be when she was gone, how hawks and orchids and Chopin would stab at me like weaponry.

We sat at Melinda's small kitchen table; it had a vintage cloth with a map of California on it. She had made poached salmon, salad and baked potatoes but I didn't want any of it. The thought of fish or other animal protein made my stomach turn. I realized, and not really until then, that I hadn't eaten any meat since Halloween, since I'd been to the house in the hills. I tried to eat the potato but even that got stuck in my throat, a mealy mass of poison whiteness.

"Can I make you something else?" Melinda asked, but not defensively; I could tell she wasn't taking it personally.

"I'm sorry. This is lovely. I just don't eat fish."

"Are you a vegetarian? Vegan? Raw? I'm sorry. Everyone eats so differently here. You should have told me." She moved the platter of fish to the other side of her. "Can you eat the salad?"

"Yes, thanks."

She frowned. "Are you sure you're okay?"

"I'm good, really," I told her. "It's just been a little stressful."

"School can do that. Are your classes okay?"

"Yeah. Except Portman. He thinks I kind of suck."

"I would guess you aren't the one who sucks in there." Melinda grinned. "But seriously, you're a good writer, Ariel." I had given her a few things I'd done, including the description of my first Halloween in Berkeley. "Portman can be tough on the ones he thinks have potential."

I wasn't so sure about that but I thanked her anyway.

After dinner we went into the living room. There was a statue I recognized as the Chinese goddess of compassion, Quan Yin, surrounded by many photographs of a younger Melinda with an Asian woman. The woman was tiny, with a round, sweet face. Melinda picked up one of the framed pictures and handed it to me.

"Who's she?" I asked. "She's so pretty."

"That's Annie." Melinda lowered her voice when she said it. I understood that tone; it was how I would have sounded if someone asked me about a picture of Jeni.

Melinda went on. "When I wasn't eating much, a few years ago, it had to do with what happened to her."

Suddenly cold, I reached for my sweatshirt that was draped over the arm of the couch.

"What happened?"

"I'm not telling you this to scare you. I want to bring it up to show you that I've been where you are and that things can get better."

Melinda's usually dreamy eyes were focused intently on my face. "She was my girlfriend. We were living together as undergrads. She disappeared."

My mind began to race, trying to put everything together

so it made sense. But I sucked at puzzles, I always had, especially when most of the pieces were missing.

"What?"

"It was six years ago now. She was out running and never came home. They questioned her ex. She hated him. But he was cleared."

"I'm so sorry." Words were lame sometimes.

"Thank you. It was really hard." Melinda had that flat tone people use when they're repeating something shocking for the five-hundredth time but she blinked a film of tears out of her eyes and wiped it away with the back of her hand.

"I became a machine," she went on. "Did really well in school. I wanted to stop feeling."

I nodded.

"But it doesn't work. The only way is to feel it."

I wanted to tell her about John, Tania and Perry. They were a way I could stop feeling fear and sadness about my mom and Jeni. But I didn't know how to begin.

"I'm in therapy," I said, just to get her to stop. "And I have a good support system of friends."

"I wanted to let you know I'm here if you need me."

"Do you think there's a connection? With Jeni?"

She leaned forward as if she were going to touch me but then drew back. "I almost didn't tell you because of that. I don't think there's any connection."

"Why?"

"It was a long time ago. And when that happened to your friend. To Jeni. I spoke to the police. I do whenever something . . . happens. They didn't think there was a link."

I shook my head. "Everything keeps getting worse."

"I'm so sorry," she said. When it came from her mouth or from John's it didn't sound empty at all.

When I left, Melinda hugged me. "Be careful getting back."

But I decided to run instead of taking the bus. I didn't know if it was safe or not. But I was motivated by the same thing that John and Tania and Perry made me feel, the last thing, the thing it was hard for me to say, even to myself. The desire to escape.

The next day I went to see Officer Liu. I had to wait for almost an hour before he invited me into his office.

"Anne Berman-Chang," I said as soon as I sat. I had Googled Melinda's Annie.

He folded his pale fingers under his chin. "Yes?"

"I was wondering if you think there's a connection."

"You're a tenacious young lady."

"I can't stop." I lowered my face; the tears behind my eyes felt boiling hot but it would not help to cry. "I'm sorry."

He leaned forward. "Listen, I understand how hard this is. But have you ever heard the expression about accepting what you can't change? This is one of those times."

"The case is unsolved!" I tried not to scream; it seemed I was always trying not to scream at cops. "Annie's! Maybe they're related. Has anyone looked into that?"

He shook his head. "We always check into past incidents. There wasn't anything. Between you and me"—he leaned closer—"and I do mean that. There was allegedly a boyfriend involved. On the football team. We haven't been able to pin anything on him but this is an entirely different kind of murder—" He stopped himself, but too late. "Missing-persons case."

Murder. A chill of nausea spread across the surface of my skin.

His phone rang and I got up and ran to the ladies' room, where I knelt before the toilet and vomited up what little I'd eaten of Melinda's dinner.

16. I lay here before and he watched over me

The flowers were strewn across both beds; they were in glass jars on the desks and dressers. Daisies, lilies, dahlias, freesia, jasmine. All white. There were even long-stemmed roses covering the floor. The smell was overpowering; I felt slightly faint.

Lauren came up behind me as I stood in the doorway looking around.

"Oh my god!" she squealed. "Dallas! Thank you so much."

He was behind her and I stepped inside, trying not to crush rose petals.

"What the fuck," Dallas said.

Lauren was hugging and kissing him. I began picking stargazer lilies off my bed. The pollen left a sticky, rusty dust on my hands and on the bedspread but I didn't mind. Why had Dallas put flowers on my side of the room?

"Chill out," Dallas said, moving her away from him.

"What's wrong, baby?"

"These aren't from me."

They paused for a moment, staring at each other. I kept gathering up the lilies but I could feel Lauren's evil eye boring through my back.

"Maybe you've got some secret admirer or some shit," Dallas said. The words *secret admirer* brought back the memory of the tampon note. Hooves kicked inside my stomach as Dallas crushed the roses under his feet. I resisted the impulse to stoop down and move them away from him; I didn't want one petal to be bruised.

Lauren put her hands on her hips. "I have no idea who that would be."

"Why? Because there are just *so* many guys who want

you?" Dallas's shoulders were up around his ears and a vein in his neck looked ready to explode.

"Maybe they're for Ariel." Lauren laughed. But her laugh was as nervous as it was sarcastic.

"Yeah, right." He turned and walked out. Lauren followed him.

I picked up the phone and dialed my parents.

"Did you send me something?"

Now I didn't feel ambivalent about them giving me flowers, even if they were the only ones who did; I wanted anything they could give me.

"Oh, honey, I'm sorry," my mom said.

"No, it's okay."

"We just have been so busy. I didn't think about it." She paused. "It's Valentine's, isn't it? We were at the doctor's all day."

"Are you okay, Mom?" My mother might not have sent me flowers in her condition, but she never forgot holidays. I reached for a rose and ran my fingers along the smooth stem. Someone had removed all the thorns.

"Oh, yes, everything will be fine. I'm just a little tired. Did you have a nice day? Are you going to do something with your friend tonight?"

I had managed to keep the Bean myth alive all this time but sometimes it caught me off guard when my mom brought her up because it made me think of John. "Oh, yeah. No. I'm just going to go to bed soon."

"But you got a present from someone?" she asked.

"Well, there were these flowers in the dorm room but I think they're for Lauren."

She was quiet for a moment. "We used to give you flowers all the time. I don't know what's wrong with me."

"Mom. Stop. You have other things to think about."

"But you're my valentine," she said. "I love you, sweet-heart." Her voice sounded pale.

"I love you, too. I'm going to get ready for bed now."

We said good night and the click of the phone echoed down through my body as if I were hollow.

I gathered up all the roses that weren't in water and put them in the vases with the other ones. The scent of the flowers filling my head made me dizzy. I could taste them on my tongue. Suddenly, as I was putting the last ones in water and sweeping up some stray leaves, I felt it. The crushing mass that I'd been carrying in my chest breaking up into shards. I put a hand to my heart and slumped down on the floor with my back against the bed.

My mom had said she'd been at the doctor all day and that everything *would* be fine. That wasn't how she usually talked. Nothing was fine.

The thought of being alone in the room, even with all the flowers for company, made me want to run. I took one white rosebud that had broken off and tucked it inside my shirt, in the lace trim of my bra. Then I locked the door behind me and fled downstairs into the night.

The atmosphere around the house in the hills was charged, almost ionized for me in some way. The air felt different, alive on my skin as I walked up the path, and a bluish mist seemed to gather in the trees. It was John Graves who answered the door. He was unshaven, a scratchy-looking dark stubble on his cheeks and chin, and his lids were puffy, with shadows under his eyes. No glasses this time. He wore a white pleated tuxedo shirt and black jeans. There were tiny rhinestone buttons on the shirt and my eyes fixed on the bright dots to avoid his gaze. One button was missing and I could see his chest. I reached inside my bra and pulled out the rosebud.

"Greetings," he said, his eyes lingering for a discreet moment on my breasts.

I gave him the flower and waited.

"Come in," was his only answer to my unspoken question.

The house felt even more current-filled than the garden; the air seemed to vibrate. There was a large bouquet of white lilies and roses in a glass vase on the table.

"So you got them," he finally said.

"They were from you?" I looked into his eyes for the first time since I'd gotten there. He smiled a small, nervous smile and nodded.

"Thank you. They're beautiful." I looked around the room, wondering where Tania and Perry were, if they'd pop out at any moment.

John was watching me carefully from a few feet away. Then he came forward, reached out suddenly and grabbed my hand. "Come upstairs," he said. His voice was a rumble.

I let him lead me. I wanted the sharp feeling in my chest to go away. I wanted him to make it go away.

Even as I followed John up the stairs I told myself that I should be doing something else, be back in L.A. spying on Kragen, talking to the cops, tracking down people who had been on the trip with Jeni. But it was pathetic. What did I think I was? Some kind of amateur sleuth trying to investigate what had happened? If so, I had failed miserably so far.

His room was a low-ceilinged sunporch. Leaves hung over it, casting shadows through the glass panes, branches tapping lightly as if they wanted to get in. Light from many candles shimmered into the illusion of more candles reflected in the glass. We sat on a futon. There was no other furniture except a low lacquered chest with dark flowers painted on it and hundreds of drawers fitted with silver rings.

"You look so sad," John said.

I lowered my eyes. All I could think about was being in my dorm room surrounded by white flowers and my mom's voice on the phone, fading from me like a ghost.

I had almost never been away from her, even overnight, for seventeen years unless I was at Jeni's. Once I had tried to go to sleepaway camp but I had cried so much, paralyzed with loneliness in the dark, that my parents came and got me after two days.

"May I show you something?" He spoke softly and moved closer, turning so that I could have collapsed against his chest if I let myself. My spine felt weak; I wanted to sink into him.

He poured a glass of water from a pitcher and held it up to the light, turned it slightly. Clear. Then he pulled a blue silk scarf out of his breast pocket and draped it over the goblet. I sat mesmerized by his hands, his eyes half-closed with concentration. When he removed the cloth red crystals, like pieces of ruby, sparkled at the base of the glass. He passed his hand across it and the glass was filled with red liquid. He handed it to me.

It smelled like poppies, growing wild on a summer hill. A cold version of the winter brew. I took a sip and every sinew of my being loosened right away.

"How did you do that?" I asked. This time I wasn't drunk or high yet; I was sure I'd seen the water transform.

"Tania showed me some tricks. She's been studying magic since she was little. Her stepfather taught her."

"Lucky."

"Not really," he said. "There was a price."

I remembered Tania's question about sexual abuse. *My stepfather.*

"What happened to her?" I asked.

"What happens to every kid who's abused, I guess, in one way or another. He lured her in until she trusted him. In this case he used magic tricks. She was just a kid. And then he messed with her."

I saw John's eyes turn hazy, blue-gray dazed, thinking about little-girl Tania being hurt. I felt sorry for her, too, but I wanted him back with me, here.

"But how did you do it?" I said. "The magic trick."

John's fingers lightly touched my left wrist where Jeni's bracelet was. He was back with me. "We all have secrets," he said.

I tapped him in the same place, where the tattoo was, dark shapes that resembled small hieroglyphs of birds and flowers. I could feel his pulse underneath. "Like this? What does it say?"

"It's the name of someone important to me who died."

"Can you tell me?"

"Not now. Someday."

Then I was crying, for both of us, the sharp pieces in my chest shaking around. I was afraid they'd cut me. I pressed my face into his chest, spilling a bit of the wine on my T-shirt. He gently took the wine from my hand.

I heard his voice through my sobs; it seemed he was singing something, some kind of lullaby with words I wanted to possess, like weird gems, but didn't understand. Through my tears the room glowed like liquid gold.

When I was quiet again I kept my face against his chest; I could feel his heartbeat. He moved his hands through my hair, gently sliding the ponytail holder off so that the loosened strands spilled down. He played with them, tugging softly, wrapping them gently around the thickness of his fingers. I slumped forward so that our foreheads touched and I heard a soft gasp escape him as I nuzzled my cheek against the scratchy surface of his. My finger found the cleft in his chin; I realized that every time I had seen him I had wanted to do this. Then I pushed my face up like a baby animal so that the tips of our noses touched. In that moment of met cartilage and flesh a squeezing sensation went through my lower body. John's fingers moved down over my cheekbones, along my neck, explored the beating pool at the base of my throat, the hardness of my clavicle. He slid his hands around behind me and placed his fingers on my shoulder blades, touching the bones reverently, as if he had discovered wings.

Then John Graves pressed his lips to mine and the veils between this world and the others disintegrated in places, like ancient lace, so that I could glimpse through.

The other worlds are not something you can describe in regular words. That is why poetry was invented. I can only say I saw golden rooms with vaulted ceilings carved with the faces of madmen. I saw rolling balls of flowers gathering flowers. I saw a woman with eyes like leaves and tendrils of green hair that grew around her body. A river came from her mouth and her hands were on fire. I saw children running through dark streets, shrieking, stumbling, bleeding, and after them came the shuddering crash of hoof-like feet.

Through it all, John Graves held me. And we spoke, too, though I don't remember exactly what we said. Except at one point I told him what I had seen when he kissed me.

He held me closer and I felt his heartbeat through the wall of my own chest. "I can't tell if you are outside of me or inside of me," was all he said.

"Where did you come from?" I asked, but I was only

partly asking out of suspicion this time. "Did I make you up?"

He smiled softly—my eyes were closed but I could feel it with my fingers as they traced his mouth. Then he told me the stories.

His father had met his mother while traveling in Ireland. She was beautiful, much younger than he was. But she never spoke. They married and returned to America, where she got pregnant and gave birth to John, then disappeared.

Or: he was adopted. He cried at loud sounds and bright lights and refused to drink milk or eat meat or fall asleep without a light on. His parents did not understand him. He left home at seventeen and never saw them again.

His father beat him. He ran away from home at fourteen and lived on the streets, panhandling, Dumpster diving, reading his poetry in the subways for change. One day a young couple found him, took him home and he never left.

And the real one, or so it seemed: he was a trust fund baby, like Perry, the youngest of three sons, from one of the Victorian mansions in Pacific Heights. The brothers went to law school and he studied English, wore weird clothes and hung out with Tania and Perry, disappointing his family, who were happy to give him a monthly stipend as long as he didn't bother them too much with his eccentricities.

I fell asleep, finally, fully clothed, in the bed of all these different versions of John Graves. Part of me never wanted to awaken and face the world again.

I did wake, though. It was morning and John lay beside me, reading. He put the book aside but I glimpsed the cover. It said *The Philosopher's Secret Fire*. Before I could ask him about it, he brushed the hair out of my eyes with the tips of his fingers.

"How did you sleep?" he asked. Sun filtered through the glass walls of the room, touched a crystal on a low shelf and scattered rainbow prisms on the floor. I stretched my body; it felt as if I had permanently gained an inch.

"Mmm. Babylike," I hummed. "You?"

He shook his head. "I'm a night owl."

I let my fingers catch his shirt collar and stroke his Adam's apple. His cheeks were rough with whiskers. I liked how they grew over the cleft in his chin, not obscuring it yet. "Doesn't that get difficult sometimes?"

"Only if I have to get up early. People ask me how I can be in relationships with anyone who doesn't stay up but it's easy, really. You can watch over each other. If someone wakes with a nightmare, the other person is always there."

I pulled him back down and pressed my nose into the pit of his arm. He smelled strong, musky. I breathed deeply.

"You had a nightmare, you know?"

I shook my head. "I don't remember."

"You cried out. You were waving your hands around, like warding something off."

"What did I say?" I asked, not really wanting to know.

"Ariel, you said her name."

I covered my face with my hands. I had let too much time go by without thinking of her. She was reminding me of this.

"If you want we can help you look," he said. "We can look for clues."

I curled up against his warmth and silently thanked him.

He kissed the top of my head. "Do you know it's eight?" he said gently.

"Oh my god, I have to leave." I forced myself to get up and put on my shoes.

"May I take you home?" he asked.

"No, you rest. You must be tired, night owl."

"Ariel?"

"Yes?"

"Thank you for letting me watch over you."

In spite of the dream, in spite of everything, a warmth filled my center, like the sun pouring into the room, spreading out through my veins into my fingers and toes. "Thank you, John Graves. Someday I will do the same for you."

I did not run that time, even though I was going to be late to class. I walked down through the North Berkeley hills among the maple and oak and lemon trees, past the houses with their rambling gardens, though none that rambled down into flowery grottoes like John's. I could smell a sweetness in the air as if spring was finally calling to me from across the expanse of too many terrible autumns.

He will help me find you, I promised her.

17. The city that already looked like a place you would go after you died

After that, everything was different. Was it the kiss? I only knew that I felt the warmth in my body, the warmth that had begun in John's room, all the time. I read and wrote effortlessly. All my senses seemed to have sharpened but the experience was not painful as it had been before. The brightness of the light no longer hurt my eyes and the sound of the leaves soothed me with their songs. I could smell John Graves on my clothes and in the wind. I could taste him when I ate. I felt my hands becoming his hands when I stroked myself beneath my blankets in the night.

But this only lasted for a week.

Then I began to go through withdrawals. My skin twitched;

it only smelled of me. I palpated my lower belly where the strange marks reminded me of his presence. I sniffed the shirt I'd worn on Valentine's and, though I hadn't washed it, I couldn't smell John there, either, anymore. Food lost its taste and my tongue felt coated, almost furred. I wore sunglasses all the time during the day and even thought of getting ear-plugs to keep the whisperings of the natural world from agitating me. The winged woman and her companion seemed to be waiting for me on every street corner. The dreadlock man wore branches in his hair like antlers. Every time I left a class my heart beat faster, hoping John was waiting there. I remembered a poem my mother read to me as a child, Christina Rossetti's "Goblin Market," where a young girl eats the forbidden goblin fruit and must be rescued from death by her sister.

I was that addicted; I needed the goblin fruit of John Graves's kiss.

Did I want it more than I wanted to search for Jeni? I certainly didn't want it more than to find her, but to search, not knowing what I would find? There was no escape in that. The question haunted me and maybe it was one reason I didn't go to the house. Besides, it seemed pathetic for me to show up again. He had come to me once, I told myself; he would come back.

But I did wonder why I felt so compelled to be near him and one day in the laundry room, about to throw in the T-shirt I'd worn to John's on Valentine's Day, I noticed a stain on the fabric. From the wine he'd given me. I remembered something then, something Coraline Grimm had said to me when I found her putting up missing-person flyers in her room.

There's some weird shit in that drink they serve.

Yes, John, Tania and Perry were beautiful and enticing

and seductive but when I left them I felt more obsessed than seemed appropriate, even for me in my strange state. I threw the stained shirt back in the hamper.

I found Ian Larsen in his dorm room. Luckily Tommy wasn't there; I wasn't up to seeing him or having to explain why I was coming to see his roommate.

"You're Ian, right?"

He nodded, watching me shyly behind his glasses. His hair was standing up in back. The origin of the term cowlick had never seemed so clear.

"I'm Ariel."

He nodded. "Hey. What's up?"

"Are you a biochem major?"

"Yeah." He seemed pleased I knew. Lauren had mentioned it in some freak/geek reference about badly matched roommates and how Ian could bust Tommy with a urine sample if they got into something.

"If I gave you a sample. Of an alcoholic drink? But it's just a stain on a shirt. Could you test it for me?"

He didn't look at me like I was crazy so I took the shirt out of my bag and handed it to him.

"What do you think it is?"

"Just this drink I had at a party. Do you think you could test it for me? I'd pay you."

He shook his head. "No, I'll do it for you. What am I looking for?"

"Something to make you hallucinate, something addictive."

He nodded. "Cool."

"Not really. But the alternative is even more fucked up."

"What's that?"

"Magic. Insanity."

"Cool," he said.

A few days later Ian texted me: *grapes sugar yeast pectin*. It was hard to believe that there wasn't more in that wine. It meant I was jonesing for John, just John, not something he'd given me. I wasn't sure which was worse.

I was coming home from the library late one night when I noticed a large white car parked in front of my dorm. The car was ungainly, finned and familiar. I stopped and stared at it.

Tania leaned her head out of the passenger seat window. "Sylph!" she cried.

I was overcome with longing, then, and not just for John— for his kisses and his wine—but for Tania, and Perry, too. Even for their tests. I wanted to prove myself; I wanted to take off my clothes and have them look at me again.

But instead of moving toward the car, I took a step back and hugged my poetry books to my chest like a shield of words.

"Don't be scared," said Tania.

Perry poked his head out of the backseat. His grin reminded me of the crescent moon dangling mischievously in the sky.

"Hi, Ariel," John said from the front. "It's the equinox."

I could only see him vaguely in the darkness, lit by the streetlamps. His strong face with the almost severe cheekbones and chin. I couldn't see his eyes at all.

"We're going to the city to celebrate," said Tania. "Come with us!"

I hesitated and looked up at the dorm. I could make out

my room from below. The light was on; Lauren and Dallas must be there. I didn't want to go back.

Tania climbed into the back as John jumped out, wearing a vintage smoking jacket and ascot, came around and held the door open for me gallantly, with his head bent.

"Please join us," he whispered. And then, just in case I wasn't yet convinced, he added, "I may have someone who can help. With your friend."

That was all it took. I slid onto the cracked leather seat, sawdust poking through.

"To Elfland," Tania said as John started the car.

The bridge glowed like the Milky Way as we rode it into the city. Tania handed me a large box from the backseat. Then she sat back, stretching out her bare, shiny legs in the gold stilettos across the seat between me and John.

"The only catch is you have to change now," she said. Her eyes were catlike in the hazy mist-glow of the city light.

Well, I would be getting naked again after all. But I wanted to please her. Maybe they really did have some clue about Jeni? I frowned at Tania and opened the box. Inside, among layers of Tiffany-blue tissue, was a dress of thin cream-colored satin with small roses adorning the draping fabric.

"Put it on," Perry said. "We won't look."

He and Tania giggled. John was staring straight ahead, his large hands firmly on the wheel, his shoulders a little hunched. I wanted to show them I wasn't scared. As we drove I unbuttoned my flannel shirt and took it off, slipped the fragile dress over my head. It was too dark in the car for any of them to see the marks that were still on my abdomen. With the dress on, I unbuttoned my jeans and wriggled out of them. Tania whistled softly and handed me a second box with a pair of cream-colored lace-up boots in it. I busied myself with putting them on so I wouldn't have to think about either her or the men looking at me. Although John wasn't looking. He still stared ahead of him and I saw the sweat on his temples. I wondered if he had told Tania and Perry about this person who might be able to help with Jeni.

The air outside smelled warm and yeasty, like fresh-baked bread. We drove into the city, just kept going along the sharp angles of broad, twinkling streets, up the steep hills of the residential sections, past storybook gingerbread houses and the shadowy shapes of trees, hedges and gardens. There was something so lonely about San Francisco—maybe it was the cool weather and the fog. Maybe it was the threat of earthquakes and the proximity to the rocky coast; you never felt entirely grounded. Maybe it was the ghosts of bohemians and prostitutes and sailors and AIDS victims, none of whom ever really wanted to leave a city that already looked like a place you'd go after you died. That's what we talked about as we finished our tour and drove into the Tenderloin, the city's "worst section" according to the guidebooks. John parked in an alley and we got out.

He came around and draped a black velvet coat over my shoulders. The street smelled like ammonia and I heard cats screaming in an alley as we walked up to a small door and knocked.

Identical young men in top hats and tails, with the thin faces and sinewy bodies of junkies, glared at us from the stairwell.

John said something to them, something I could hardly hear and didn't understand—it almost sounded like a different language—and they exchanged a look, then turned back to us, frowned menacingly and moved the velvet rope that barred the way. We descended into a dark room that vibrated with industrial sound and prisms of light. John handed me a small flask and I took a large gulp to wash away my anxiety and self-consciousness among so many beautiful people.

Some girls swayed in a circle, half-clad, long hair braided with flowers like the three graces from a Botticelli. A boy dressed as a court jester leapt around ringing bells and pelting everyone with petals. Tall men with shaved heads and long sheer robes strolled arm in arm. Boys wearing fur loincloths wrestled on the floor. Go-go dancers of indistinguishable gender gyrated on pedestals, casting rainbows from their fingertips. Everyone was covered with a sheen of glitter and perspiration.

We danced together for a while, the four of us, and then John led me away to a smaller chamber with red velvet walls.

"There's someone I want you to meet."

The woman was tall and thin with thin wisps of black hair, a receding chin and deep-set, unfocused eyes. She wore a long black dress, high platform fetish boots and a chain leash around her neck. A man with a black Mohawk and slashed black clothes was holding her leash blithely while he chatted with some women at the bar.

The woman's eyes looked as if she were trying to light me on fire with them. She said, "You don't belong here. You have not caught any souls for us."

John said, "Catalan, this is Ariel. She belongs with me."

The woman stared from him to me and back again. "What does she want?"

"She has someone she needs to find," he said. He turned to me. "Catalan can sometimes help with these things."

The woman began to laugh, a high, sharp sound, and the man with the Mohawk jerked her chain. She shut up and hung her head but John whirled around and took the leash from the man, who, to my surprise, let him without a fight. Then John tried to hand the leash to Catalan but she shook her head and wouldn't look at him so he let it drop to her side.

"You shouldn't have done that," she said. Her hands worked the air like she was doing some strange origami.

"Sorry." John looked back at the man, who had his hand on the bare ass of one of the women at the bar. "Can you help us? Show her the picture, Ariel."

I always carried one in my purse. I took it out. The woman grabbed it from me, brought it close to her face. She shook her head, biting her lip with small, sharp-looking teeth. When she stopped biting there was a bead of blood on her chin.

"No," she said and her voice was lucid now, the mineral-glitter of hysteria gone from her eyes. "I can't help you." She looked at me. "I'm sorry," she said.

John grabbed my hand and pulled me close to him before I could turn away. "Why did I do that? Fuck. I'm so sorry. Let's go."

When we drove back it was almost dawn. The sky, as we crossed the bridge, glowed with pink, purple and gold clouds and there was a breath of warmth in the air but it could have been storming and black. I wondered if John would take me back to the dorm, or at least offer to, but he went to the house instead. I was relieved; I wasn't ready to be away from him after what had happened. I didn't blame him; he had tried to help but he had only made things worse.

Tania and Perry scampered obliviously inside holding hands, tossing good-byes like bright scarves over their shoulders. John led me up the stairs and into the house, then upstairs again but not to the sunporch room.

This was another room I hadn't seen before, much darker. Heavy pale green damask drapes covered the windows, a mirror with an ornate frame hung on the wall and there was a large carved bed painted with faded wreaths of flowers. John sat on the bed and pulled me down gently beside him.

"I'm so sorry," he said again. "She's crazy. It didn't mean anything. I don't know why I did that. She helped me once . . ." He trailed off.

"How?" I asked. I wanted to be angry at him but I couldn't find it in me.

"She told me to leave Tania and Perry for a while. Things were very hard and it helped. Then she told me to come back, that someone important was coming into my life through them. That was you, Ariel."

I was so drawn to the hollow of his armpit, the warmth and the smell, that I had to struggle not to fall down against him.

"She's known as being an intuitive but she's wrong a lot. Jeni could be okay still. You can't listen to that psychic bullshit. I'm an asshole. You've been through too much."

Without thinking, trying not to think about anything anymore, I took his face in my hands and leaned in so our lips were touching. Then as we fell to the mattress I slid back into the otherworld.

There was a path wandering up a hill among the shattered stone ruins of what looked like some kind of mansion. It was overgrown with roses and trumpet vines. I smelled spicy leaves and heard water rushing in the distance. Shadowy figures watched me with luminous eyes from behind pale pink, green and silver peeling trunks. Were the creatures animals? One of them lowered its horned head and lapped at a shiny trickle of water on the ground. My body shivered with pleasure and anxiety. I was looking, looking for someone . . .

On the bed, John took me by the waist and lifted my body easily onto his. Our forms locked together, every hollow met with fullness, every sharp edge finding a curve to settle into. I could feel his hardness through his pants and I rode against it. He was saying my name over and over again, as if it hurt him. I gasped for breath. Tiny jolts of electricity moved back and forth between us and I shuddered.

"Are you okay? Is this okay?"

"Yes," I breathed back. I could feel his heartbeat inside of me. I didn't want it to stop.

"Is it just me or can you feel the energy between our bodies?" he asked. "I mean, I can almost see it."

I moaned a yes; it was getting harder to speak.

"I could hold you like this forever," he said.

We did not take off our clothes, only kissed and kissed, traveling to other worlds in the dim room, until I finally fell asleep on top of him as if I were floating there, completely weightless.

I woke to John hushing me. There were tears on my face.

"Oh, God," I said. "I was talking in my sleep again?"

He kissed my forehead. "You were asking for your mom."

"Damn. I'm such a mess. I'm sorry."

He shook his head. "You're not a mess. Under the circumstances. Believe me."

"I'm so scared of everything," I said.

He paused and I could feel his thoughts welling up, filling the room. Then he said, "I don't want to upset you, and I know you're worried and you have the right to be but it seems, from the little you've told me, as if you've gone pretty far in the direction of this thing with your mom having a bad outcome."

I tensed. His expression showed he noticed, but he went on anyway. "But do you think there is room for some hope?"

I wanted to clutch onto him but I turned my face away a little instead. "I'm afraid," I said. "If I hope and then . . ."

"You can prepare yourself but you can come from a place

of hope," he told me. "I know it sounds so cliché to say it, but I think it might help."

There were tears in my eyes again and I didn't try to hide them.

"I shouldn't have said that?"

The obstruction in my throat burned. "No. You're right."

"Because there is magic that protects, that you can't see. Everyone is entitled to some and I know there are a lot of good spirits around you."

He pulled me down beside him and I curled my legs up with my knees against his hip. As he stroked my hair I pushed my face into his neck. "John?" I said. That was all I could say. But I meant, *thank you I need you are you really here? should I be afraid?*

We fell asleep like this and I woke again later, disoriented, trying to remember where I was, who I was, once more. The old-fashioned clock on the wall said six and when I parted the thick curtains of the strange room, the wild garden was dim with evening. I checked my reflection in the mirror. A pale girl with long, brown hair. Ariel Ilana Silverman. Then I looked at the man lying asleep on the bed. John Graves. His face seemed much younger in repose, except for the thick, bristling eyebrows and the shadow of whiskers on his cheeks and chin. His eyelids trembled in sleep and I leaned over and kissed both of them before I changed into my own clothes and left.

By the time I got to my room there was a text from John. It said, *if u need co. 4 spring b. we can drive u 2 l.a. 2 c yr mom.*

18. If you partake of the food of fae can you ever leave?

John Graves and Perry and Tania did drive me to Los Angeles for spring break. They picked me up at the already nearly deserted dorm late at night and we took the highway, riding fast so the lights blurred, loud music—a mix of industrial, punk, gothic and the mysterious stuff they played at home—making the dashboard vibrate. The air got warmer as we traveled south. I opened the window and let the wind run its fingers through my hair. I smelled scents animal, vegetable, mineral and poisonous. There was a queasy feeling in the base of my belly. I wasn't sure what it meant, though I could have called it fear, but fear mixed with hope. Maybe John was right; Jeni was still gone but I had not given up on her yet and my mother was still alive. Who was to say she couldn't stay that way for a long time still?

They dropped me off at my house. The eucalyptus-lined street was dark and quiet except for the crickets chirping wildly in the bushes, seeking their mates.

"You have a good home," Tania mused, surveying it. "Good parents who love you. You're luckier than you realize."

"We'll call you tomorrow night," John said.

They'd told me they'd be staying with friends but that was all I knew. Tania and Perry leaned over from the backseat and kissed my cheeks.

"Blessings, Sylph," she said.

John got out of the car and hauled my bags from the trunk. He carried them up to the front door. I wished we weren't illuminated (illumined was a better word) in the spotlight of the front porch like that, where everyone could see—Tania and Perry in the car, my parents inside, if they were watching. John hugged me quickly and then ran down the steps, the path, out the gate back to the car.

My parents hadn't waited up, which surprised me, but only at first, since I was getting used to this different behavior from them. There was a note on the kitchen table telling me they had tried to wait up but had finally gone to bed and that there was some soup in the refrigerator. I heated up a bowl. It was watery and thin; I was sure my dad had made it. I poured most of it down the sink, then went up to my room, got in bed in my clothes and went to sleep.

The next day I spent sitting on my mom's bed with her, reading my term papers out loud and watching *The Red Shoes,* which was one of our favorite old movies (and Jeni's). The girl on the screen danced and danced while outside in the garden the jacaranda trees were blooming with purple flowers that seemed surprised at their own intense color and concerned about their brief life span, and the sunlight shifted through the feathery leaves. My mom still looked fragile and pale and seemed distracted but she told me she was glad I was there with her and she asked questions about my papers as if she were really interested, the way she always used to be. She also asked me a little about what was going on with me and Bean, whom I hadn't mentioned in a while. I told her that Bean had recently hooked up with a boy but that I'd made some new friends. I thought that talking about John, Tania and Perry might show some hope in the situation, like John had suggested, a way to express that I hadn't given up on my mother.

"Who are these people now?" she asked. She sounded a little suspicious. At least I hadn't made them up.

"They're really cool. I met them at a party at their house."

"Are they students?" she asked, peering at me over her glasses.

"Grad students."

"So they're older?"

Part of me was glad she was asking this way; it meant she felt well enough to worry about me the way she used to. But part of me wanted her to drop it. "Not that much older."

"And they have a house? Those places in the hills are expensive."

"They're kind of independently wealthy. Trust fund kids. And they're very artistic," I said. "Their house, the way they dress and everything."

My mom was frowning. I knew how idiotic I sounded.

"I used to know everything that was going on with you." She stroked my ponytail. "You seem far away from me, Ariel."

I wanted to tell her it was she and my father who were far away but I didn't want to upset her. "It's okay, Mom. It's normal. The way we were before was too close." I tried to smile.

"Just promise you'll take care of yourself," she said. "I wish I could do a better job of it."

"I do."

"You look thin."

"These guys? They cook almost as well as you do. They feed me all the time."

She smiled. "Well, that's good to hear. I haven't been cooking much lately."

I pulled my T-shirt over my knees and sat huddled like that, looking out the window. She kept watching me. Then she said, "I didn't want to bring this up, but that thing you said about Jennifer Benson a while back, about looking for her before you started therapy? I was wondering if you're still doing that."

I could tell by the tone of my mom's voice that she really didn't feel like talking about it but had worked herself up to ask me anyway.

"I was freaked out when I got there. It's better now. I'm sorry if I scared you."

She smiled a little and I was glad I had lied to her. "That's good to hear. I know this has been hard."

"Don't worry about me," I said. "You need all your energy to get better." And I meant it, too. But part of me wanted her to be my mommy, to worry and fuss and ask countless questions and not let me go away again.

She did not ask questions, though, when I asked to take the car that night. Besides, she always went to sleep by nine now.

I drove by Mr. Kragen's house and parked in the shadows. His Taurus wasn't there and only the porch light was on. I wanted to run to the back, smash a window with my sweater-wrapped fist, stalk around that bookless house to find the evidence I needed. If Kragen came home I wanted to slap him in that pudgy face and tell him to fuck off before I ran. But my body wouldn't move from the car seat and my thighs were sweating so much they stuck to the leather upholstery.

My phone signaled a text and I jumped as if Kragen's eyes were peering bulbously through the window at me. When I saw it was from John, the adrenaline continued to pump, but for a different reason now. *pick u up 2morrow nite 8*.

Then a car—pulling up into Kragen's driveway; the headlights shone in my face and I ducked my head reflexively, turned the key in the ignition and drove away.

The next night I sat waiting on the front porch. It had rained that evening—an unexpected spring shower—and the air was still fresh. The streets were greased with rainbow puddles and the roses were hung with quivering drops of water. I didn't smoke, but sitting there made me want to take out a cigarette and light it, watch the tip smolder against damp darkness.

They pulled up—it was all of them. Part of me had hoped it was just going to be John. They were dressed up as usual and I was prepared this time. I'd rummaged through my mom's closet and found a velvet dress with an embroidered corseted bodice that she'd worn to the Renaissance Faire when she was young. She even had a pair of brocade slippers. I'd curled my hair and put it up on top of my head with some loose strands falling around my face. I'd also found some fake pearls to decorate it with.

Perry whistled as I lifted my skirt a little around my ankles to get into the car.

"You look beautiful," John said.

I smiled at him and he leaned over and kissed my cheek. I was blushing right away, thinking about Tania watching us.

"Where are we going?" I asked. I felt bold and free, much less self-conscious than usual. This was my world now, I thought, a city whose secrets I knew, not the dreamworld of the house where they had all the control.

"Our friends are having a party," John told me.

We headed east down the broad, flat expanse of Ventura Boulevard. If you came from outer space you'd think all we did was drive and eat and shop; perhaps it was true—then south up Laurel and into the canyon itself where the road narrowed, twisting among the trees where water had once cut out a path in the rock.

"Wait," I said, "this is one of the secret places I was going to tell you about."

They were all quiet and I looked back to see Tania and Perry regarding me calmly. Of course, they already knew. I had nothing original to give them. In Laurel Canyon there were the haunted-looking ruins of the mansion where Houdini had once lived and there were castles and cottages where rock royalty had stayed in the 1960s and '70s. Neil Young. Jim Morrison. Frank Zappa. Joni Mitchell. Fleetwood Mac. Everyone had lived there. Now bands still rehearsed in ramshackle buildings, hoping to channel the music that had been made before. Evening primrose and poppies covered the hills. There were rumored to be underground catacombs. Deer and coyote ran, sometimes to their death, darting across the road in darkness.

But where we went wasn't like anything I'd seen before.

The house tumbled down the hillside, a cascade of crumbling stone steps. There were thick balustrades lining the front and stone lions crouched on either side of the entrance, guarding it. Thick, squat palm trees crowded around and morning glory vines clambered over the terra-cotta-tiled roof. Bougainvillea and oleander bushes added splashes of bloodred and pink color. Luminarias in paper bags lit our path as we climbed up to the front door.

We heard laughter and a young woman answered. She had elegant features and her long hair gleamed in the candlelight that filled the house behind her. Her dress had the same dark sheen.

"There you are!" She hugged them all, John last, her fingers tightening around his shoulders so that I found myself tensing with the same force she exerted.

"Claudia, this is Ariel," he said, extricating himself.

She took my hand regally and raised her thin, arched eyebrows. "Ariel. So you're the missing piece?"

I blinked back at her and Tania swept past me, pulling me into the house. The paint was peeling off the walls, the lace curtains were torn and the Persian rugs on the tiled floor were faded and threadbare but the whole place still had a feeling of grandeur. Large old oil paintings of vibrant fruits and flowers against dark backgrounds—I thought of Danish still lifes I'd seen in museums with my parents—hung in chipped gilded frames on the walls. Like in the Berkeley house, old books were everywhere. The air inside the place had a cool, piney scent.

We walked into a large room. There were more paintings on the walls but these were portraits of young people—pale, and with large, haunted-looking eyes. I felt a chill go through me like a ghost on its way across the room.

"What are those?" I whispered to John.

"Eamon made them," he said, nodding at a tall blond in a white suit who had walked in.

Eamon hugged and kissed Tania, Perry and John, then greeted me the same way. He smelled minty and his hands felt cool.

"I like your work," I said, looking back anxiously at the paintings, although "like" wasn't exactly the right word.

He smiled thinly. "Thank you, Ariel."

John took my arm and led me toward the open window. It looked out over the canyon below, what had once been a gorge made by rainwater now overgrown with wildflowers and eucalyptus trees and built up with houses. The lights of cars and windows shone out of the darkness. Crickets chirped a mating song, creating a vibrating wall of sound. A breeze with a slightly citrusy scent, and fresh from the rain, came in and cooled my neck.

I wished John and I were out there, in the night, alone, away from this place.

"Come eat!" called a voice and a girl with rather large ears sticking out from her short red hair appeared at the door of the room, waving her hands around. She giggled hellos to everyone and gestured for us to follow her into the dining room. Large picture windows overlooked a rectangular tiled pool, aglow with blue phosphorescence in the night, and, beyond that, the distant lights of the city.

The smell of the food made me ache almost like the thought of John did. We took our seats and Claudia, the woman who had answered the door, came in with another young man, also very tall, dressed in black and with long black hair like hers. Both of them were carrying plates of food.

He and the redhead were introduced as Demitri and Fallon. I smiled vaguely at them, eyeing the food; I hadn't eaten dinner and my stomach was growling. There were an array of what looked like Italian dishes, bruschetta, polenta, pasta salad, grilled vegetables, fettucini in a light green sauce. There was also red wine to drink, like the kind I loved in Berkeley. I hardly paid attention to anything except the food and the wine. Even the fascinating faces around me seemed to fade—even John's face seemed to fade.

Then, as my stomach ached full and I leaned back against the green velvet chair in a stupor, I heard someone say, "If you partake of the food of fae you can never leave. Isn't that how it goes?"

I woke in a candlelit bedroom, in a large canopied bed. I sat up, startled, and looked around, trying to place where I was.

"It's okay," I heard John's voice say. "It's okay, sweet one, I'm here."

He was beside me, I saw, fully clothed. I could smell a warm, sleepy scent wafting off of him. His hands stroked the hard lines of my back. My bare back. I realized I was only wearing my underpants and a thin cotton nightgown. My hands reflexively covered my breasts as I sat up.

"Tania undressed you," he said. "I hope that is okay. The dress seemed so heavy and hot."

I could hear the worry line on his brow in his voice. "It's okay," I said. "Thank you for staying with me. What time is it?"

"About five in the morning."

"Shit! I have to call my mom."

He handed me my bag and I found my cell phone and called. No one answered so I left a message saying I was fine, still out with my friends. Then I dove back against John's side, snuggling up to him, winding my bare legs over the rough, heavy fabric of his jeans.

"Who are they? Your friends?"

"They're old friends," he said. "Eamon and Fallon are brother and sister. Eamon's the painter like we said. Claudia's an actress and Demitri is independently wealthy, although no one knows exactly from what."

"I'm sorry I passed out again," I said. "I don't know what's wrong with me. Maybe I should see a doctor."

Now I could hear the smile on his lips. "You're fine. Just sometimes it takes a while to get used to us, especially the drinks."

"But I felt like I was going to pass out the night I met you."

He stroked my hair, pushing a strand behind my ear. "Maybe you were overcome with wonder at my charm, as I feel when I am with you."

"Weirdo!" I said, poking his rib cage.

He slithered down so we were face-to-face on the pillows. "May I kiss you?" I tilted my face up and his lips fastened to mine with a gentle pressure that made me feel as if I were falling, falling down through the earth among the roots of a tree, in a cascade of leaves and flower petals. I clutched at John's shoulders through his shirt. I didn't think I could wait much longer to have him naked beside me.

"I want to feel your skin," he said as if he'd read my mind. "May I?"

I nodded and pressed my fingertip against the pad of his

lower lip, staring up at the planes of his face. A glimmer of light was coming through the curtains. My hands traveled down to his collar, to the buttons of his shirt. I slowly pressed the button through the buttonhole with my thumb and forefinger. His chest was smooth and hard, very pale with only a little hair. He winced slightly.

"Are you okay?"

"My heart is very open right now," he said.

"Should I stop?"

He took my hand and moved it back to his heart. "No."

I finished unbuttoning his shirt and slid it off his shoulders. They curved white and defined as sculpture against the dim background of the room. I gasped to see him and he silenced me with his lips again.

I could feel myself going to the otherworld but I didn't want to go. I wanted to stay here with him. I held onto his back tightly, trying to remain in the room.

My hands found his belt buckle and fumbled with the metal.

"I should take that off," he said. "I don't want it to hurt you."

I laughed. "Yes, that's a good reason."

He unbuckled it with one hand, the other still holding me close to his chest, then pulled the belt out of the loops. I could see the long, hard shape in his jeans. My hands went there of their own will, my fingers running along the ridge of his zipper. Now, in turn, he gasped.

"I need to lie with you," he said. "I want you so badly."

I nodded, suddenly mute. Words seemed impossible to find.

John took off his jeans and lay naked on the large bed. His body gave off a pulsing white light. There were framed mirrors all over the walls and they reflected us again and again.

I put my arms around his chest. He was broad enough that I couldn't encircle him, but I tried, stretching myself out. He shuddered softly. He was erect and I wanted to stare at him but I kept my eyes on his face. I pulled myself closer, lying on my side, my legs over his. I couldn't tell if the shaking came from him or from me.

"I will make love with you soon," John said. "If you will have me. But I want this part to last as long as possible."

I nodded and kissed him again.

In the woods a small thatched cottage shone with firelight. Smoke swirled like ghosts from the chimney. I walked up, leaves crunching dry under my feet. An owl whoo-ed in the tree above me. I saw it take flight, a span of white wings ruffling the darkness.

An old woman opened the door. Her hands were gnarled and she was smiling toothlessly. She beckoned me in. The room was small and cozy with large pots of boiling liquid on the stove and bunches of dried herbs and flowers hanging from the ceiling.

John was there, seated by the fire, hunched over with his back to me, holding something in his hands. I came and knelt before him. He kissed my forehead. His lips felt cool on my burning skin. He offered me the object he was holding and I took it—a locket on a chain. I opened the filigree heart. Inside was a portrait of a girl, very similar to the paintings Eamon had made.

The girl, with her soft-looking hair and big dark eyes, was Jeni.

I gasped and reached out my hands in the dark and John held me close to his chest so that I felt the reverberations of his voice.

"I'm here. We're here," he said.

We lay in that bed with the thick canopy, in that room of mirrors, and kissed and touched each other and dozed and woke and kissed again throughout what was day but felt more like a timeless floating. I went in and out of the otherworlds. John, he tugged the nightgown down over my shoulders and kissed my breasts, massaging them with his hands, his tongue flicking against my nipple, then his whole mouth sucking. I groaned and threw back my head and his fingers found my throat, lightly circled it so that when I swallowed I felt the slight pressure of him there. I kept thinking, *This is John Graves here with me. This is his body that contains his brain and his lungs and his heart. This is where his soul lives. This is not just sex; this is us going somewhere together. This is us finding each other. Again.*

He lifted the hem of my nightgown up over my thighs and kissed my legs slowly. I felt the roughness of his unshaven chin against my skin. I was slippery wet, entirely ready, when he got up between my thighs. He parted them gently and rested his hand there. His cheek lay against the place where the marks from the concert still showed on my belly. I had gotten used to the increased sensitivity around the shadowy prints but I flinched a little and he moved his head to look. "What's this?" He squinted at the marks. "It looks like a bruise or something. Does it hurt?"

"I think it's from you."

"What?" He sat up with a start and I reached to bring him back where he was.

"They just won't go away. They came after the concert."

He looked into my eyes. The candlelight reflected so that there was a thin shimmer beneath the rim of his eyelids. "They've been there the whole time?"

I nodded.

"I don't know what those marks are or how you got them but I promise I would never hurt you." He paused. "Ariel? Do you hear that?"

"Yes." I pulled him back to my belly and this time he let me, careful not to lean on the bruises. We lay quiet for a while. I could feel the pulse beneath my hip beating against his cheek. Slowly his fingers began to move over my abdomen.

"Is this all right?"

We were both panting.

"Yes."

"You tell me if something hurts now."

I felt his fingers touching me in ways I'd never known anyone could touch, soft but with just the right amount of pressure, tips circling on the small hard knob of me, then sliding down and up inside where I was opening to him. He found a place I'd never felt before, a soft, padded, aching spot and he played it again and again like an instrument that gave off different notes, which came out through my mouth.

That was when the otherworld and the room with the canopy bed became the same place. There was nowhere further to go than this.

It was night when I woke from a fitful dreaming. More candles were lit around the bed and the flames were reflected in the many mirrors. They reminded me of the eyes of spirits. I smelled a sweetness—night-blooming jasmine?—through the open casement window. John wasn't there. I wondered for a moment if I'd dreamed the whole thing between us.

My skin was sticky and damp, I realized, as I threw back the covers and got out of bed. I wanted to shower. My dress was on the floor and I put it on, but my underpants were gone.

I walked out of the bedroom and into a dimly lit hallway

with faded green-and-gold wallpaper. As I took a step into the hall something scuffled away among the shadows. A cat, I thought, but I couldn't see it. I could hear soft voices speaking somewhere below me.

My heart still beating from the surprise of the creature in the hallway, I leaned over the banister and listened. I could hear Tania's laughter—or maybe it was Claudia's?—and the deeper voices of the men. I couldn't make out the sound of John, though.

I suddenly felt abandoned by him. Why hadn't he stayed? The thought of him down there with the others made my face heat up with shame, although I wasn't quite sure what I had to be ashamed of. The memory of his touch made my thighs watery so I steadied myself and then I walked as quietly as I could down the staircase.

I could see them through glass doors, sitting in the large room with the paintings. They were drinking wine and laughing. Claudia and Eamon lay on one sofa, legs tangled. Tania was there, too, sitting on the ground while Claudia stroked her hair. Fallon sat on Demitri's lap in an armchair. Perry was cross-legged on the floor beside them. John sat in another armchair a little bit away from the others. He was reading, his head lowered, glasses on.

My heart was trying to rush to him.

I moved closer. They didn't see me.

Then I noticed a tiny painting on the hallway wall I had missed the night before. How had I missed it?

Because the painting looked exactly like Jeni.

I stepped into the room. "What the fuck!" Everyone turned to look at me. "Is this why you brought me here?" I shouted. "Because of this?"

John jumped up. "Ariel, what are you talking about?"

"Jeni!" I said. "What do you think?" I pointed to the paint-ing. "Where did you get this image?" I demanded.

Eamon observed me coldly. "It upsets you? I'm sorry."

"Where did you get it?"

"The obits, the papers, missing-children posters. I don't recall with that one. I make so many."

"What are the chances you'd actually have seen my best friend? And drawn her?"

Tania stood and approached me carefully, her voice a ca-ress of sound. "It's okay, Ariel. I promise. Everything's okay."

"Don't talk to me!"

"Listen, sweetie, I know you're upset. But there's an expla-nation." Perry was behind Tania now.

"We won't let anything bad happen to you," John added.

"It already has!"

He went up to the painting and examined it. "I'm sorry, Ariel. It looks a little like her but it could be anyone."

"Oh, Ariel." Tania shook her head; her eyes looked like the oil paint of an Italian master in the candlelit room. "It could be her," she said. "Eamon paints every missing child he can find. I'm so sorry, Sylph."

"It's a sick world," Eamon said. "I try to see the beauty."

Tania pushed his shoulder and hushed him with her mas-terpiece eyes.

I wanted to vomit. "Shut up," I said. "Stop talking about her. You have no right!"

John put his arms around me and I let him, but stayed rigid. How could they have brought me here?

"Let's go," he said.

On the car ride home they tried to explain to me that—if the image were even Jeni at all—Eamon painted everything he could find for inspiration; how Jeni's picture had been in the papers a lot for a while; how they had not meant to upset me, had not known this was there, would not have brought me if they had. I let them talk but I felt myself drifting away from them.

It's better, I told myself. I needed to stay focused on my task. When I got home I looked up Eamon on John's Facebook page. Eamon R. Collins. There was a Web site of his art—all those dark, candlelit Caravaggio-esque portraits of young faces. The Missing, they were called. Jeni's portrait wasn't there and, for a moment, I wondered if I'd imagined it. But I e-mailed the link to Rodriguez anyway, asking if he had any concerns about what I'd seen.

John texted me five times the next day but I didn't respond; I had to clear my head. The following day I wrote back and said that I was going to be spending the rest of the vacation close to home, to be with my mom, and that I'd be flying back before school started. (By then I'd also received an e-mail from Rodriguez politely dismissing my latest "clue.") John tried calling me but I didn't answer. His voice on the message sounded worried and he said he hoped everything was okay and that if I changed my mind he'd be happy to drive me. But I ignored him. I couldn't get the image of Jeni's eyes, depicted in oil paint, both luminous and dark, out of my mind.

19. As if we were starving

But she wasn't the only one who haunted me; when I got back up north I was missing John so much that my whole body—bones, joints, sinews, tissues, even weirdly my blood—ached with it.

I was almost always swollen with wanting but no matter how long I touched myself I never quite found relief. It only exhausted me and made me miss him more. My fingers traced one of the marks that still showed on my lower belly. I hated them and, at the same time, hoped they would never fade.

I did okay in school, using my studies as a way to block out everything else. I was going to be spending the summer in Berkeley, staying in the dorms again, taking a Shakespeare in film class and European art history and looking for signs of Jeni. I had made the decision a few months before, with the thought that I'd get to see John, and now I wondered if it was a bad idea. I had found no trace of my friend and any interaction with John had taken me more off-course. The incident at the house in Los Angeles had disturbed me; even if the explanations were true, there were so many things about John and his friends that I didn't understand and I still couldn't face them. But being back with my mom and dad wasn't really an option, either. It had felt too strange to curl up in the bed where I'd been as a child, just down the hall from where my parents slept, half-listening for my mom's moans even in my dreams. I missed her but I really missed the mommy I'd had before she got sick, even though I hated to admit it. The mommy who was always able to take care of me and who seemed invincible and who was never in pain. And I couldn't help Jeni from Los Angeles, even if Kragen was somehow involved in what had happened. I decided that until I figured out what to do next I'd stay with the summer-school plan and just use some self-control when it came to the house in the hills, even though I could feel it singing to me every night.

I might have been able to keep away from that singing siren house longer if Lauren hadn't done what she did.

A few weeks after I got back I opened my drawer and found the underwear covered with dark red stains.

When I looked closer I saw that the blood had to be fake, ketchup probably. But it brought tears to my eyes anyway and my heart started pounding like an animal's under attack. Just the fact that Lauren had gone to the trouble of taking my underwear out, pouring anything on it and putting it back in made my whole body feel as red as the mark she'd left.

Worst of all the blood reminded me, as blood always did—though I didn't let myself acknowledge the thought—that whatever had happened to Jeni must probably have involved it in some way.

I sat down on the bed, trying to figure out what to do. Then I picked up my phone and texted John.

He wrote back right away.

Come over. Do you want me to get you?

Yes, I wrote.

I met him in front of my dorm and he drove me to the house. We hardly spoke the whole way. I was afraid I'd start crying or screaming if I even looked over at him. When we got to the house I looked at it with almost the same relief and trepidation that I had felt when I had seen his face as he pulled up in the dark. Its windows were glowing, heavy-lidded eyes and its front door was open, pouring out music like a mouth. John took my hand and I let him; we walked inside and up to the room with the damask drapes and the carved bed. He shut and locked the door, flicked on the green shaded art nouveau lamps and came to sit with me on the mattress.

"Talk to me, lady," he said. "I was worried."

I had to resist the impulse to put my head in his lap. I wanted him to stroke my hair forever, feel his fingers moving through the strands, touching my scalp. I would have shaved off all my hair to feel him hold my head even more closely.

"I still don't get what happened at that house," I hissed.

I thought that by being away from him the intensity of my feelings would have dulled, but instead they seemed even sharper. John paused, tugging on a lock of his hair.

"I know. I'm sorry. It's really strange. I asked Eamon more about it but he just said he wanted to paint the image when he found it. He literally has hundreds of clippings of those things."

My body was studded with goose bumps in spite of the warmth of the room. "Those *things*! That was her!"

"I'm sorry, Ariel. I'm sorry you're in pain but none of us meant to hurt you. It was just a really horrible coincidence."

I wondered again if what had gone wrong was my own mind, warped by a tragedy that I did not understand. My sinuses prickled.

"Are you upset about something else besides the painting?" he asked. "About what happened with us?" I couldn't see his face but I knew I'd find the anxious expression if I looked up.

"No," I whispered. "Not that."

I felt his hand on my shoulder and my whole body relaxed. I hadn't realized how much effort I'd been using to hold myself rigid, how much tension there was all the way down into my bones.

"Ariel," he said. "What happened to your friend must have been so scary. It's going to haunt you for a while. But it gets easier. I promise. I've been there." He hesitated and it was as if I could feel his thoughts forming before he spoke them. "I've been better just since I met you."

He stared off into the distance. I couldn't help it; my hand reflexively reached up and played with the strands of hair at the nape of his neck. His hair was always so cool, no matter how hot everything else was.

Then I let myself slide down so my head was in his lap. My

cheek rested against the thick denim of his jeans as he stroked my hair.

"Why did you want to talk to me tonight?" he asked.

I drew my arms around his thighs and squeezed. I felt a tremor run through his body.

"I fucking hate my roommate," I said. "I'm sorry; I sound like such a baby but I hate her. She's a total bitch and I can't get away from her and I don't know why she hates me so much." I rambled on, not making sense, and he listened and made compassionate sounds.

"You didn't tell us," he said when I had finally shut up.

"I didn't want to sound like an idiot. Like I do now! I didn't want to bother you with it." I thought, but only fleetingly, *Why did he say you didn't tell* us *instead of you didn't tell me?*

"Look," he said. "Humans are cruel. They just are. I don't really get it but you have to accept it on some level and then just stay away from the ones that won't stop. It's like if you look at animals. They're stuck with people most of the time; they have to put up with it. But if they are with someone cruel they find ways to shut it out."

I nodded, my cheek against his thigh, and he went on.

"This sounds random, as they say, but it's not . . . There was this llama I saw once, at a petting zoo. It was so beautiful and perfect with these little cleft hooves and these long eyelashes and beautiful, long legs. She looked a little like you, actually. And she was in this pen with flies buzzing around her feet so she had to keep lifting her knees. And people were trying to pet her and feed her and she was staring off into space, ignoring them, not getting near to them, making this sad, high-pitched sound. I wanted to set her free so badly. I felt sick about it. But I saw that she was protecting herself in her own way. At least I hope so."

I closed my eyes and saw the llama in my mind. John was holding a little girl in his arms, holding her out to see the creature.

"Ariel." The way he said my name, in his deep voice, with such urgency, delighted and startled me at the same time. He lifted me gently off his lap and held me against his chest. "I want you to know that Tania and Perry and I have already discussed this and we want you to stay here with us if you want to. There's an extra room. You can move in whenever you want."

That was all I needed to melt the rest of the way. Any resistance was gone. "Thank you," I whispered.

He took my chin in his hand and brought my mouth to his. The sweet, salty warmth of the kiss flooded my entire body. I clung to him and we fed as if we were starving. My hands flickered over the breadth of his shoulder, down his back; there was a pool of dampness that had soaked through his shirt at the base of his spine. I held onto his hips, massaged his thighs. He moaned and his head went back a little. I kissed the cleft in his chin, his throat. My face was prickling with the scratch of his stubble. He rolled me over on my back and gently lifted my T-shirt up, kissing my belly, which convulsed with pleasure at the touch of his lips. It seemed as if my organs were right beneath the surface of his hands, that he could almost touch them.

As he moved toward my breasts they ached the way I'd imagine a new mother's felt and I forgot about the marks. If anything, I was glad to have a reminder of him on my body. He kissed my nipples, sucking gently with his lips, then using his whole mouth and his hands to massage the flesh. I arched up, offering him more. I felt energy crackling back and forth between us like lines of electricity. I gasped, louder than I'd meant to.

"Are you okay?" he asked. "Ariel?"

"Yes. Yes."

"Can I keep kissing you?"

I put my fingers deep into the cool of his hair in answer, guiding his head lower down.

He sighed, working his way over my belly to the patch of hair between my legs. I had always kept it natural until once when Lauren, who shaved almost everything off, had stared at me in disgust when I was changing. I'd started shaving then, although not as much as she did. I was glad that he'd be able to get to more of me, though, and I thought, *I'm actually grateful to Lauren right now,* and then I had to repress a laugh.

"Does it tickle?"

I took his face in my hands. "No, it doesn't tickle. Don't stop, please."

He put his head back down and ran his tongue lightly over the top and center of my opening. *Raspberry Swirl,* I thought, like the Tori song. I pressed up against him, everything that was me focused in that one part of my body that was now his. With one finger he delicately parted me and felt inside for the swollen inner wall while he continued to kiss . . .

The girl crouched at the edge of the cliff. She was shrouded in a dark cloak, her head bent so I couldn't see her face. She was shivering. The sky was filled with stars like pieces of broken jewels and the sea below the precipice was like tatters and shreds of dark silk. The girl was weeping and her tears mixed with the drops of saltwater that the wind lashed against her cheeks.

Then the girl was in the room with me and John. She sat in the corner and I could hear her weeping.

I realized that she was a part of me, a lost part, the part that had left when Jeni did.

I wanted her to come back—I stretched out my arms as John kissed and caressed me—but she shook her head.

Tears slid down my face and I tried to stifle a small sob. John stopped kissing me. He lay his cheek on my pelvis, then slid up and took me in his arms, held me until my breathing regulated and I snuggled closer against him.

"How are you doing?"

"Still scared."

"About Jeni?"

I nodded against his chest.

"I know." He paused, stroking my hair. "Are you scared of this?"

I shook my head.

"Because you're safe here," he said. "Maybe we can help you look for her."

I sighed and buried my face into his neck. I was only eighteen years old but it felt like I had been waiting for John Graves for centuries. I had found him but the waiting was not over.

After we had dozed for a while we woke at what seemed like the same time. The candles he'd lit had almost burned down to nothing, their flames flaring defiantly in the last moments of their lives, but the lamps were still on, bathing the room in verdant light.

John propped himself up on his elbow. His chest seemed paler than usual, almost glowing in the darkness. There was a vulnerability about it, especially at the center. He looked very thin suddenly in spite of the breadth.

I felt the hardness in my throat that was the first sign of more tears and I tried to dry-swallow it down like a pill but it wouldn't move.

He sat up the rest of the way and gestured for me to come into his arms. I wriggled up and pressed my head on his chest. Our eyes met and I felt a tremble of emotion move through my body, from deep inside, out.

And then Tania came through the door.

She stood in the doorway, silhouetted by the light from the hallway. Her hair was combed back away from her face and she wore a long red satin slip trimmed in lace. The roses clambering over her shoulders looked almost real. I had never seen her so beautiful and I wanted her to leave and I wanted her to come and sit beside me.

"Am I interrupting anything?" she asked. Her accent seemed slightly more noticeable than usual.

"Yes," said John but she entered anyway and one of my wishes came true; she sat next to us on the bed and flicked off one of the lamps so that the room darkened. Somehow this seemed odd to me—why did she want less light?

"I'm sorry," she said. "I was feeling lonely. Perry went out." Her natural pout was even more exaggerated.

John pulled the sheet up over his stomach. "You can't just walk in like that," he said spikily.

She ignored him and turned to me. "Sylph? Are you all right?" She stroked the side of my face with her soft hand. I felt myself leaning into her without meaning to. "Are you still upset about Eamon?"

"Of course she is," said John, the barbed tone of his voice catching on the air.

"Tell me what you're feeling, baby." Tania tucked her feet up under her in a cross-legged position and watched me carefully. She had never called me that before. I realized for the first time that I was naked and I reached for my T-shirt and held it over my breasts.

"It doesn't make sense."

Tania touched my leg under the sheet. "That must have been terrible for you," she said.

"Tania . . ." John's voice had a warning tone but she didn't pay any attention.

"I'm so sorry," Tania went on, speaking just to me. "I think that when things happen like that it can do weird things to us. To our minds. It's a kind of survival mechanism. That happened to me when . . ." She paused. "We've all had losses," she went on, her eyes flicking sideways at John, who turned his face away. "I think when people leave it does things. Believe me, I know. You can even have actual visions of the eidolon. It's very powerful."

"Eidolon?" Like on the flyer from the Halloween party.

"It's from Poe. The image of someone that appears to us after they die. A kind of ghost. Perhaps a psychological phenomenon. Though, some would argue, not."

"Are you saying I didn't see her in the painting?"

"No, I'm not saying that. Eamon could have seen her picture in the papers. But I'm just saying that the mind is a magician, too. Especially the truly artistic mind."

My mind, the artistic mind, like hers. How did she always know exactly what to say?

She stroked my hair again. "Johnny? Did you ask Ariel if she wanted to come live here?"

I was suddenly afraid he'd retract the invitation so I spoke quickly, too quickly. "He did. Thank you so much."

"And you'll stay then? Dorms can be nasty. I was miserable until I met my kin here."

John reached out and held my wrist, right at the pulse. "She needs to think about it," he said. "Right, Ariel." It wasn't exactly a question.

I looked over my shoulder at him. His brow was creased with worry. If I lived with them I could have every sensual pleasure I had ever wanted. "I want to stay," I said. "If it's still okay with you."

"Of course it is," she said. She stood up and smoothed silk slip over sharp hip bones. "Now I'll give you two some privacy."

And she was gone.

After Tania left I fell asleep in John's arms. We slept restlessly, heating up under the blankets, tossing them off, our bodies reaching for each other while we dreamed and then woke again. Arousal shimmered along the surface of our skins until it was overcome by fatigue and dissipated for a little while again.

I fell asleep thinking, *You are going to live here; you are going to be free.*

The next evening we woke and John wrapped me in a blanket, lifted me in his arms and carried me into the bathroom. He had run a tub full of bubbles that smelled like lavender.

"What time is it?" I asked, yawning.

"Almost dinnertime."

"I slept all day."

He smiled. "You're catching on to our schedule."

"It won't work. I have to go to class. And finals."

"We have something that will help with that," he said. "Besides, I won't keep you up all night all the time."

He pushed his boxers down off his hips and stepped into the water, then lowered himself modestly beneath the bubbles. His eyes watched me closely. I put my arms over my breasts, turned my back to him and got in, too. I leaned back against his shins and closed my eyes. The room was filled with steam, smoking the mirrors. This was the bathroom where I'd gone when I'd first been looking for Jeni in the house. I could vaguely make out letters written with a finger on the glass. It looked like it said *Diaspora*.

"What's that? Are you guys trying to improve my vocabulary or something?"

He smiled. "Tania might be. It's one of her favorite words. She says she feels like she's not quite human. Like we're all part of this other race that's been displaced and relocated."

"I get it," I said. "Sometimes I feel like that."

"You're one of us."

I sank back against him, sighed and closed my eyes. He soaped my shoulders and back and I put my feet up on the edge of the bath and studied my toes. Even they suddenly looked like sex to me. John moved his legs and put them around me so that I slipped back against his chest. I could feel his erection pressing; I tilted my mouth up and he bent over and kissed me with a succession of deep but light kisses, moving his mouth away slightly for breaths between them.

"You gave me so much pleasure," I said. "I want to do something for you but I'm scared I won't do it right."

"There's no right or wrong."

I sat up and turned to face him. His hair hung in his eyes and his cheeks were flushed.

"I want you to show me," I said. "Please show me." I took his hands and pressed the palms together, kissed his fingertips. Then I gently moved them down onto his groin.

"You want me to touch myself?" he asked. He sounded shy. I felt my nipples tingle.

I nodded.

John's eyes stayed focused on mine as he took himself in his hand and stroked lightly, then more firmly and quickly, his thumb moving back and forth over the underside of the tip, other hand working, too. I was wet again, feeling the slickness even in the surrounding water. I licked the drops of water off my lips and kept my gaze on his face, then let it drop to his moving hands.

"Will you kiss me?" he asked. He shuddered softly and his eyes rolled back.

I slid toward him and took his face in my fingers, brought his mouth to mine. He suddenly seemed so helpless. It scared and excited me; what was this I felt—power? I kissed him harder. He sighed like a girl and whispered my name.

When he came I could feel it rocking my own body from the inside out, even though only our mouths were touching. Relief coursed through me. It felt, again, as if I had been waiting for him forever but also as if my own body had been pent up, holding semen that was only now being released. I had forgotten who was who.

We rested in the bath for a while and then we got out and wrapped each other in large, soft towels and dressed. I wore a white shirt of John's with my jeans. We entered the parlor barefoot, our hair still wet. Perry and Tania were sitting on the couch. The evening light through the windows had a white glow, against which the branches of the trees looked stark and black.

"There you are! We made dinner," Perry said. "No more malnourishment for you, young lady."

"Shall we eat outside?" Tania asked.

We took our vegetable curry, samosas and cucumber raita out into the garden. I hadn't been there in the light before. It looked much less haunted than the night I had stood naked before them. There was a small table set up in the gazebo of worn latticework, under the cascading wisteria and trumpet vines, and we ate there. Berkeley in the spring smells like flowers—roses and jasmine and fruit blossoms. The air was almost as delicious tasting as the food. I looked around at the ornamental plum, persimmon and lemon trees, up at the sky starting to twinkle, and I realized that this was where I would be living, in this house, with them.

"How do you grow plants like this?" I asked them.

Tania grabbed Perry's hands and held them up. "Old green thumb, here." So that was what the green nail polish was. I should have known. "He can make flowers bloom with a wave."

Perry wiggled his fingers almost lasciviously at me until I laughed.

After dinner we sat on a blanket on the mossy ground drinking our wine and Perry took out a joint and lit it, passed it to me. The smoke was smooth and fragrant in my lungs.

"This will help you through finals," Perry said. "We'll give you a stash."

"You guys think of everything."

"Here to serve." The look John gave me made me feel like he had slid his hand between my thighs.

"So you'll be our roommate?" Tania asked.

John took a hit of the joint and smiled at me, then stared up dreamily into the branches.

"I'd be honored," I said.

Perhaps, you may say, it was the wine (grapes, sugar, yeast, pectin) and the joint, or perhaps it was Perry's magic, but when I woke from a brief doze, something had changed; the fairy lights were on, the air smelled of vanilla and candy and the night garden was filled with flowers—fragile white ones, dripping golden angel trumpets, soft purple blossom clusters, spiky cactus moon blooms—I had not seen before.

20. Whatever I could retrieve of his soul

I promised Jeni I would return to my search after I had settled into the house. There were things I had to attend to—getting through finals, telling my mom that I was moving (in with Bean—who had broken up with her boyfriend), packing up my few possessions.

I didn't pay attention to much that week but there was one incident that stood out.

It was Tania, on campus, walking along with a small group of freshmen. She was wearing a printed 1950s sundress accessorized with rhinestone jewelry and very high black peep-toe pumps. The students were animated, trying to get her attention, but her face was quiet, composed. Among the groupies I noticed Ian Larsen. Tania didn't see me but, at just the moment he passed, Ian turned his head. And then turned quickly back to her.

The next day I went to Ian's room. He was packing his suitcase.

"Hey."

"Hey."

"You know Tania De la Torre?"

He frowned at me. "Yeah."

"How do you know her?"

He rocked back on his heels and pushed his glasses up on the narrow bridge of his nose with his middle finger. "Why? What's up?"

"I saw you with her on campus."

"Yeah? She's my psych T.A. She's doing an experiment with us. Why?" For the first time he sounded impatient with me.

"I'm moving in with her," I said. "What kind of an experiment?"

Ian's usually narrow eyes seemed to widen. "You're moving in with Tania De la Torre?"

"What kind of experiment?"

"She'll tell you about it if you're all BFFs. It has to do with how people react to substances depending on who administers them. Basically, if Tania administers them everyone feels all good and shit."

I wondered what this meant but more importantly I wanted to experience again what Tania had made me, and could supposedly make everyone, feel ("all good and shit") if she chose to do so.

John came in the evening on the last day of school with a U-Haul attached to his car and we loaded up my things. On the way to the house we stopped at the copy store and made more Jeni flyers, which he promised to help me distribute.

Later that night, back at the house, John showed me to the room with the draped bed.

"This is yours," he said.

"What about you?" I was hoping he would stay with me. Hoping wasn't the word. My body was so heavy with desire for it I could barely move.

"I'll be in the glass room. It's nice in summer. It stays cool." I couldn't ask him to stay; he had already turned toward the door. "Make yourself at home. The only room that's off-limits is Tania's storeroom in the basement. She likes to keep it locked."

"Why?" I asked him.

He shrugged. "I have no idea. She likes to create this aura of mystery around her. She says it's part of her thesis."

"Her thesis?"

"Magical thinking, parapsychology, magic and influence. I can't ever keep up."

"Never a dull moment in the House of Eidolon."

He came back toward me and my heart beat faster with hope that he'd stay but he just kissed my forehead and said, "Let me know if you need anything." Then he was gone before I could tell him even one of the things I needed from him, let alone list every part of his body and whatever I could retrieve, even briefly, of his soul.

I got in bed and shoved my hand between my thighs, just held it there, not moving, afraid someone might hear me. Moonlight shimmered over the garden like white fruit blossoms and the trees themselves made long shadows—the legs of giants. I closed my eyes and breathed myself to sleep.

I woke some time later to feel a body sliding into the bed next to me.

"May I put the lamp on? I want to see you," John whispered.

I could tell he was naked. His skin was cool at first and he pressed up against my back as if he were trying to absorb the warmth from me. I scooted back so that my haunches were tucked into his groin, his hardness heavy against me, and he smoothed his hands over my hips, slipping one into my panties. I arched back and turned my head to kiss him. His lips were ready, moist and parted the way it felt between my legs. Every orifice was waiting to receive him. We kissed and stroked each other and as we did I saw a girl with sad, dark eyes and wisps of brown hair watching us.

But what of me? she might have said.

21. When couples married and drank mead

One afternoon in late June, the light honeyed, the air smelling sticky with plums, I came home from class and they were all up waiting for me in the front room. I could tell by the way they were dressed—the men in white tuxedo shirts, Tania in a white silk 1960s dress printed with red roses and hemmed short to show off her tan legs and red cowboy boots—that they were ready to go out, although they rarely were awake or even left the house by daylight.

"What's the occasion?" I asked.

Perry grinned. "Solstice, you silly sylph. We're going to the city."

But they hadn't said Golden Gate Park. I wouldn't have come if I'd known we were going there.

I faced Jeni's palace of whiteness and glass filled with rooms of rare blooms and humid air. John put his arm around my waist and I leaned into him, unable to forget the words written in her loopy script. *Live here someday.* I wished I hadn't come. But what was I supposed to do? Avoid places like this forever? Stop living my life? Maybe, at least until I knew what had really happened.

I stayed close to John's side as we wandered through the rest of the park—banks of rhododendrons, camellias, magnolias, succulents, groves of trees, meadows, rose gardens, herb gardens, the Japanese tea garden with its pagodas and bridges and mammal-sized koi, the moon-viewing garden where pink petals drifted down like the tears of dryads into the shallow water.

"You should shoot your film here," Tania said as we made our way along a path under the tree ferns of the cloud forest. I had to film a scene from a Shakespearean play for school and I had chosen *A Midsummer Night's Dream,* with Tania as Titania, John as Oberon, Perry as Puck and myself as the fairy.

"*'How now spirit/wither wander you?'*" Perry said, tousling her hair.

She pulled his curls and he howled and chased her down the mossy path. She stopped under a tree, ignoring his caresses, and raised her hands to the sky. The soft, misty light made her hair, which was now bleached platinum and had grown out beyond her shoulders, glimmer like pale feathers.

"And through this distemperature we see.
The seasons alter . . .
And this same progeny of evils comes
From our debate, from our dissension;
We are their parents and original."

As I watched her, John Graves grabbed me in his arms. I smelled him and felt his heartbeat through my thin back. His cheek scratched against mine. He brushed his nose against me, nuzzling. And then the cloud forest became his lips and he kissed my mouth as if we were alone, while Tania continued to recite, Perry tackled her, the strange mists drifted and the trees listened.

"There's a Solstice party tonight," John told me and the rhododendrons, camellias and magnolias as we were walking back to the car.

I wasn't sure I wanted to meet any more of their weird friends, especially after being shaken by our visit to the Conservatory of Flowers. But they all seemed so excited and I didn't really have a choice anyway.

We drove to the sea and parked along the cliff. A swollen-looking moon hung low over the dark waves. The word I thought of to describe it was effulgent—radiant in a full, pregnant-sounding way.

"Honey moon," said John. "The first full moon in June. When couples married and drank mead."

He took my hand and we followed Perry and Tania down a steep, rocky path to the sand. Since I wore only a thin sweater I was glad for any protection, even the shield of my backpack thumping against my spine. The cool, salty air seemed to be seeping into every part of me. A breeze whipped my hair around my face and the grasses at my calves so that my skin stung. Down by the shore four people were beating hand drums and dancing around a bonfire. The flames leaped with them, silhouetting the graceful flail of their bodies against a burning backdrop. When they saw us they all ran up, whooping and with their arms open. Four of them again, like the four in L.A. Two men and two women. They were mostly half-dressed—the girls in silk slips in spite of the cool, the boys in ripped shorts—with flowers in their hair and wreathed around their necks. They hugged Tania and Perry and John and then they threw their arms around me, too. Their bodies were warm and wet with sweat and they smelled like crushed petals and like fire and ocean.

I didn't really feel like dancing but they pulled me in with them and I couldn't say no. After a while I was glad of it. The flames bathed my face in a hot glow and the salt-chill evaporated off my skin. When I looked at John moving his spine in a sinuous way, eyes closed, mouth in a half-smile, I couldn't tell if the heat was coming from inside me or out. A voluptuous young woman with black curls danced up to me and put a large garland of spicy-smelling flowers around my neck.

"Solstice we wear flowers to protect from evil spirits." She laughed and her eyes slanted elvishly under lashes so thick I wondered if they were real. She had piercings in her regal nose and all the way up the cartilage of her ears.

There was a tall young man covered with intricate tattoos that I couldn't fully make out in the darkness; he passed around a polished drinking horn, threw back his shaved head and howled from his throat, but his voice got lost as the waves crashed against the shore.

"Honey moon," John whispered in my ear as I drank the mild, sweet liquid. "Honey is considered an aphrodisiac. The couple drank it for a month, one moon, after their wedding."

I handed the horn to him and our eyes were drinking each other, too. Honey seemed to be pouring out of me. John danced behind me and I leaned back, resting my head against his shoulder. His hands encircled my waist, fingers lightly touching my hip bones. The world was a spangle of sea and stars and fire and dancing bodies.

Besides the woman who had given me the wreath and the bald guy with the horn there was a delicate girl with a shaved head, too, and an amber-colored man with dreadlocks. Did all of my housemates' friends have to pass some kind of extreme beauty requirement? They whooped and danced and banged their drums and drank their mead around the fire.

Then when we had tired, were nestled in the sand, Tania whispered in my ear, "Show us your magic now, Sylph."

If you had asked me at any moment before what I would do, in answer to this challenge, I would not have known. But, suddenly, then, in that solstice moon time, in the midst of these bewildering creatures, I knew. I lay down on my back with my head on my backpack in Tania's lap and closed my eyes. "I levitate," I said.

They gathered around and I could feel their hands on me,

gently touching my skin, seven sets of hands, fourteen sets of fingertips. I tried to tell which were John's—perhaps those on my left, near my heart? The warmest, biggest hands.

I had done this with Jeni at sleepovers, like all kids, using it as an excuse to touch each other, to play with the mysteries. But there had only been the two of us then; we wouldn't play games of this import with just anyone. We believed that if we had the rest of our secret "family" we would have been able to float, perhaps to fly.

Now I believed in it. I had seen Tania's hands catch on fire. Perry made flowers grow. John turned water to wine. Why not me?

I breathed with them, listening to the waves so that I felt as if I were floating on the sea, buoyed up, the moonlight skimming along my skin, making me translucent, revealing my very organs to their gaze. Lifting lifting.

"Sylph," Tania said gently. I felt her lips on my forehead and I opened my eyes with effort, as if I'd been asleep for hours. "You did it. You are the one. You are ours."

As I sat up, just at that moment, a breeze blew in like icy breath on my neck and I watched some pieces of paper fly out of my backpack and toward the fire. It took me a moment to realize what they were; a moment was too long. They were the flyers of Jeni. I scrambled after them but when I got to the flames, tripping on the wet, sagging hem of my dress, the papers were already alight, curling up into pieces of fire. I held out my hands, watching them die. I looked at John.

He took me in his arms and eventually we sank to the sand together, among the group of bodies entwined under blankets, now. When the flames had died down, he led me away from them, to an outcropping of rocks at the base of the cliff.

I saw Tania raise her head from the belly of the tattooed woman, who, all curls and lashes, was kissing the man with the dreadlocks. Perry was holding the slender bald girl against his chest and the bald guy was massaging her dainty, sandy feet. She had features that all seemed to turn up slightly and I thought of how sorrowful my face in repose must look in contrast to hers. But it had not turned John away from me.

"It is the time," Tania shouted over the surf as we walked away. "It is the time, my darlings."

Sea grass screened the entrance to the cave. Inside the sand was so cool as to feel almost wet, but it was dry. John spread his jacket out over it, then sat, took my hand and pulled me gently down beside him. The sea was glistering with a pewter light seen through the last mirage-like shimmers of smoke from the dying bonfire.

"Those were Jeni," I said.

"I know. I'm sorry. We'll make more."

"I shouldn't have come. I should be looking for her."

"We will. I promise."

I stared through sea grass and smoke at the six figures nestled by the fire that had turned Jeni's image to ash. "Who are they?"

"Shoshanna, Steadman, Erin, Sage." He gently tugged his fingers through the wind tangles of my hair.

"Four of them," I said. "Two men, two women. Why is it always groups of four?"

"Tania started it. She has this thing about everyone in the group representing a different element. Fire, earth, water, air. It's one of her fancies, as she calls them. Everyone complies because it's kind of interesting."

"Kind of weird."

"That would probably be an accurate description of us."

He leaned over and kissed my neck, his lips pressing against the tendon, then down into the pool of pulse. I was instantly hot. I ran my fingers along his wrist, pulled up his sleeve and traced the letters of his tattoo.

"John?"

He stopped kissing, held my chin in his hand and looked at me. "Are you cold? Do you want to go somewhere else?"

"No. I want to know about the name on your wrist."

There was a pause. Sound of wind and sea.

"My daughter's," said John. "Camille."

I pulled away from him and looked into his eyes. Aqueous, I thought. Sad water eyes. The waves crashed against the rocks. He had said the name on his wrist belonged to someone who had died.

I put my arms around his shoulders and pulled him close to me. I didn't know what else to do. I pressed my face into him, clung to him. I didn't know how to make it better but he made me feel better every time he touched me.

"I'm so sorry," I said. I thought about the graveyard, the grave of the little girl we had seen. I still remembered her name: Lucy. He had brought me there. Maybe he was trying to tell me then.

"What happened?" My fingers touched the marks on his wrist. "Can you tell me about her?"

"It's hard for me to talk about," he said.

"Can I ask you one question?"

He didn't say yes and I could feel his body tense but I kept talking.

"Do I know who her mother is?"

John shook his head. "I can't talk about it, Sylph. Sorry. Not now." His voice was firm.

I dropped down so that my cheek rested on his chest and my breast pressed into his abdomen. I shut my eyes, wishing I could disappear.

"I'm sorry, baby," he said. "I don't want to upset you."

But I didn't have to ask John; I already knew who Camille's mother was. I saw her perfectly pouting, always ravenous-looking lips on his. His hands grasping her flowered shoulders. They were younger then, even more beautiful, if that could be possible. Perry was there, too. John's hands in his faunish curls.

I knew the answer to my question.

Camille's mother was Tania; that I knew.

I remembered Tania coming into the room, sitting on the bed with us, talking about loss. *We've all had losses.* She knew grief, Tania did. Maybe the loss of a child, maybe that was what had messed with her, besides the fact that she'd been abused as a kid. It was her baby, too. And Perry's, somehow.

I could have pressed the point but I let John keep his silence. Part of me didn't want to know. More sadness, always sadness. I was relieved to have found him—that's what I wanted to focus on. I had him. I was living in the house with him. Tania slept in bed with Perry and John was with me every single night. Now, with this secret, I had been initiated; I was one of them.

"Ariel, it's all right now. I can't talk about it right now but it will be okay now that you're here."

A chill went through me, maybe coolness from the sand penetrating the cloth of his jacket. He sat up and opened his arms. I wriggled myself into the familiar space, my head under his chin, my shoulder against his chest.

"Can I tell you a story?" he asked.

"Of course."

"There was a man who captured his true love by holding onto her as she shape-shifted into a dog, a snake, flames."

"What does it mean?"

"In order to have bliss you have to be able to accept all the parts of the other, all the wildness and the darkness. You have to be able to hold on." He paused. "I can hold on."

"I can, too," I said.

"I want to be inside you," he said. "Please. I brought protection."

I nodded; holding onto his T-shirt I slid onto my back and pulled him on top of me. He was hard through his jeans and his breath came in gasps. I could feel his heart beating, too, almost frantically against mine. The flower wreaths we wore were crushed in our embrace, releasing their peppery scent. John pulled up my skirt and slid my underpants off my hips, tugged them off my legs. His fingers stroked me almost prayerfully but I was wet already. Then John undid his jeans and held himself rigid against my opening, one hand lightly massaging my clitoris. As he unrolled the condom along his length with the other hand he closed his eyes, bent his head and filled his chest with breath.

"I have been waiting for you, Ariel," John Graves said as he pressed inside.

Blue kaleidoscope butterflies made a sound like shaken bits of glass and refracted beneath my eyelids. I felt a tight squeezing sensation and then rings of release, like those on the surface of the water when a stone is thrown. I grabbed his hand and opened my eyes so wide I thought I might consume him with them. My whole body trembling.

"John John John. You don't understand! It's happening. You don't . . ."

"Yes, my baby," he said.

The portals to the otherworlds were opening.

There was once a different world before this one. Eve's hidden children, the fallen angels, lived in houses made of willow branches with earthen floors. They ate fruits ripe from the trees. Roses grew wild, melons and gourds strewn along the ground with their curling vines. Animals roamed freely. We understood their language. The air was clear; it shone blue. At night the stars told stories in clear voices. There were bonfires and dances. The trees were sacred then. The wine was sacred. Sex was sacred. Sacred music played. Nights came and then dawns and noons and nights again, all a rush of light and dark and work and sleep and prayer.

This wasn't another planet; it was Earth. What more enchanted land than this? And then somehow all that had been, was gone.

The devastation came.

But there are still daughters to be found.

John and I continued to make love almost every night after that one, after he got home from wherever he went. When I asked he told me that mostly he just liked to walk around in the dark and think, make up stories. These he told me while he kissed and touched and entered me. A buck and a deer making love by a stream. A man stroking the crevice of a eucalyptus tree until it changed into a dryad. Elves weeping in a field where trees had been cut down—hundreds of will-o'-the-wisps on the hillside weeping for the dead tree spirits and finally making love in an orgy of sorrow and desire. A strange woman who took a sleeping man and made him her horse, riding him through the night as he slept; he woke with sore muscles, an aching back, tangled hair and a quenchless desire. A beautiful girl dressed in bells and crystals with the hooves of a goat instead of feet. Because I was half-asleep they seemed like dreams I'd had.

I lived for that time of night, those stories, our bodies finding each other in the warm bed, sliding together so easily, all the nerve endings responding. I hadn't known what it would be like but I had sensed it since those first kisses with Jeni. I had known I would love it when the time was right. I wasn't afraid with John, not the way I'd been after Jeni disappeared, when I thought I'd never make love with a boy without fear.

I thought of Jeni, that strange summer, I thought of her often. I hadn't forgotten her and I told her so. I asked her what I could do to help her besides passing out the flyers John and I made but she was silent. And though I asked, if I am honest, I will say that I did not demand an answer nor make any real promises.

Part II

Sophomore Year

22. Because I am

I wasn't ready to go back to my classes when the time came. The air was cooling just a bit but to stay warm I had to swaddle my bones in layers of clothes that itched my hypersensitive skin. It was hard to concentrate on what the professors were saying. I doodled through the lectures—large staring eyes and swirling leaves, flames and raindrops and flower petals scratched in ink around the margins of my notes and then encroaching over the things the teacher said so they became illegible. My favorite words written over and over again. Effulgent. Radiant. Illumine. Scintillate. Pellucid. Luminous. Mellifluous. Lunatic. Aquatic. Gloaming. Mercurial. Infinitesimal. Beryl. Vernal. Amulet. Anthropomorphize. Corinthian. Columbarium. Eldritch. Elvish. John. John. John.

As if these words might ward off the words I dreaded: Phlegmatic. Unctuous. Holocaust. Immolate. Conflagrate. Decapitate. Disembowel. Dismemberment. Sever. Renderer. Murderer.

My grades were dropping. In every class, it seemed, was someone I wanted to avoid. Kyle Langley snickering in English. Lauren Barnes gossiping in abnormal psych. Coraline Grimm in women's studies.

Yes, Coraline Grimm was back after her breakdown,

calling herself Rebecca now. She had gained some weight, cut off all her hair and stopped wearing the goth eye makeup, but she still looked just as sad.

When I asked how she was doing she came and took my hand in both of hers. They were even colder than mine were. I fidgeted and tried to pull away but she held on.

"I was in the hospital."

"I'm sorry," I said.

She bit her lip as if she was trying to keep words inside her mouth. Then they came out, a bit too loudly. "I heard you moved in with them."

"Who told you that?" I tried unsuccessfully to keep any defensiveness out of my voice. "And who are *they* anyway?"

"You tell me." She flicked her eyelids open and closed like a plastic doll's. "I spent some time with them myself and I still don't know."

"Really? What happened?" I tried to sound lightly bemused but my heart was beating faster, like a wind-up toy monkey with a drum. I pulled my hand away.

"They invited me into their lives. Well, it was only one party, but still. I loved them. But I wasn't the one. They told me I wasn't the one and they let me go. I was so sad. What's the word? Bereft. Like I wanted to die."

"I'm sorry to hear that, Coraline, Rebecca." I spoke each word deliberately, like I was speaking to a child. "But there isn't a problem, really."

She shook her head quickly back and forth. "I'm trying to help you. Don't you see that?"

I winced a fake little smile as I backed away from her. "Okay, thanks." I turned, blinking my eyes in the harsh, cool light of the day and looked around. The campus was crowded with students hurrying to classes. A man wearing clown shoes was shouting about the thousands of troops being sent to Afghanistan. Sky and trees and buildings and the round memorial called Ludwig's Fountain, in honor of the campus canine, spouting its jets. The bell tower chiming. Everything was normal—except for Coraline.

But *them*? There was nothing wrong with them. She was just jealous that she had been cast away. They weren't trying to be mean; she wasn't the one.

No offense, Coraline, you can't be.

Because I *am.*

23. Giantess boudoir

One day John picked me up from school. It was already getting dark and the sky was streaked with brilliant, foreboding blue light. The air smelled bright and electric. We drove back to the cemetery where he had taken me once before. The ginkgo trees were turning swarthy autumn colors and in the light that promised rain the crypts on the hills looked like bewitched mansions whose glamours had been removed so we could see them. John took my hand and we ran up the hillside and into the sky-lit columbarium, where the ornate shelves were lined with glass boxes full of ashes; it looked like a giantess's boudoir. The air was pale with chill and the light there was marble-white. John noticed I was shivering and drew me inside the folds of his wool coat. His body was hot though his cheeks were colder than mine. His unshaven chin scratched my face like the finest sandpaper. I closed my eyes and he pressed his lightly chapped lips to my eyelids almost prayerfully.

"I am yours," I whispered.

I thought I heard him murmur, "You are all of ours," and I

opened my eyes, startled, and asked, "What?" sharply, I guess, because his eyes changed for a second.

"What did you think I said?"

"I'm sorry. What did you say?"

"I said, 'You are all I want.'"

"I'm sorry." I buried my face in his collar. He smelled of sage, smoke and rain. "You are all I want, too." But it wasn't entirely true; I wanted Jeni, though I wasn't proving that to her much anymore.

"Come with me." He took me by the hand again and we ran outside. The sun was setting and the strange blue tints in the sky had changed to the lurid reddish pink of certain lilies. We stared out across the grounds and I remembered how we had come here months ago, how nervous I had been with him, how we had seen the grave of the little girl. Lucy, her name was. He had been trying to tell me something, then, and I hadn't been able to hear him.

Now he led me past some muscular wisteria vines, barren with the coming of winter, and knelt down in the dirt and leaves. I joined him. He reached into his book bag of cracked black leather and took out a small bouquet of slightly wilted pink and white roses. He laid them on one of the graves.

OUR CAMILLE. IN LOVING MEMORY. That was all it said on the plaque.

I didn't want to look at him too closely, see the pain that I knew was carving his face. I didn't want to hear him weep. How could I comfort him? But I made myself look.

His features resembled the angels that guarded the cemetery—chiseled and smooth as ever. But his eyes were burning with tears I'd never seen in them before. He shook his head so that his hair fell across his face and bit his lip. "I'm sorry," he said.

"No. No sorry." I flung my arms around him and felt him stiffen for a second, then melt into me, his chest heaving quietly against mine.

"I don't understand it," he kept saying. "I don't understand why."

"Maybe there is no why. It's just how we manage to survive it."

He nodded against me. His tears were on my shirt. I kneaded his shoulders through his coat, trying to loosen the knots of hurt. Then, in moments, his lips brushed mine; then, in moments, it changed.

John was kissing me, fierce as a beast so that I felt the edge of his teeth under his lips. I took his head in both my hands and tried to calm him by stroking his temples with my thumbs. He had me on my back in the earth and I felt the pressure of him forcing between my legs. Desire shot up through my groin. I groaned and he reached down and undid my jeans, then his own. I didn't tell him to stop. He was so large and hard I almost couldn't take all of him. He didn't ask me if I was okay the way he usually did. He didn't have to. Sparks of light shot through me; I was panting so hard I thought I might faint. His fingers, jammed between us, rubbed so that I tightened even more around him. Tighter tighter tighter like a bud ready to explode. Then I was a flower in time-lapse, opening my petals all at once. Big, pink, velvety tongue-like petals dusting his sex with their russet pollen. And then he was coming and coming and I could feel all of it without any barriers between us, just John inside of me as the sun set and we clung to each other and wept on his baby's grave.

John apologized immediately after for not using a condom and I told him not to worry; I'd been just as carried away, I said.

But what if I were pregnant? What then? I'd always had a silly fantasy that if I accidentally got pregnant too early I'd have the baby and my mom would help me raise her. Of course, now my mom couldn't do that at all. I imagined living in the house with John, Tania and Perry. Raising the baby with all of them. I had a sudden, disturbing image of sitting in a bathtub with Tania, passing the child back and forth between our breasts.

Even so, the blood that came brought some disappointment, because I felt pregnant, pregnant with feeling for John Graves. It formed deep in my belly. It swelled my breasts with pleasure. It pressed up against my heart. I remembered my mom telling me that she had read somewhere that having a baby was like walking around with your heart outside your body. I felt that way about John. I also felt that way about Jeni, though. So what did it mean if that heart, that missing heart of mine, no longer beat?

24. You'd better change

On Halloween the rain came down. Not the kind of rain that makes you want to snuggle under the covers and read and dream but the kind of rain that feels like the end of the world. It beat on my brain. I didn't understand how my housemates expected anyone to come to their party in that storm but they didn't seem fazed by it; they went about getting ready—or Tania and Perry did; John was out—as if it were a balmy spring evening while I sat huddled on the sofa in front of the fire, nursing my tea, my socked feet tucked up under me. I smelled something sweet and warm coming from the kitchen and went to see.

"The fees danced on it in the night!" Tania exclaimed, showing me the pockmarks dotting the surface of the cake she had made.

"The what?"

"Fees. Another term for fae. It's lucky! They wore high heels."

I looked at her blankly and sank into a chair. She didn't sound charming to me, then. My head hurt and the smell of the cake was making my hands shake and my mouth water. I wanted to eat the whole thing all by myself right then and there. I'd been losing weight again, sustaining myself mostly on my housemates' wine, but occasionally I'd get ravenous.

"Sylph!" Tania said. "You'd better change. You're not wearing that, are you?" She had on a long vintage gown of cream mesh encrusted with bronze, gold, silver and red sequin flames. On her back were a pair of large angel wings made of precisely layered red feathers.

I ignored her and she came and sat beside me, took one foot onto her lap. She massaged it gently but strongly enough that I could feel the pulses rise up to meet her touch. "What's wrong, love?"

I shook my head. "I don't like this rain."

"It's a magical shower. Our guests love the rain. Come on. Let's get you dressed."

She took me upstairs and I remembered the first time I had gone with her like this, to put on the blue dress and then came down to eat and dance with her and Perry and John. I was such a different person then. I hadn't made love with anyone. No men looked at me. I kept my head down. I did well in school. But some things were the same. Jeni was still gone. My mom was still sick. As in love as I believed I was, my heart still ached as if it had been brutally broken, even in the midst of the most ecstatic lovemaking with John.

Tania dressed me in a white bridal gown that night. It was of lace so fragile it was almost disintegrating, like cobwebs. It made me want to hold my breath. She painted my face white and put a veil over me.

"A dead bride!" she chirped. "Perfect."

I adjusted the crown of the veil—a circlet of tissue-thin green leaves and golden roses—and it caught in my hair, tearing precisely at my scalp. "What are you? A fairy? An angel?"

"Me, an angel?" She laughed. "I'm an elemental."

"A whatamental?"

"A nature spirit. A bit like a fairy but that word's been done to death, don't you think? The elements. I'm fire. Perry's earth. Johnny's water. That's why we needed you, Sylph."

John had mentioned this before but it seemed stranger when she said it. I shivered in the cold lace dress. It could have been made of clouds.

"You're air," Tania said, handing me a cup of warm punch that smelled of cloves and cinnamon and something else I couldn't place—like smoke and rain and minerals and light. "The fourth."

"What does that mean?" I asked.

"You'll see."

"I don't want to *see*. I want you to tell me."

Tania knelt by my side. Her scent was like vanilla and honey.

"It just means you were meant to be here, with us," she said. "John loves you. He's coming back to life."

John loves you.

I could feel the familiar warm prick of tears coming and I didn't want her to see me cry.

"Okay?" she said. "Does that help?"

I let her hug me. Her body always surprised me; it felt so small and thin and so steely at the same time. Her fuller breasts pressed against mine. They'd gotten smaller lately but John didn't seem to mind; he kissed them just the same. I thought of his mouth on me and mine on Tania's nipples, sucking like a baby. Then I shook my head to make it go away and took a sip of punch.

I was drunk by eight o'clock. "Why don't you lie down," Tania said. "No one will be here until ten anyway."

"Where's John?" I asked her as she walked me to my room. "I want John."

"He'll be here."

When I woke up the rain was still pouring down. My body felt leaden and my eyes were heavy as well; it was as if they had sunk deeper into my skull. I pulled myself up and shivered in the lace bridal gown, then got out of bed. A girl was staring at me.

I jumped back before I realized it was my reflection. Even then, I still half-expected her to start speaking in someone else's voice.

Damn.

John.

Where was John?

I picked up Tania's piano shawl, wrapped myself in the embroidered roses and peonies and silk fringe and went downstairs. I left the crown with the veil on the dresser.

The party was like a live thing raging through the house. The walls shook with music. Bodies filled the parlor—young men and women in top hats and tails, biker leather, furs and skins, purple wigs, monster masks; the only light came from candles so that the room was streaked with melancholy, flickering shadows. I recognized the friends from the Solstice party—Shoshanna, Sage, Erin, Steadman (even their names were like supermodels) standing in a circle, wearing elaborate headdresses made of twigs, leaves, flowers, bones, feathers and fur. Their eyes were closed.

I was headed back upstairs to look for John when someone grabbed my arm.

"Where are you going, ducky?"

It was Eamon, the painter from L.A.

I pulled away reflexively.

"I'm sorry my paintings upset you," he said.

"What the fuck was that anyway?"

Eamon's fine, white hand clutched the banister. "I think we should get you some help." His voice was tight. "Really."

I pushed past him and ran up the stairs.

They were lying there, on the bed. Tania in her metallic sparkled dress. Her wings were tossed on the floor but there was a red feathered mask over her eyes. John in a suit covered with iridescent blue-and-green scales, a tangle of what looked like real seaweed in his hair and around his neck. Bare feet covered with sand. (Had he gone to the beach?) Perry—was it Perry? He wore brown fur trousers and a mask that looked so much like a real goat that it could have been taxidermy. The hinged jaw clattered as he turned toward me and fixed me with the yellow slitted eyes.

Tania extended her hand.

John's eyes were sunken with worry.

Perry's goat jaw clacked.

It looked as if they had been waiting for me.

"What's going on?" I said.

"It's okay, baby," Tania said. "Come here."

Instead, I backed away, pulling her shawl around my shoulders.

John got up and approached me the way you would a wild

animal or someone with a weapon, stepping tentatively, hands outstretched in front of him, fingers down.

"Come sit with us and we'll talk," he said. "Please, Ariel."

"We need you," Tania said, getting up, too, coming toward me and taking off the feathered mask so I could see her eyes better. "Just the way you've needed us all this time. Now we need you. We can't really explain it that easily. It won't make a lot of sense to you. But we need your help."

She turned back to Perry. "Take that thing off. It's scaring her."

Perry lifted the goat head off and it fell to the floor with a loud thud. The jaw continued to chatter for a few seconds.

"We had a baby," Tania said. "Camille. You can imagine what that is like because you are close to your mother. It's loving someone so much you want to die if they go away. She was only here for a moment and then she went away and none of us have been the same." Tania's voice was rising in pitch and she was crying, tears melting makeup down her face. "We know about death. We know that souls continue on. But we can't bring her back. Unless you help us."

"What are you saying?" I backed toward the door, reaching for the knob, but my hand only touched air and I stumbled. "That you want to bring back souls?" I stared at John. I could smell the electricity burning in the air. "Or maybe I'm just losing my mind. Is that it? Because I hope that's it. Otherwise I've been living with three psychos and fucking one."

John's face winced like I'd slapped it. "Don't say that. You're not crazy. We may be a little crazy. With grief. But we would never hurt you. And what Tania says is true, Ariel."

It felt like everyone was silent for five minutes, although it might only have been seconds.

Then Perry said, "We need you, Sylph." I saw he was crying,

too. His bare chest glowed, every golden muscle and sinew defined.

"What do you mean you need me?" I looked to John. Wanting him to make it stop, to make things go back to how they had been before—just us in the big bed, our pulses pressed together so that they vibrated through our bodies, no talk of soul retrieval or resurrection.

"We need you to make love with all of us," Perry said slowly. He looked at Tania. "Right?"

She nodded. "You're the fourth. It's the only way to bring her back."

"So that's why I'm here," I said. "I should have known that's why you let me in. And you've all been sleeping together this whole time, haven't you? I'm just some missing piece for you to use, right, John?"

I turned toward the door. "No!" John shouted. "Ariel. No!"

As my hand touched the cold metal of the knob I turned back one last time. "Fuck. You," I said. The bracelet spelling Jeni's name, the one I had never removed all these years, caught and pulled and broke, scattering four white baby beads across the floor.

In the ballad, Janet, or Margaret as she is sometimes called, picks the double rose and a strange man appears to her and demands it back. When she arrives home she finds she is pregnant and goes back to where she had first met him to pick an herb to abort the child. He appears and tells her she must not get rid of his baby. "Were you ever mortal?" she asks. He says he is not an elf as she suspected but a mortal man who had been captured by the queen. He believes she is going to sacrifice him as an offering to hell that Halloween. The only way the girl can rescue him, he tells her, is to catch him at the crossroads, as he rides by on his white horse, and hold him while he shape-shifts into the form of many beasts and, finally, a piece of burning coal. So she does and he becomes himself again, naked as if reborn. The fairy queen wails that if she'd known he'd escape her she'd have taken out his eyes and replaced them with plugs of wood from an eldritch tree. But it was too late.

But that Halloween I knew I could not hold onto John Graves and still have any piece of myself left.

I had to let him go.

As I stepped outside I saw the giant, swaying back and forth on the porch, making soft, moaning sounds. He reached out one hand, like a slab of meat.

I went to Melinda Story's that night because there was no place else to go. She came to the door in her robe, blinking at me with worry, and I asked her, panting, if I could come in. All I told her was that my boyfriend and I had broken up. She made me tea, ran a bath for me, gave me some dry clothes and let me sleep on her couch.

My mom and dad arrived the next afternoon to drive me back to Los Angeles. I didn't let them stop at the house in the hills to get my things. I hardly owned anything anyway— almost everything I had belonged to Tania. And I didn't want to see John's face again.

That was it.

Everything was over.

The lovemaking, the sprawling garden dinners, the dancing, the music, the dreams, the dresses, the fairy tales told while John kissed me in the dark.

And also the not knowing whom I slept with, the living in the land of the dead.

It wasn't that I was so shocked that they'd asked me to

sleep with them. I'd seen it coming—I'd desired it in one way, though another part of me wanted to keep John to myself. But I'd run because of *why* they had wanted me.

Now it was all over and I told myself I was relieved. And my heart hurt just the way they say it does—as if it had been pierced with something sharp.

Along I-5 there weren't many trees but I tried to remember which ones had elves in them according to one of the books I'd read in John's library. Birch and cherry and oak, I remembered. Elm, ash, willow, cypress. There were no elves of the oleander bushes, that deadly poison with its deceptively cheerful flowers that crowded the islands on the highway and lined it on either side. I found myself yearning for tree elves and books. John had so many books. Books on Kabbalah and Gnosticism, Norse and Greek and Celtic mythology. Fairy tales and books of poetry and philosophy. I wanted to lock myself up in the house in the Berkeley hills and read every book there instead of going to school, instead of going back to Los Angeles. But it was too late. And even the stories in the books were changing, becoming as poisonous as the oleander.

The sky was gray with haze and there was such a bleakness everywhere that I found myself sinking into a kind of stupor. I thought of all the tales John had told me. But I remembered them differently now. The girl who didn't believe in the Fates and had a spindle stuck into her heart. The wood spirit who was captured in a wild hunt and nailed bleeding to the door of a man who did not believe in fae. The witches with sugar candies for fingers who lured children into their wells and ovens. Why hadn't I pondered those tales before? I only heard the beauty, saw the glamour. Whom had I been living with?

My mom sat in the backseat with me and cradled my head against her breast. She'd had reconstruction and you couldn't tell. I heard her heartbeat through her thin sweater. She called me baby.

When I was born, she told me, she rode home from the hospital in the backseat so she could be with me. She thought it seemed wrong, somehow, to bring something so tiny in a car. She had kept the clothes I wore that day—a little gown that made a pouch around my feet and a tiny pink knit cap that they'd given to me at the hospital. The gown had pink, blue and yellow ducks on it.

We didn't talk about what had happened to me that night in Berkeley. My parents played *Little Earthquakes*, not realizing that it made me think of Jeni. They stopped at a Fosters Freeze and bought me a vanilla soft serve, not seeming to know that I had given up sugar and, more recently, dairy. I licked it to its demise anyway and then promptly put my head down on my mother's lap and fell into a deadly sleep. Like Beauty.

But she only pricked her finger.

I had a spindle through my heart.

25. Deep as marrow

In the weeks after I returned home, Melinda Story called me a few times and John Graves called me many times but I didn't answer. I never even listened to the messages on the cell phone. They, the messages, especially John's—the rich sound of his voice, the voice that had whispered to me in the dark— would only have drawn the spindle deeper in. Besides, I didn't want John anymore. I wanted nothing because I was nothing.

Except that, from the moment I saw my bed, with the little-girl butterfly quilt cover, I wanted to sleep.

Sometimes I got up in the mornings and went jogging with what little energy I had left, returning home to take a bath and collapse back into bed. My bones ached and my back felt hollow, like the elf girl in the tale whose husband caught her pouring food into it and sent her away. One smoggy day, much too hot for November, I felt my phone vibrate in my sweatshirt pocket, against the jut of my ribs, as I ran on my spindle legs along the cement wash near my house. It was John. I took the phone out and watched it move in my palm like a creature. Then I lifted it above my head and threw it over the chain-link fence into a trickle of dirty water at the bottom of the L.A. river. My arm trembled from the effort. My phone was gone. But, more significantly, John was gone. I was gone.

I didn't get a replacement.

On another run I went farther than usual, past the house where Fritz Kragen lived. His car was in the driveway and I stopped for a moment, panting, pulsing, the day white in my eyes. My clothes were sopping wet and even under sun I shivered.

Slowly I turned and stumbled away, knowing I wasn't strong enough to fight with anyone. Except myself.

In December, my parents sent me to a therapist they were also seeing, a tall, blond woman named Elise Ronan with an office waiting room filled with *People* and *Us Weekly*. I didn't like her from the first moment. She gave my dad a bright smile and then turned to me and took my hand.

"I've heard a lot about you," she said. Her lips looked puffy, like a fish's.

I stared blankly at her. I could feel my father staring at her in a different way. I could feel Angelina Jolie and Brad Pitt staring, too, from the cover of one of the magazines.

"Please, come in." She smiled at my dad again and led me into her office. It was decorated in pastel colors. I sat on a mint green couch and crossed my arms over my chest.

"This must be a hard time for you," she began. "With your friend gone like that. Your mom being sick."

I shrugged and picked at my cuticles. I didn't trust her, not at all. There was an ugly floral print on the rug and I stared at it. The flowers seemed to have eyes.

"Do you want to tell me how this whole thing is making you feel?" Elise Ronan asked. Although she was probably in her forties, there were probably more lines in my face than hers when I smiled.

"I don't feel much," I said. "I'm just really tired."

"Are you eating?" she asked.

I shrugged again. "Yes. I'm not really that hungry."

"You know, a lot of women your age have body issues. I know I certainly did," the therapist went on. "I always thought I was fat." She smoothed her skirt over her narrow hips.

I blinked at her. Was she really talking about her weight?

"You know," she went on, "when the mother is ill it can really affect how the daughter feels about herself. It's very natural. How do you feel about yourself in general?"

I shook my head. Tears were coming to my eyes and I didn't want her to see them. I couldn't believe my mom had sent me here; if she hadn't gotten sick it would never have happened.

I stood up. "I can't be here," I said.

My dad was waiting in the lobby, waiting for me. He looked worried but his face brightened again for a split second as Elise Ronan followed me out.

"What's the problem, Ariel?"

"I need to go home," I said.

He turned to the therapist and made an apologetic gesture with his hands. Was this my father?

"It's okay," she said. "We can try again next week."

"What the hell was that?" I asked on the way home after my fuming silence didn't provoke any response from him.

"What the hell was what? You walked out on her. I don't really appreciate that. Her time is valuable," my father said.

I wanted to bang my forehead against the glass. "Who is she? She's scary. I can't believe you and mom picked her."

"Actually she's a very good therapist," my dad told me. "She's very caring. Your mom wanted us to be in good hands . . ." He stopped.

"What are you even saying?" He came to a sudden stop at the light and I slammed my foot forward on an imaginary brake. We went on in silence for a while.

Finally, he spoke. "I'm sorry, Ariel." He pulled the car over and leaned his head against the side of the car. "I don't know what to do."

"Neither do I. But not this. I'm not going back to her and I don't think you should, either."

"That's not your decision."

I looked over at him. It was as if he'd aged ten years. I wondered if he was imagining having sex with Elise Ronan. I hated him. And I didn't.

"Just take me home now," I said.

That night my mom came into my room in her bathrobe and sat on my bed, took my hand. Her hands were always cold now and the flesh looked as if it would stay in little peaks away from the bone if you pinched it gently, like there wasn't any moisture left in her.

"What happened today?" she asked.

"I can't stand that woman. Who is she?"

"My oncologist recommended her," my mom said. "Dad really likes her."

"*Dad* really likes her? What about you?"

"She's very practical. I just want someone who can handle things." I could hear the fragility in her voice and I didn't want to make it worse but I felt like I was about to scream.

Instead I pressed my head against her chest and she held me but she seemed very far away already.

"I have to have some more surgery," she said, finally.

I pulled away. "What? What's wrong?"

"There's another tumor." She was managing a smile but her eyes were shining with tears. Illumined. But the word didn't matter. "I'm sorry, baby."

"Why are you saying sorry?" I turned away from her. "You don't have to be saying that."

But I was lying. I wanted her to be sorry. If she was responsible for this then she could be responsible for making it go away. And she would do that for me, of course she would.

My mom's surgery was scheduled for after the first of the year. All we did, all of us, was wait.

My parents had given up on trying to get me to see a therapist for the time being. They let me lie around and sleep, as long as I promised to eat three meals a day. I did as they asked, although the thought of having food in my system just seemed wrong, like making a plant eat a sandwich.

I felt a lot like a girl in a tower or one who slept in a briar-covered castle or a glass box. My skin was always clammy and my hair was tangled. I slept and slept on soft pillows, seeing almost no one. But if I was the spellbound princess I was also the witch who had put myself in that place of icy isolation. One thing I was not, though: the faithful prince with the sword and the kiss, the rescuer.

I thought about John a lot but in an abstract way, the way you would think about a character in a book, an actor in a film, a singer whose voice haunted you or a shadowy figure in a masochist's wet dream. I watched candelabra-lit videos in my head of him dancing with me through the house in the hills, wearing a dark blue velvet suit and a carnival mask over his eyes, Chopin nocturnes coming out of his mouth and into the whorls of my ears. Even though it wasn't real, the desire was worse than reality. Deep as marrow.

The tree has a hollow in it. That is where the children live. The dead children.

Sometimes you can hear them crying.

The tree grows up from the water. Its leaves fall into the creek. The water shines at its roots, a thin sheen over the mud. Light twinkles off of the wetness. You can see your face if you look closely enough. You can see their faces.

The children walk in a procession. They drink from the cups of flowers. They weep their songs.

There is one of them, a girl, who visits me.

She has small bright eyes, like little lights in her face, and tiny dimpled hands.

"They only wanted you to help them," she tells me with her telepathic baby voice. "They did not want to hurt you. They did it for me."

Sometimes I see her holding a large flower.

"What is that?" I ask her.

She shows me the drops of liquid glistering among the petals. "It's Mommy's tears," she says, holding it out to me. "Drink."

26. Whether they are ghosts or memories

Sometimes I think I dreamed it, at least some of it. Like this:

New Year's Eve day there was a knock at the door.

I was lying in bed in my pajamas, watching the rain shaking the trees outside my window, making them look like frightened children. I didn't move.

The knocks grew louder, more insistent. My dad was out and my mom was sleeping. I didn't want her to wake up; she needed her rest.

I pulled on jeans and walked into the hallway.

Even with the rain outside, there was a strange winter afternoon stillness to the house. I shivered, barefoot on the wooden floor. I wondered if I listened closely enough, could I hear my mom breathing through her door? I was always listening for her breath.

I walked slowly to the top of the stairs and held the banister like I was eighty years old.

The knock came again. I went down the staircase and asked who was there.

"John Graves," he said.

My heart was beating so hard it felt as if it could animate the rest of me—a stern puppeteer—but my limbs were frozen. I had to force myself to open the door.

It was the way I felt when I'd seen Jeni on the streets of Berkeley. He couldn't be real. But there he was.

"Greetings."

I took a step back and stared at him. He had grown a small beard and his hair hung shaggily to his shoulders. His glasses and his corduroy jacket were sparked with raindrops.

I tried to speak but couldn't find any words in my throat.

"I tried calling you and you never answered." His voice rose a notch and I put my hands over my face as he moved closer. "I'm sorry," he said.

I backed away one step. But that was all. I didn't shut the door.

"May I come in?"

I shook my head.

"Will you come driving with me then? I need to talk to you." There was a heavy, lost sound to his voice.

I looked back into the house. Cold air was rushing into the warm living room. I imagined my mom calling me to her bedside, beckoning me to put my ear to her lips. My protective mommy who wanted to shelter me from everything. But there are some things from which you cannot shelter yourself.

"Wait."

I closed the door and left him in the rain. I ran upstairs and checked; my mom was sleeping. I wrote her a note, put on a jacket, jeans and boots and came down again.

John was standing exactly as I had left him, with his hands in his pockets. I regretted for a moment having shut the door on him like that, not asking him in, but he didn't seem to mind. We walked out to the car. He leaned over and put the seat belt on for me, reached and locked my door. I could smell him, which meant he was too close; it didn't feel safe.

"I'm not a child," I said.

"Sorry. I know."

I turned to look at him. He was slumped in the seat. I wanted to pound his shoulders with my fists but they looked so defeated already.

He let his hand drop onto my arm. Even through the fabric of my coat I could feel his heat, as if without the cloth between us he would burn me.

"Why did you ask me to sleep with you?" I asked. "What was this thing about bringing your child back?"

"Tania said that was the only way it could work. If we really love you."

"What the fuck are you even talking about?"

"Ariel, I'm sorry. I should have told her no. I was wrong. But I want you to trust me now. Please."

I shook my hair around my face, scattering rain, and bit my lip. "How can I trust you? You kept these secrets from me all that time."

He reached over and started to touch my arm, then drew his hand away when I flinched. "I wasn't sure if I believed it. I left them for a while about two years ago because I didn't believe it, I thought she'd lost her mind, but I came back because I thought, what if in some crazy way she was right? Or maybe, even if it didn't work, it might help us all go back to how things were before. I wanted to try. But it was fucked up. I'm sorry."

"The way things were before? When you were with Tania? You kept it from me that you needed me for something. You pretended to love me."

His voice was deep and crackled like wood in a fireplace. "I do love you. And I'm glad I came back to them because otherwise I might never have found you. You're who I want, Ariel. I left the house again. I got my own place."

"You left?"

He nodded.

"I don't want to talk about it," I told him, swiping at the betrayal of moisture leaking from my eyes. "I want to forget about all of it. I want to forget everything tonight."

He paused, his palms open to me. "I do, too. How can I help us forget?"

I looked at him for a second before I spoke. There was a

warm feeling spreading through my chest in spite of myself. "I'm hungry," I whispered.

John took me to a Thai restaurant with pink booths where we ate soup and rice, noodles and dumplings. We hardly spoke, just stared at each other across the table the way you might watch an apparition. By the time we left the restaurant the rain had stopped. The air sparkled with moisture and Christmas lights. We drove around until we passed an out-door ice-skating rink. John parked.

"What do you think?"

"I haven't skated since I was twelve." It was with Jeni.

"Like riding a bike," he said. He got out of the car, came around and offered me his hand. I let him baby me. He rented the skates and knelt before me and tied them on. He held my hand as I went tentatively onto the ice. I let him. My legs felt like a fawn's, tiny and weak, especially on the slick surface, wobbling on the narrow blades. I let John Graves lead me around and around the rink of ice while lights flashed, pop music played, soap bubbles filled the air and the world be-yond our magic circle grew dark and still. For once I was awake. And the demons slept.

Later we drove through the canyon to the top of a hill overlooking the valley. John parked and we stared out at the false fairyland of light.

"Do you want to dance?" he asked me. "Dance this fucked year to its death?"

So he blasted the stereo and opened the car doors and we danced in the street until we were soaked with sweat. I took off my coat and then my pajama shirt and danced in my tank top, my nipples rubbing against the thin fabric. There was a nearly full moon ringed with mist but still white-bright. Jimi Hendrix came on and John sat in the driver's seat and pulled me to him and as midnight came I lifted the glasses tenderly off the bridge of his nose and put them in my pocket and he kissed me the way I had never known anyone could be kissed. Blasts and riffs and explosions of kisses while I straddled his thigh and rubbed myself up against him again and again. Kissing to death the old year with its sorrow. Part of me felt guilty for the pleasure of the kiss after everything that had happened. Part of me thought, *Without this I am bones in the dirt, Jeni. I can't live the life we promised each other we would have.*

"White Wedding" by Billy Idol made the speakers throb.

There was the sound of an explosion in the sky behind us and a flash of light illuminated John's uptilted face.

"You thought of everything, didn't you?" I said.

Fireworks shot green, pink and white chrysanthemums out of the sky.

We made love for hours in the back of John's car, grasping for—in each other's bodies—the two months we'd been apart, and at dawn he brought me home and parked in front of my house.

"You still don't want to talk?" he asked.

I shook my head.

"Talk to me. Please."

"I'm so fucked up."

"Ariel . . ."

I looked at my house. The light was on in my mom's window. "She has surgery in two weeks."

He put his arms around me again and I had to force myself to pull away, shut the door and run into the house.

"May I call you?" I heard him say, but I couldn't find the words to answer.

One night after John's visit and before my mom's surgery I went driving by myself. The streets seemed to lead me along until I was in parts of the Valley I hadn't expected. The places I had been with Jeni. The library where we went every afternoon to check out as many books as we could carry. Sometimes we stayed there and read, in the cool, quiet room with the windows full of leaves and light. The musty smell of the books in their crackling plastic covers. The pencil shavings. The whispers. The park where we soared on the swing set, late into the evening on warm days, the sky turning pink and a little breeze starting to chill our bare shoulders. The mini mall where we got takeout Chinese in those white paper cartons with the red pagodas on them, frozen yogurt and a DVD and went home to get in bed and eat and watch. While we had dessert we took turns combing and braiding each other's hair. The elementary school we went to, looking so small and dark now. We scratched our elbows and knees, pressed secret notes back and forth, wore matching outfits for weeks at a time. Once we swapped clothes and put our hair up in caps and came to my mother's door thinking she might mistake us for each other. That was how much we wanted to change places; not because we didn't like our own lives but because we wanted to know each other that well. Now the playground looked dangerous, the tetherball poles and volleyball nets casting shadows on the moonlit blacktop. The eucalyptus and jacaranda trees hung shabbily over the road beyond the chain-link fence. There was a quiet I hadn't remembered feeling before. The middle school where we went. Parked in front of it, looking at the sign announcing the dates of winter break, the locked gate, the deserted grounds lit with a buzzing fluorescence, I shuddered.

Ghosts haunt every place we go whether we believe in them as apparitions or not, whether they are ghosts or memories. This city where I lived was filled with Jeni, but so was Berkeley. Everywhere I went she went with me and she didn't.

I could still hear her lispy laugh and see the dimples and the ways her eyes gleamed like a baby's. When someone so young and lovely vanishes they leave a cutout in the atmosphere; they don't fade. They leave a place for the sun rays to cut through and burn us, melt all the important ice to floods.

Berkeley terrified me but Los Angeles was a wild garden in its own way, where people also disappeared and blood stained the secret grottos. There was blood on the ground from the Native Americans who lived here first and had their land usurped and there was the blood of the Manson murders and the blood of the junkies dying in the streets, blood of people killed in car accidents on the highways. Have you ever seen those red stains on the cement? I felt as if the freeways were bent on leading me astray and that was how I drove them, defensive and fearful.

One kidnapped me and took me to the mall where Jeni and I used to go, a big indoor palace of mirrors and lights and music where the idea was to confuse and stimulate you into overspending. Boys and clothes and sugar, that was what we wanted. And because you could only pay for two of them you were willing to spend too much. The clothes might attract the boys and the sugar would soothe you if that didn't work. I rode the escalator up and down up and down until some security guards began to eye me suspiciously. I walked through the food court and the fried smells and sugar smells coated the roof of my mouth and made me nauseous.

So I left the mall and drove to Jeni's neighborhood and before I knew it I was sitting parked near her front door. Her parents still had the pale blue Christmas lights up and they looked like a sad attempt at cheer. I waited for a while and finally her dad's sedan pulled into the driveway and her parents went inside without speaking to each other, as far as I could tell. They turned on every light in the house as soon as they got in. I wanted to go talk to them but I knew I'd seem like a ghost, that time of night and the way I felt. I wondered if they kept her room the way it had been when she disappeared, as if, even now, she might return to sleep there once again. I thought of Jeni's room with the roses and books everywhere, the mix of flower fairies and rock stars. We gave each other pedicures and listened to music and giggled late into the night. We were girls but becoming something else. If she was gone, then so was I. If my mom left I was more than gone. John Graves stood between me and complete annihilation but, at the same time, did I really exist with him, either? Did he exist?

What had I done, ever, in my life? I had been a daughter, a student, a friend and a lover but I felt I had failed at all of them. I had suffered loss and been afraid. I had loved books and words. If I vanished like Jeni had, what would it really matter? My mom would grieve and my dad, too. John Graves might grieve for at least a little while. But besides a love of words and beauty and a strange tenderness in my heart, what did I really give to the world? I was no heroine and I would never be. No heroine at all. I was what a girl is told to be by most of the world—be passive, be quiet, be slim, don't draw too much attention to yourself. But in that way, too, I was a failure; I was a skeleton child who didn't even comb my hair.

I drove to Kragen's house and parked. All the lights were off and his car wasn't there. My heart beat faster, as if it had already done something dangerous.

I got out of the car, leaving my keys in the ignition, and walked quietly across the lawn and around the side of the house. There was a gate but it was unlocked and I pushed it open and went in. A sensor light flicked on and I froze. Through the back window I could see the office. There was one bookshelf and I remembered how the lack of books in the living room had disturbed me. On this bookshelf, though, there were books I recognized, even from far away. Thin-spined and brightly colored. School yearbooks.

I tried the back door—locked. But I didn't have to smash glass with my fist, either; there was a small window and it was slightly open.

I was sick of myself for doing nothing. For waiting and wondering and crying and forgetting.

I stood on a low wall and pushed the window. It stuck at first but then slid up. I hoisted myself onto the ledge and pushed my body through and slithered inside.

I wasn't even scared anymore. The light in the yard was still on and it shone into the office. The yearbooks on the shelf were organized chronologically so it was easy to find the one with me and Jeni in it.

It was especially easy to find Jeni's picture. Because it was the only one that was circled.

The silence around me was thick and deep. I ripped the page out of the yearbook and then had to steady my hand with the other one to keep it from flapping like the wing of a dying bird.

The car pulled up then. I heard it in the drive. I bolted out the back door into the yard, through the side gate, into my car. *Go go go.* I got away but the paper was not in my hand—as if I had imagined it, as if I was insane.

Detective Rodriguez was in when I came by the station the next morning looking like an avenging demon. He didn't seem particularly happy to see me.

"Miss Silverman. How are things?"

I followed him into his office and he adjusted his large body into his chair. Held out his hands, waiting.

"I saw something," I said.

"You saw?"

"Something. At Kragen's."

"At Kragen's." He narrowed his eyes at me, trying to tele-graph something. *Ramifications* was the word that came to my mind.

"Let's just say someone found a yearbook in someone's home."

"A yearbook? In a teacher's home?"

"And a picture of a missing person was circled."

He cleared his throat. "Let's just say that what *she* found was taken illegally by forced entry from someone who had absolutely no criminal record and a solid alibi." He leaned forward on his desk. "Miss Silverman. Ariel, right? I have three daughters. Not one—three. Your age. If anything happened to them I'd be out of my F-ing mind, excuse the French. I'd be busting through walls without warrants, the whole nine yards. I understand, believe me I do. I'll have my men look into this. But you can't go chasing after Fritz Kra-gen just because he seems a little odd to you."

I wanted to jump across the desk and he could tell.

"Okay, very odd. But he's clean and I'll just say this—if you get yourself into any trouble, I won't be able to help you. Understand? No matter how much empathy I may feel.

"Now, I strongly suggest you get yourself some help deal-ing with all of this and I promise if anything new turns up we'll be on it."

"You'll investigate, then?"

He cut me off. "Meanwhile, I'm sure there are some impor-tant things you can attend to in your own life."

My own life? But he was right. There was.

Jeni, the living need me.

But what if she did, too?

27. Vigilant, our magic

Rodriguez called me a week later and told me they hadn't found anything at Kragen's. We were right back where we started and I was even less sure of my sanity. Had I seen that circled picture of Jeni at all? But, as Rodriguez has said, I needed to attend to my life now, and my mom's, from which, at this point, with the surgery ahead of us, I could hardly distinguish my own.

I had never been to Duarte, where the cancer hospital was. That was all I knew about Duarte. Long streets lined with low buildings, a suburban emptiness. And the hospital. Which had well-groomed gardens, fountains and impressive-looking buildings designed to make you feel reassured. But I didn't. I just felt small and numb.

I went with my parents for the initial consultation and sat quietly in the corner while the doctor talked about the tumor that had grown through the wall of one organ into another. No one cried; we were getting used to this. The doctor had a calm voice and steady, cool hands. He told me when we left that I should make sure I got cancer screenings as early as possible. I just stared at him, not sure whom he was speaking to.

On the way out I passed a young Asian man, not much older than I was, shuffling along, wearing a colostomy bag. He stared, challenging, and I met his eyes for a moment, then had to look away.

He could have been me.

The night before the surgery my dad and I stayed in the waiting room. I curled up in the chair with one of my mom's shawls draped over me. It had butterflies on it and smelled like her. I wanted to capture her scent inside of me so that it would never dissipate.

My dad fell asleep with his legs stretched out in front of him, his arms crossed on his chest and his mouth open. His shirt was wrinkled, there were crumbs on his pants and his face looked terribly pale and crumpled like fabric in the fluorescent lights. I tried to imagine what it would be like to have only him. There was no one else alive in our family; it would just be us. *And Elise Ronan,* I thought perversely, and promptly wanted to vomit.

At midnight the new iPhone my dad got for me rang and I walked into the long glass corridor that ran between the two main buildings and answered. It was John.

"I'm here," he said.

"You're where?"

"I'm at the fountain at the main entrance."

I had told John that the surgery was going to be here and the date. We'd been e-mailing and texting since I'd seen him on New Year's Eve. But the idea that he had come here made no sense to me. It was as if someone had told me an elf prince had come, accompanied by a hundred fairy children to sing to me and bring me cakes.

Still, I ran down the stairs and crossed the plaza to the fountain. It was lit up in the night, glowing a greenish white, and the air was moist with it. I saw a tall, shadowy figure standing on the other side.

It was John.

"Why?" I asked him. "Why do you keep coming to me? What have I done for you?"

He grabbed my shoulders and pulled me into him. I could smell him—his smoky sweat—and I wanted to bury my face into that smell, drown in it.

"Ariel. Stop. I think about you all the time. I wanted to be here." He paused and rubbed his cheek against my hair. "Do you want me to leave?"

I grabbed him tighter. His muscles were hard, tensed under his coat. Everything was so quiet, except for the sound of the fountain. Without that it seemed as if we could have heard the stars.

"No," I said. "Don't leave."

"I got a hotel," he told me. "If you want I can go there and wait for you or you can go there with me tonight and sleep and I'll bring you back here in the morning."

I went back upstairs and left a note for my dad, then drove with John to a cheap hotel a few miles away. The lobby smelled of cigarettes and the man who checked us in looked right out of a zombie horror movie, without the rotting flesh. He gave us the key and we went upstairs, past a door with something fastened on it. I jumped back against John. The thing was the head of a man with a pointed beard and horns.

"What the hell is that?" I said.

"We can go somewhere else if you want . . ." He put his body between me and the door with the carved head.

I was too tired to go anywhere else; he saw that.

"Sometimes those things are just there to remind us that we have to be vigilant in our magic," he whispered, taking my hand and leading me down the hall.

The room had ugly, scratchy curtains and bedspreads but it could have been a boutique hotel full of stargazer lilies and silver champagne buckets as soon as we got in bed. We lay there fully clothed and held each other so closely it was hard to tell who was who.

The alarm clock woke us at five. My eyes hurt like they'd been replaced with glass ones when John turned on the light. We didn't take the time to shower or get breakfast but John had brought a blueberry muffin, an apple and a banana, which I didn't eat but held carefully in my lap as we drove back to the hospital.

"Call me when the surgery is over," he said. "I can give you a ride if you want."

He closed his eyes and pressed his lips to my forehead as if he were praying.

My mom lay on the gurney, looking fragile as a child in the hospital gown. Her hands were shaking when I held them but she smiled.

"It's going to be okay," I told her. For some reason, this time, I believed it and I could tell it relieved her to hear the confidence in my voice, although I hardly recognized myself. I thought of the devil head in the hotel hallway and then of John, all the beautiful and frightening images I'd seen since I had known him. *Vigilant in our magic.*

Whatever was between John Graves and me, it had the quality of something otherworldly—maybe I'd go as far as to say magical—and I was going to believe in it now. How could I choose not to? If nothing else, he had infused me with a calm and confidence about my mom that I hadn't felt before.

It frightened me that Tania had wanted me to sleep with her and Perry and John because somehow they believed they were involved with the retrieval of souls. But what was that if not some form of magic? Insanity, maybe. But could I dismiss it so easily? And wasn't cancer, and the loss of Jeni, a kind of insanity, too? A much worse kind.

I went back into the waiting room with my dad and curled up under my mommy's shawl again. The smell of her was already fading.

Jeni, I whispered in my brain, *please keep her safe. And I will help you, too.*

When I woke up, the craggy-faced doctor was standing

over me talking to my dad, who was wiping his eyes with his rumpled shirtsleeve.

"She did well," the doctor said. "I think we got it all."

He smiled at me and in that moment it was the most beautiful smile I had ever seen.

John Graves told me later how he had spent the night in Berkeley before he came to be with me:

He had gone out into his garden, lit candles all over and strewn red roses and poured wine on the ground around the pond. He had put a wreath of leaves in his hair and taken off his clothes and danced under the moon and spoken to the mysteries. I don't know if that is part of why my mom's surgery went so well or not. But it made me love him even more. And I was indebted no matter how I looked at it. To John, and Jeni, too. But I was still afraid.

I was there when my mom opened her eyes. She patted her lips—delicate as parchment—together and stared at me.

"Who is this?" she said.

I smiled at her. "It's me, Mom." They had told us that the meds might make her hallucinate.

"It's my angel!" She tried to smile but then groaned and the nurse showed her how to squeeze the control to administer more medicine.

"You did great," I said. I was surprised at how rich and warm my own voice sounded, the way a woman's voice would sound when comforting someone she loved, not the voice of a frightened child.

My mom blinked at me and clutched my hand. "Thank you, angel," she whispered.

My own gratitude buckled my knees. I knelt beside the

bed and closed my eyes and thanked the gods and goddesses and spirits and guides.

While my dad slept in the chair I fed my mom ice chips and when she shuddered with pain I helped administer more of the I.V. medicine. She dozed off, waking to reach for my hand.

"I think I saw her?" She spoke it like a question, her eyelids flickering.

"Who, Mommy?"

"Jennifer."

"What did you see?"

"She was looking for you."

"Tell her I'm looking for her, too," I said, but I wasn't sure, though I wanted it to be, how true it was anymore.

When John drove me home from the hospital I sat with him in the car, staring at the yellow house and wondering how it would be possible for me to go inside and leave him. But I couldn't ask him in either. For some reason John was still too much a part of my imagined world to bring all the way into my real one. I was afraid he might vanish if we crossed that threshold.

"Thank you," I said, because the language I loved hadn't invented more accurate words yet.

He reached over and took my hand, put it in his thick denim lap. "I'm here for you."

"But I haven't been there for you."

"You were scared."

"I still am." I told him about Kragen and the yearbook, about how no one would listen. About how I had to find out what had happened to Jeni.

As I spoke I stared out the window into the leafy street where she and I once rode our bikes, oblivious to terror.

"So you think he did it?"

"I'm not sure. He has an alibi." My voice snagged on phantom nails in my throat. "I don't know what I think anymore. I don't even know what's real."

He squeezed my fingers so that it almost hurt. "I know how hard this is for you. I'll help you. In Berkeley. Just come back to me."

I moved my hand away as gently as I could. "I can't. I don't understand what happened. With anything."

His eyes, behind the glasses, were so full of all the things I feared and wanted.

"I know," he said. "I'm so sorry. It's not an excuse, but when we lost her, it made us sick with grief."

He meant Camille. "I can't even imagine what that's like."

John got very still and lowered his head. "She was really, really tiny. She fit in the palm of my hand. But her eyes were like little lights." He took off his glasses and wiped away the steam that coated them and put them on the dashboard.

"I can't come back," I said. "I'm sorry."

"Ariel," said John. "Even if you run away again, my love will follow you."

It reminded me of a story from a picture book my mother read to me when I was little. I had to get out of the car, fast, or I never would. I pulled my hand away and kissed him quickly on the lips. And then I was gone.

Just days after John left I got the call.

"Did you hear the news today?" she asked me. I wasn't sure who it was for a second.

"Katie?"

She was speaking too fast. "I knew there was something fucked up about him."

"Are you talking about . . ."

"Kragen! He was arrested for child molestation," Katie Leiman said.

Fritz Kragen had been taken into custody for fondling an unnamed female student. Rodriguez called me this time. He sounded warmer than before.

"How's it going, Miss Silverman?"

"Is there any proof?" I asked.

"About Jennifer Benson? *Nada.* The same. But we got him on this one. I know I'll sleep easier. And your instincts were right on the creep factor, I'll give you that."

"What about Jeni?" My teeth chewed on the inside of my lip; I wondered how hard I'd have to bite down to taste blood.

"Case is still open. I promise we'll let you know if we get anything."

"Okay."

"Oh, and you ever want a job on the force and need some advice, you come to me. But no more breaking and entering, understand?"

Even if it hadn't been proven Kragen was the one, at least now he was behind bars.

I wasn't sure what I was supposed to feel. Substantiation? Acceptance? Closure? I felt mostly only a fierce agitation that slowly dissipated as I directed my attention to my mom and her recovery.

I drove to the hospital every day, memorizing the freeways until I wasn't afraid of them anymore, and sat at her bedside reading to her or watching movies and feeding her pudding and soup.

One day I took her out in the wheelchair and we went to the Japanese garden tucked away behind bamboo, a minia- ture version of the magnificent one in San Francisco. A woman and her three children were leaning over the koi pond, feeding the fish. The oldest child was bald and pale and I tried to imagine how the woman must feel, how every day she must have to fight her terror with each breath. I gave my mom some fish food and we tossed it over the bridge on the other side of the pond. The fish came surging toward us—huge, wiggling, meaty bodies that fought for the crumbs of food we tossed into the water, their mouths opening obscenely. They made me think of Fritz Kragen and I wanted to throw up.

My mom must have noticed the look on my face. "Let's go back," she said. I hadn't told her about Kragen yet. It wasn't something I wanted her to have to deal with.

We brought her home after a week and when I saw her back in her room at home it changed something in me. In some ways Kragen's arrest was part of this change as well. I didn't feel like sleeping anymore. I did the shopping and the cooking and ate more food. I started running again. I even took some yoga classes at the studio near my house. It was as if the combination of my mom surviving the surgery and my time with her afterward and Kragen's arrest had given me some part of myself back. Sometimes I imagined returning to John but I was still afraid of losing the self I had lost once before in that house of fae.

Six weeks after her surgery I went with my mom to a consultation about chemo. The handsome Persian doctor didn't look much older than I was. He was the one who had treated her before. My mom shook her head at everything. When we left she said, "I don't want it!"

She'd had it before, lost her hair and whatever curves she'd had left on her body. Now her hair had just begun to reach the length it had been before she'd started.

"No one wants it," my dad said.

"Yes!" Her voice was thin as ice. "Yes, some people do. He said so. They go right into it after their surgery."

"They don't want it," I said. "They want to live."

My mom sat very still in the front seat. I could only see the back of her head.

"I want you to live," I said. "I'm not letting go of you again."

"Me neither," said my dad. He reached for her hand and at first she stayed stiff but then I saw her shoulders slump.

"We're going to help you through this," I said. "I'm going to be here this time. It's going to be different."

A week later she came into my room and sat on my bed, where I was reading one of my books of fairy tales.

"May I talk to you?" she asked, and I put my arm around her waist and leaned my head on her shoulder. She stroked my hair.

"I'm not sure I can go through it again," she said.

"I know. But I know you can do it."

"I don't want to lose my hair. I know it sounds vain but . . ."

"It'll grow back, though."

"The treatments aren't even guaranteed."

"But the chances are better if you try it. Can you just try it? Please." I didn't want to cry in front of her again. I didn't want to scream at her but I could feel emotions seething inside of me.

"Your dad wants me to do it."

"Of course he does. He wants you to live." For a second I had a sickening flash of my dad standing at my mom's gravesite with his arm around Elise Ronan. "I'm going to shave my head, too," I said. "Just so you know."

She took my face in her hands and I struggled not to pull away. "No you're not."

"Yes I am. I want to. It's no big deal for me. I want to support you. And we'll get you some medical marijuana this time. We'll get all toasty. It really helps."

She smiled. "You're crazy, you know that?"

I wrinkled my nose at her and shrugged. "I'm your daughter," I said. "And it's going to stay that way."

So my mom agreed to the treatments and over the next few months I made her miso soup and smoothies and helped her with the bong. When my dad was out we put on *This Is Spinal Tap* and smoked and giggled until she fell asleep. I knelt with her on the bathroom floor and held her forehead while she vomited. I drove her to her doctor's appointments. Every time I got tired or depressed I told myself that the only thing that mattered was that I was spending time with her, getting her through this to the other side.

When her hair started to fall out again I asked her if she wanted me to take her to a salon to get it cut short.

"I can't handle going to one of those places," she said. "Will you do it for me?"

We smoked some weed and I cut her hair close to the scalp, the soft tufts falling to the ground.

"Shave it," she said.

"What?"

"Shave it off. Then we don't have to watch it fall out all over the place."

So I cut the hair even shorter, got the razor and wet and lathered her head and held the razor up. What if I cut her? But I couldn't let her feel my fear. I took a deep breath, the kind I'd learned in yoga class, and steadied my shaky hand. I thought of all the times my mom had washed, cut and braided my hair for me. One day I might take care of a little girl. I thought of shaving myself, how sometimes I nicked my shins and little lines of blood appeared on my skin. But that was when I wasn't concentrating. And now all of me was going to be focused inside the blade I held until there was nothing left of Ariel but eyes and a hand with a purpose.

I didn't cut my mom. When I was finished I put mascara, blush and lip gloss on her, then held the mirror up for her to see. That part was even harder than the shaving; her eyes filled with tears, as if I *had* cut her. I suppose I had.

"Wait," I said.

I left her and went into the bathroom. My hair was in a braid down my back and I held it at the nape of my neck and dug the scissors into it—they made a dull, sick, saw sound—and cut it off. I threw the braid to the ground, suddenly a dead thing. Then I chopped around my face—these sounds were light and sharp and free. And then I took a razor to my head; my hand didn't shake at all this time.

Baldness didn't bother me. I didn't care about looking attractive to anyone; it was the last thing on my mind. I just wanted my mom to see, every time she looked at me, how much I loved her. Perhaps, too, it was a sort of penance. For Jeni.

I got in bed next to my mother.

"Ta-da!" I said.

Even though I'd warned her, it made her cry once more, much to my dismay, to see my tiny naked head, my crazy, looming eyes. When she could tell I was okay with it she kissed my face again and again and I placed my head on her chest and closed my eyes and slept to the sound of her heart.

As she recovered I enrolled for the spring semester at UCLA. I rode the bus there from Ventura Boulevard, over the 405 pass. But I wasn't really there in the smog and traffic. I was tripping out to Björk on my iPod—the music I'd been listening to when John came to campus to find me; I might as well still have been at Berkeley, walking among thousands of rose-bushes in the amphitheater-shaped garden on top of the hill or in the park with its volcanic outcroppings at Indian Rock. That was where I imagined myself to be until I was disturbed from my reverie.

There was a boy at my bus stop with large angry pustules on his face and a precarious walk. He stared at my head, the hair just beginning to grow back—I'd continued to shave it until my mom stopped her treatments—pointed and said, "Ugly. Bald."

This would have mortified me even a few months ago. Now I smiled and told him, "My mom was very sick. I wanted to show solidarity with her. I'm sorry if you don't like it but it really has nothing to do with you."

He stared at me (as did some other bystanders), patting his lips with his fingers, but he never said anything about it again.

If I'd been a ghost at Berkeley now I was even more invisible, even with my bald head. It was easier to be a ghost here. I was more invisible in the bright sunlight, and no one was on the lookout for ghosts in West Los Angeles. I went to the lectures, alone. At lunch I escaped the crowds and the heat of the open brick courtyards into the sanctuary of the sculpture garden and ate under the purple shade of jaca-randa trees with Maillol, Matisse, Moore and Rodin as my only company. I never hung out at the restaurants, shops and movie theaters at the edge of the campus in Westwood. I came home as soon as my classes were over, did homework, took a run, helped my mom with dinner, read and went to bed early. I didn't have any friends at all, not counting Jeni, whom I talked to all the time in my head.

———

I was baking loaves of bread. The dough was soft and alive-feeling in my hands as I kneaded it, cool but with the potential for warmth, quiet but, I thought, perhaps with the potential for song. I hadn't baked bread in years, not since my mom had let me help her when I was little, forming the dough into funny fat bunnies and birds, but in the dream it felt natural and familiar. After I had baked the loaves I took them out of the oven and put them on a table with a blue-and-white checked cloth where they began to sing. Then I picked up the phone to call my boyfriend but I couldn't remember his number or his name. So I went out searching for him. I was on Melrose Avenue where all the hipster shops are and I was walking along past all the beautiful people but none of them seemed to notice me. I was embarrassed by the pimples on my chin and my hair looked bad. I kept walking, looking and looking for this man I loved whose name I could not remember.

At last I found him.

"I made you bread," I said and he put his hands on my hips and kneaded his fingers into my flesh.

"You are my bread," he said.

When I woke from the dream my hands were gripping my abdomen, my fingers pressing into the spot where John's marks still lingered.

That spot. It was always a little tender, though I hardly noticed the feeling anymore. I believed John had marked me. But maybe, all this time, I had been marking myself.

After that, slowly, over months, those marks, made my him or by me, or first by him and then, again and again, by my own fingers, faded all the way away.

28. A man happened by

People usually change in small, incremental ways over time. You don't see it overnight, even after a trauma, not usually. People fall apart or fall in love or grow up or die slowly, most of the time. Children's brains take years to develop and diseases usually do, too. That was what was happening to me for all those months living with my parents, taking care of my mom, separated from John. I was changing. When I went away to school I had thought I was a grown-up but now I realized that even at twenty I was still a child who was just learning who she was and how to take care of herself.

Change comes in the way you serve food and water, administer medications, clean up messes, do errands, read the words of masters—prophets and poets—listen to music, listen to each other. It comes in the way you say *I love you* over and over again, as if you won't be able to say it in the morning, and the way you say *I'm sorry* as soon as possible after you have hurt the person you love. I hadn't said either of those things enough times in my life but now I said them to my mom a lot as her cancer went into remission. And I said them to Jeni because I had not gone to Berkeley with her, because I had neglected my search, because even though Kragen was in jail there was no solid evidence linking him to her.

It had been nine months since I had been with John in the house in Berkeley. I was ensconced in the window seat staring out at the night. My parents were asleep in their room. My mom had gained the weight back, her hair had grown back thicker and curlier this time. Most days we didn't even think the word cancer.

I thought the word John, though, still, and Jeni.

As I came downstairs I looked at her photograph, the two

of us smiling goofily at the camera. In the background was her house. Her mom had taken the picture of us. I had been there only once since it happened. I had meant to go again. I had never gone.

Go now, a voice inside me said. What are those voices? Shall we call them intuition? Shall we call them angels? Shall we call them ghosts?

Jeni's mother, Joanne, answered the door that night. She took a step back when she saw me and I wondered if I'd made a mistake.

"I was driving by," I said.

"Do you want to come in, Ariel?"

We sat on the couch and she made tea. I remembered the mugs from when I used to come over after school on rainy days to drink hot chocolate and eat cinnamon toast with Jeni. I could still feel the slight burn of the spiced sugar on my tongue.

"I almost didn't recognize you," she said.

I smiled, a little stiffly, and ran my fingers over my scalp. My hair still felt prickly, growing back.

"How are your mom and dad? I haven't seen them."

I realized she didn't know that my mom was sick. "Oh, they're okay. How's Mike?"

"Fine, thanks."

There were lines carved around her eyes, like with a knife, and I wondered if, and how, she ever slept at all.

"I'm so sorry." These were the words I'd been dreading. They sounded so cliché and trite. But what else were you supposed to say? I loved language but not in moments like this when you couldn't use poetry to explain how you really felt.

"Thank you," she said, kindly. She probably knew that no

one thought the words sufficed at all. But that we were all trying our best, even if it was ineffectual, and much too late.

But then I did something I had wanted to do for two years. I reached out and hugged her.

Joanne Benson was a runner, she'd always been in great shape; now she was bony and hunched, like a tiny old woman. Like when I hugged my mom, I wished my body was softer for Joanne, too, comforting in some way. She pulled away first.

But at least I had touched her, finally.

"What do you think about Fritz Kragen?" I asked.

"The teacher? I heard about that. They said it isn't connected. Why?"

I didn't want to push; the strain showed on her face—more questions, more visions of her daughter in pain. It was enough.

"I'm sure the police are on top of things," I said.

There was an awkward silence. I could hear the hall clock tick. Joanne adjusted her thin frame on the couch as if her tailbone hurt her.

"Well, I'm glad you came by. There's something I've been meaning to give you for a long time."

She went upstairs and came back holding something.

"This was hers, you may remember? I think she would have wanted you to have it. I couldn't part with it before but I think it's time now."

My hands tingled and I didn't want to touch it. But I took it anyway.

"Thank you so much," I said.

I had heard that Blythe dolls were discontinued because they frightened children too much with their big heads and eyes that changed colors. This one's were amber; reflecting the color of the sofa cushions they looked almost red, like blood.

I showed my mom the doll the next day. She examined it closely, smoothing out the long brown hair and straightening the blue-and-white gingham dress.

"You still think of her. Jennifer. All the time."

"Yes," I said. "Can you call her Jeni?" I tried a yoga breath, sipping air from the base of my throat, to keep from crying.

"Sorry—Jeni. You know, Ariel, I think of her, too. It's hard for me to talk about but I do. You know you can speak to me about it."

"I don't want to upset you."

"I know."

"I don't know what to do anymore," I said. "How to help her."

She looked different, my mother. She was better, her hair had grown back, but sometimes her eyes would get a faraway look that I didn't want to think too much about.

"You know, I didn't want you to go back there. To Berkeley. But in some ways I think it might help you to come to terms with what happened."

"Why are you telling me this now?"

"It's weird," she said. "I didn't ever believe in these things before, but since I've been sick . . . . I had a dream. She was in it. She was asking you to come back."

That night I dreamed, too.

A girl rose up from out of the water. Her hair looked green, woven with seaweed and shells. She was naked, with perfect tiny white breasts, but her eyes were ravaged.

A man happened by. He was an unassuming man with a paunch, and balding. You wouldn't have looked at him twice on the street. You wouldn't have suspected him.

The girl pointed her finger in his direction and opened her mouth in a silent scream.

———

The girl lay asleep in a nest of straw and feathers under a blanket of green foliage. Her hair was wild, a tangle of leaves, twigs and flowers. She was sleeping peacefully but around her neck was tied a rope.

A man came by. His eyes were red-shot. His hair shone like it was metal-made. He bent down and pulled. Rope. Taut.

The girl wore a wreath of flowers and a long white dress. She danced among the stalks of grain under the fullest moon. A man arrived. He was a tall man, too tall, and there was something terribly wrong with his eyes. The eyes of a zealot. Or worse.

The girl smiled at him and beckoned.

Dawn came, lighting up the field as if it had caught fire. Conflagration. Immolation.

A boy walking there saw something in the dirt and picked it up, then threw it down, his whole body convulsing with disgust.

It was a severed hand, ragged at the edges and rubbery-white like the kind you find in a Halloween store. But real.

Other parts were strewn across the field. Bloody parts. Body parts. Rendered.

The boy heard a voice like wind, blowing through the stalks of grain. A woman's voice.

Laughing.

This dream, combined with the revelation of my mom's, was what made me decide, finally.

I had to go back up north; I had to find out. Something, at least. I'd failed Jeni long enough.

Part III

Junior Year

29. A woman? Was I that?

I could have called John when I got back; I had his phone number and even his address—he was living in a hostel on Piedmont. But I wasn't ready to see him. I purposely avoided that street when I arrived with my parents at the end of the summer but I couldn't help turning my head after every tall, dark-haired man who hurried by.

My parents and I looked at a lot of places for me to live in that first semester of my junior year. There was a corpulent guy who interviewed me while clipping his toenails. He kept pet rats and explained that I had to be very quiet at all hours so as not to disturb them. An entomologist and his girlfriend kept bugs in their refrigerator and told me, while eyeing me up and down, that I wasn't exactly what they were looking for; I assumed they meant something besides my skills as a housemate. There was a slim, tawny, red-haired girl who lived by herself in a two-story Tudor-style house and was offering me the filthy garage for almost two thousand dollars a month if I also agreed to clean for her; I guess she was in pretty high demand. There were three punk rock guys living in a dilapidated house with graffiti all over the walls; they were renting a room the size of a closet and painted black; it was cleaner-looking than the beautiful girl's garage but smelled of piss. One guy lived in a beautiful house in the hills, but besides the fact that it was in too close a proximity to the house I wanted to avoid, he told me he made "erotic films, well, some call them porn but whatevs," and asked me if I minded naked women lying around the yard.

And then, while my parents went for lunch, I met Pierrette, who liked to be called Pierre, a tall Swiss woman with a smoky voice and smokier blue eyes who came gliding out to meet me, a batik sarong tied around her hips.

We sat on cushions on the floor and talked for about half an hour while her three-year-old son, Michelangelo, ran around, chasing the cat and four kittens that also lived in the Oakland apartment. Michelangelo's skin was dusky brown and his eyes were sweeter than chocolate. His father was a Rastafarian man Pierre had met in Jamaica but now she was dating an African doctor. She supported herself by making fabrics and jewelry. There was almost no furniture in the apartment that had been part of an old Victorian house, divided into separate units, but the floors were polished wood, the walls were hung with masks from all over the world and the big, clean bay windows let in the sun. Slender columns flanked the front door and in the small garden there was a chicken coop and a vegetable patch.

The tiny room I was offered had lace curtains Pierre had made and an old-fashioned frosted pink glass fixture shaped like a breast, even down to the nipple tip. Right away, I wanted to live there.

"Do you need any references?" I asked her, although I wasn't sure who I'd ask for one, except maybe Melinda Story, and I hadn't spoken to her in almost a year.

Pierre said, "You always know when it's right."

I didn't argue with her.

I loved her right away.

It reminded me of how I felt when I met John, Tania and Perry. Except different. This was love without any attachment, therefore without any real risk. I wanted to be near Pierre and Michelangelo but not really involve myself with them. I wanted to feel their quiet presence as they drew on large pieces of paper on the floor of the living room, collected eggs and picked vegetables, ate their omelets and homegrown tomatoes at the kitchen table, sang each other songs at bedtime. In the first few weeks we shared meals and occasionally Pierre and I shopped at the Co-op together. She suggested foods and supplements to add to my diet—like flax oil, probiotics and a green powder to make smoothies with. But often I shopped and ate alone in my room and I was content.

I was taking classes and doing art projects in my spare time. The collages I'd started to make were really all for Jeni. I got large black poster boards from the art supply store and glued on photographs, then decorated them with ripped pieces of fabric from dresses I'd worn, with glitter and dried petals, safety pins, plastic insects and tea sets. I used the collection of greeting cards my mother had given me over the years—paintings of fairies and dancers and angels and flowers and reproductions of great works of art—as well as a few photographs of my mom, of Jeni and of John. With a silver pen I wrote bits of my stories and poetry on paper that I then ripped and scattered over the surface of the collages. In one piece I used matchboxes with tiny white plastic skeletons inside of them and covered the whole thing with black tulle and black glitter. Sometimes Michelangelo came into my room and made collages with me. He covered his black poster board with gobs of glue and then sprinkled on white feathers and silver glitter.

"Angels are stars in the air," he said.

"Angels are little boys named Michelangelo," I told him.

I didn't spend time with anyone besides my roommates and in the first few weeks I rarely even saw the people I'd known from before. But when I felt settled I did go to visit Melinda Story.

During office hours I knocked tentatively on her door. She smiled when she saw me and we hugged. She'd cut off her braid into a short pixie; it made her look even younger than she already did.

"I was so worried about you," she said. "But I heard you had come back. How are your classes?"

I shrugged. "They seem okay. I'm trying to focus on the writing."

"I'm glad to hear it. I think you're so talented."

"Portman didn't really."

She gestured for me to come and sit at her desk. The light through the windows of Wheeler had that familiar dusty glow, making dust particles ignite.

"It can be an old boy's club around here. They don't always know how to handle a strong woman."

A woman? Was I that? A strong woman? "I don't feel strong. I've been afraid to come back but I had to."

Annie's picture was behind Melinda on the shelf. I hadn't noticed it there before, facing outward, completely visible to anyone who came through the door.

"They arrested someone," I said.

"They found who did it?" Melinda's eyes looked rounder than usual.

"No. They arrested the teacher who escorted them, on something 'unrelated.'" I made quotation marks in the air. "Child molestation. But they say he's innocent."

"Doesn't sound clean to me." As Melinda spoke, Annie's eyes in the photograph wouldn't stop watching me. I couldn't tell if they were challenging or just sad.

I thought of the homeless woman who had spoken to me when I first came here. *You think you're fine now,* she said. *But just wait. It gets harder. Then you'll be transformed. Then you'll be just like us.*

No one was sure if Kragen had done it. What if it was someone else? What if I found out what happened to Jeni and lost my own soul in the process? Is that what I had been afraid of all this time?

"I guess in some ways I'm scared to know," I said. "I almost want it to be him so I can just let it rest."

"I get it," Melinda said. "But it's better to know. No matter what, it's better."

If I lost my soul in this so-far fruitless searching, perhaps it would be for the best. Who else deserved it but my Jennifer, my friend?

One day Lauren Barnes came up to me, suppressing an embarrassed smile.

"Where've you been?" she asked. "We were worried." She only looked curious; I had been elevated to the level of prime gossip material.

"Lauren," I said calmly. "I've just been through what could be described as a fucking nightmare and I'm just now trying to come back here and have a life again."

"Wow," she said. "Chillax. What's all the attitude?"

But I went on, ignoring her. "There is no reason for you to treat people the way you do except because of some serious and fucked-up personality disorder. I am hoping that you will refrain from speaking to me again, unless you have something sincerely kind to say. Otherwise I may be forced to hit you in the face."

She took a step back and put up her hands but by then I was walking away.

There was one other person from the past that I saw sometimes: Tommy Leeds. He was in my modern art history class. We never said hello but one day he sat next to me for the lecture. He wore eyeliner and his hair was spiked. The plugs in his ears had stretched.

"Hey," he said.

I thought of John Graves and the way he greeted me.

"Greetings."

Tommy gave me a split-second squint of *what the fuck* and then asked, "How's it going?"

I wondered why he wasn't avoiding me.

"Okay."

"Heard you were in L.A. for a while."

I nodded.

"I'm playing with my band in the city this weekend if you want me to put you on the list," he said.

"I thought you thought I was a freak."

He grinned. "Do. But I also get that you went through some pretty bad shit with all that."

I shrugged. I realized then how desperate I still was for any show of sympathy, anyone who would recognize what I had been through. I accepted his invitation.

Pierre asked me where I was going.

"You look good," she told me while she stirred the spaghetti sauce.

I was wearing eyeliner and lipstick, which I usually avoided now. I'd also had my nose pierced on Telegraph by a jewelry vendor and I'd just switched out the original sterile silver stud for a tiny diamond chip. I thanked Pierre and told her about Tommy.

"But that's not who you are really thinking about it, is it?" she said in her dusky voice. I hadn't told Pierre about John but she'd seen photographs of him in the collages I'd been making.

"The man with the dark hair, in your art?"

"Yes."

Her gaze was gas-flame blue. "May I ask who he is?"

"I don't know," I said.

"Perhaps you need to find out."

As I headed for BART I saw the man with the dreads.

"I was once like you, my friend," he said. "You could become me easy, walk out into the street covered in hair and filth and people would look at you with disgust, sister, and think you were born like that, that you never were a little child, clean as a small tree, quick as water, bright in the mind and breathing sweetly. When you walk as long as I have you'll see too much, things you don't want to see. They can kill your mind, yes they can, kill it dead. I hope I can teach you by who I am. You'll go like me if you don't watch your back. Those souls, they keep coming no matter what we do and you will always have to hear them until you or someone, some damn thing else takes your life, but you don't have to let them make you ill in the in-between."

He moved his hands in the air so the dirty red poncho he wore gave him a winged look. His eyes were rolled up in his head. "There is a sickness, child. You must put it out."

I took BART into the city and came to the club where I'd first met John Graves. I almost wanted to turn back; I hadn't realized how it would affect me, dizzy me, to be there.

A sign on a trash bin read: DO NOT PLAY ON OR AROUND. Like a warning about everything.

Just as I was standing there, beneath the marquee, deciding what to do, I felt a hand on the small of my back and gasped.

It was Tommy.

"Hey, come in with us," he said.

I followed him through the back entrance into the green room, where the rest of the band was milling around drinking beers.

"Glad you made it out," Tommy said.

I tried to smile at him but the muscles in my face felt weak, unused.

He offered me a drink and I took it since no one seemed to care. The alcohol went right to my knees at the first sip. I could feel it turning to sweat, later, as I bounced around in front of the speakers, thrashing my body to the music, my ears ringing with pain. My eyes were closed most of the time and every so often I'd open them and think, *I might see him. I might see John.* But of course he was never there.

After Tommy's set he brought me another drink and we watched the second band together. His hand snaked to my lower back, slid up my shirt, and I let it stay there. I thought, *I have never fucked anyone else.* Actually, I'd never fucked anyone. What I had done with John wasn't that.

Maybe I should fuck Tommy Leeds?

But then I thought of how I had turned down the chance to sleep with John and Tania and Perry and nothing made sense to me. Would that have been more meaningful than sleeping with Tommy Leeds? Of course it would. I loved them, didn't I? I loved John. Would it have given me "experience"? Yes, but that wasn't really what I wanted, was it? Would it have made me closer to or farther away from John, closer to or farther from Jeni; that was the real question.

Tommy leaned jerkily over to me. His breath smelled of beer and his eyes were bloodred, from speed probably—I thought of the Blythe doll by my bed at Pierre's; I still hadn't changed her eye color to blue or green, even though it would have appeared much less strange.

Even this high Tommy looked like a boy whom Jeni and I would have crushed on, like a boy Jeni might get to know on a school trip and agree to meet later, in the night.

"I have to go," I said.

"Wait, man. I wanted to hear if you found out more about what happened with that chick," he said.

I turned back and saw a smile like a hand was crawling across Tommy Leeds's face.

"What the fuck do you know?" I screamed. My palms contracted into fists and I leaped at him, wanting to slam that smile away.

"Back off!" In the laser beams of light that burned the air his expression was distorted, grimacing. "I told you I don't know shit. You need some serious help, man."

I felt thick arms gripping. A security guard smelling of cigarettes and menthol dragged me away. I was trying to explain it all to him but the words coming out of my mouth didn't make any sense. He deposited me on the street in front of the theater. I was too stunned to run off; night had never looked so vast. I leaned against a wall for support, wiping the sweat from my face with my T-shirt, and watched four skinny, decadently dressed kids huddled around a cigarette—two boys, two girls, like a group to which I had once belonged.

I heard some commotion and turned to see a young man being hoisted out in much the same way I had been. He was holding his glasses, which were broken.

"Ian?" I said.

He looked at me curiously and began to laugh in a wheezing

way through his nostrils. He had lost a lot of weight and his hair was long and lank with grease.

"What happened?" I asked him.

"Aren't you the one who wanted to know what they put in that wine?" He stopped laughing and his eyes were suddenly suspicious.

"Ariel," I said. "From the dorms."

He put his finger to his lips. "It's a *secret*," he said, drawing out the word.

"But not from me," I said, with as much authority as I could. "I'm their roommate, remember?"

He giggled. "Oh yeah. Whatever." He blinked at me. "Cannabis, ephedra, opium. It's intense stuff. She gave me a lot of it and now it's all I think about."

Intense stuff was right. Weed, speed, heroin. "Who?" I asked. "Tania?"

"Ms. De la Torre!" He was laughing again. "She's a fuckin' hottie. I'd have done anything she said even without all the soma."

"Soma?"

Ian waved brightly at me, turned and started to stumble away into the darkness. I went after him. "What is soma? Are you talking about Tania's wine?"

"Ritual wine," he corrected me. "Drunk as part of the sacrificial ritual! A substitution for the original psychotropic substance."

"It had weed and ephedra? And opium?"

"Awesome, right?" he said.

I knew then, in that moment, where I needed to go.

30. Other magics

My best friend had vanished into air. My mother had had parts of her body precisely and painfully removed. I had lived for almost a year on flowers, lived with a man I loved, but still didn't really know, and then I had left him and now I was back, still haunted. Perhaps I was under some kind of spell. Nothing seemed real anyway. So why should I believe what happened that Halloween after I ran into fucked-up Ian at the concert? And why shouldn't I believe it?

I wore the dress Tania had given me a year before. I told myself it was because I had no other Halloween costumes but that wasn't really it—I wanted to relive my experience in the house, so I could understand it better. I wore the fragile dress as I walked up into the hills, in the dark, even though it looked as if rain might soon fall.

It always surprised me how few people I saw in front of the houses in the hills—as if wealth implied closed doors; in the flatlands there were always kids playing, students riding their bikes, people sitting on lawn chairs, walking dogs. Here it was much more quiet, even on a night when carved pumpkins leered from porches and bowls of candy were just inside the doors. There were hardly even any trick-or-treaters in sight. You wouldn't have guessed what went on in the house where I had once lived, so maybe there were other magics going on behind these facades, but somehow I doubted it.

The house with its mess of foliage—the oak trees, the roses, the persimmon and ornamental plum—gave hints of what it held if you looked closely enough.

The curtains were pulled closed and I couldn't hear the familiar music coming from within. I stood there a long time before I finally gathered the courage to knock, and then I stood there longer still.

But no one came.

Standing there in the rain, I was now sure that it was time for me to visit John. If I could make it to him.

31. Or the Wilding

So this is how we run. We run in our pretty clothes, the ones we put on earlier to attract love. We run with our hair streaming out behind us. We run as quietly as possible, so no one hears us.

But sometimes they hear us.

It is called the Wild Hunt. When they come for us. Or the Wilding.

We are girls and women who were out alone, who were out at night, who were not rewarded for being kind to strangers as the fairy tales once taught us. We are girls and women who were unlucky. Sometimes we are boys, too.

We have no magic powers.

We have no amulets of protection.

No one has cut crosses into the stumps of trees to keep us safe.

Would that even keep us safe?

We no longer believe in fairy tales.

But we will learn to believe in monsters.

I ran that night in the rain, away once more from the house I had loved and toward the man who was the reason I had loved it. I ran for Jeni, too, though I still doubted whether anything I did could help her anymore. As I ran the rainfall grew heavier, drops of water blinded me. Soon it was a storm, roaring in my ears like the voices of giants.

I don't know if what happened that night really happened to me or how it did, if it did, in spite of the evidence that I would soon hold in my hands. But I could have been feeling so guilty about everything that had gone before—I had let down my mother, then John, and Jeni, always Jeni. Now I was back, maybe stronger, but still running, and perhaps more deranged than ever. Maybe that is why these things happened that night. Or I believed they did.

He was there before I knew as I came down into the flatlands. The car parked blocking my way and the passenger door opened. I slid to a stop. The night was so dark I couldn't see myself, except the vague glow of my white dress, plastered to my body like the marble folds of a gown on a statue. I was shivering and the car was warm—I remember that. The heater was on in the car and it felt warm compared to the night that shook me.

A hand. It pushed me down so that my face pressed into the cracked, bristling leather. Smell of cigarettes and mold. I thought, *I am going to die.*

I didn't think to scream. He slammed the door closed and I pushed myself up and grabbed for the handle but it wouldn't open. My fingers crawled madly over the door panel looking for the lock. Knobs. Buttons. Metal. Darkness. Nothing. But he was in the passenger seat now. He grabbed both my hands in one of his. His hands were that huge. There was a rope in his mouth and he used his other hand to wrap it around my wrists and pull it tight so the braiding burned into my flesh; then he pushed me down on the seat again.

"Please don't," I said. I pressed my face into the upholstery so I couldn't see his face. "I'm not going to look at you. I'm not going to scream. Just let me go."

He was silent. His silence was huge, like his hands. There was something about him that seemed familiar, like a nightmare you've had before but can't remember, like a face on the street you can't place but that makes your back hollow with fear.

I knew not to look at him.

I knew not to scream.

I knew to keep talking.

I don't know how I knew. Maybe I had imagined this before, a thousand times, without realizing it, thinking of Jeni in my unconscious mind.

What did she do when it happened? What would a little girl with no fear do when this happened? What could she have done if she had thought about it beforehand?

Maybe Jeni was telling me what to do—the spirit of Jeni. Because as I lay there breathing the smell of my own death, a voice said:

Keep talking. Keep talking. Ariel.

So I did.

"My mom has cancer. Do you know anyone with cancer?" I didn't wait for him to respond because I knew that he wouldn't anyway. "I love her so much. She's a really good mom. I'm so lucky. Not everyone has that. It must be so hard if you don't." I hesitated then, for just a moment. I could hear him breathing. I didn't want to hear the sound of his breath. "I go to school here, that's why I'm here, but it's really bad sometimes. It's not like I have the worst problems but I want to go home and be with my mom." I could feel tears in my throat and I tried to grit them back. "I'm sorry. I don't want to cry. I don't want to freak you out. You must already be pretty upset." I turned my head so that my eye wasn't pressed into the upholstery. My neck clenched with pain. Streetlights flickered over me like shiny fish. "My name's Ariel," I said. "I'm twenty. Just turned twenty. In October. Now it's November, almost, isn't it? I had a boyfriend but we broke up. I think there's something wrong with him, or at least I know there is something wrong with the world he belongs to. Have you ever felt that way? Like there's something wrong with the people you care about, with the whole world? And then you think, maybe it's me?" I heard a soft groaning sound coming from him. I peeked up and saw the huge form at the wheel. His head touched the roof of the car, even bent over, a hump on his back.

I had seen him before. Many times on the street. The giant. I buried my face down again.

"I don't want you to hurt me," I said. "I know you could hurt me if you want to. You must be so angry to want to hurt someone you don't know. You must have had people hurt you . . ."

Maybe it was worse. Maybe I'd gone too far. The car veered and I slid off the seat onto the floor. The rain was still pouring down. It seemed to be darker now, no streetlights. I could smell the earth outside, wet and thick with worms.

"Please," I said. "Please don't hurt me. Just let me go. I won't look at you. I won't report you. Just let me go. I want to go back to my mom. I should never have come back here again."

The car screeched to a halt. He was breathing heavily now. I was covered in a cold film of sweat. He was going to rape me and then he was going to murder my body, and then I would be with Jeni and on All Hallows' Eve I would return and dance with John Graves.

I should have called him as soon as I got back to Berkeley. I should have trusted him this time.

I should have told my mom more often how much I loved her.

I shouldn't have given up on Jeni. I should have done anything I could to find her.

These are the things you feel at death—the regrets more than anything else.

The giant bent down and grabbed me by my bound wrists, hauled me up to the seat again.

"They believe they can bring back the souls of the dead," I said. Tears were pouring down my face now and I was speaking faster and faster, not trying to calm him anymore. "Do you believe anyone can do that? They must be crazy. Or maybe it's true? They want to bring back their baby. They had a baby who died. I can't imagine that. How awful that must be. A baby. But he apologized, he said he was wrong. I shouldn't have left him."

There was a rushing sound, like a windstorm in the trees, and what sounded like cries. The giant cocked his head and his eyes darted to the car window.

"Please don't hurt me," I whispered. "Please. I'm sorry for whatever has happened to you."

He smelled like the wet earth and excrement. I held my breath and my heart clenched. The rushing sound grew louder—branches cracking under stampeding feet, wind tearing through the leaves, those strange voices. It seemed as if the storm had circled the car. Everything turned black and in the black lake of the window I thought, for a moment, I saw the reflection of Jeni's face. I tried to scream but a huge, grimy hand slammed over my mouth.

Then my captor reached over and I felt raw, dry lips brushing my cheek.

A kiss.

A kiss?

He unlocked the door, grunting something I didn't understand, and pushed it open and pushed me out into the rain.

And I rolled down the muddy slope away from everything that had ever gone before. Toward nothing.

32. The dead bride of nothing

Mud was in my mouth, nostrils and eyes and the only sounds were the voices of the rushing water. *I am dead. The dead bride of nothing.* But there was cold, gold light through the trees; it was morning.

My wrists were not bound and there was no sign of the rope that had cut into them. I crawled and clawed my way along the creek bed and leaned against an oak tree that grew at the bank to help myself stand. My legs were shaking like the golden oak leaves in the cool air and my dress was torn and brown with mud. Mud lined my fingernails so that they ached with it.

The tree had a hollow. Something about that hollow frightened me. I imagined I could hear children crying there.

My hand was touching something hard. I blinked at it, trying to understand. The rain had washed away the dirt, revealing what lay beneath. Pale and dense and rubbed clean of what it once knew. It was a bone. And not an animal's. I had been taking anatomy that semester.

I recognized a human femur when I saw one. But this one was very small.

I stumbled back to the path where I used to run. Some joggers passed me and looked back but kept going. When I got a bit farther a guy on a bike stopped and squinted at me.

"Are you okay?" he asked.

I stared at him. He had freckles across the bridge of his nose. I thought, *I can't be dead. He has freckles.* It seemed to make sense.

He was dialing on his cell phone. "I'm going to get you some help," he said.

I thought, *Are you going to get me John Graves? Are you going to get me my mommy? Are you going to get Jeni?*

The campus police officer checked me in to Cowell Hospital where I was examined. No serious injuries—just bruises, but they kept me for observation anyway. Pierre came by with my overnight bag and my book filled with notes about Jeni. My roommate hardly said a word, just leaned over and kissed the top of my head.

Officer Liu came later in the afternoon and had me describe what had happened and ID the giant, Burr Linden. "We've got him. He didn't go far. Was sitting in the car a few miles away from where we found you."

"What did he say?"

"He doesn't say much. Mute. Or supposedly. Why do you think he would take you where he did? You think he was aware of the bones?"

"The bones," I said, trying to keep calm even as the words clawed in my throat.

"We found some more, actually. We'll keep you apprised."

"Human bones."

Pain winced the man's face—so intense it was like I was looking into a mirror. "You just need to rest now. We'll check into everything. I promise." He handed me his card. "And call me if you need anything."

"I need you to take this," I said, handing him my notebook

filled with suspicions, terrors, rants. "Maybe there is something that will help."

"We've got him," he said.

"No. With Jeni."

My parents flew in that day. My mother clung to my father's arm as they came into my hospital room. She looked as ill as I'd ever seen her, her skin white and peeling as birch bark, her cheekbones exposed ridges, and I thought, *It's my fault for coming back here.* But I wasn't ready to leave now, not now.

"We can't let you stay," my mom said. "Not after Jennifer."

I didn't correct her. *Jeni.*

"And now this! I knew we shouldn't have let you come back."

"I promise," I said, reaching for her hand. The skin on her palm was so thin and dry it felt like it would tear. "I'll be more careful. I wasn't careful."

My father shook his head. "Ariel, how can we trust this situation? Look at the elements."

"I'll be safe," I said. "I'm safe at Pierre's. I won't go out at night alone again. And they caught him, anyway. He didn't hurt me."

"Why would you want to stay?" my mom asked. "How can you justify it to us?" She was crying. "I mean, how can I live with myself . . ."

"I promise," I said. "I'll be so careful, Mom. I have to stay now. I have to help find out what happened. Just give me until the end of the semester."

That night she insisted on sleeping on a cot in my room while my dad got a hotel. She wouldn't leave me alone, she said. I slept better than you would have thought. Because she was still there.

33. An angel, not

I checked out of the hospital soon afterward and my parents got me settled back in my bedroom at Pierre's, the collages glittering on the walls, Michelangelo playing with wooden blocks in the next room while Pierre cooked dinner. All this reassured my mom and dad and after more conversations and many instructions and warnings they agreed to let me stay.

Before they left, my mom and I sat in my bedroom and I showed her the collages in detail, describing what each one meant to me. There was one made up of greeting cards she had sent me since freshman year. Many were of angels.

"I didn't even realize that," she said, peering at a Piero della Francesca reproduction of the *Annunciation* that I had used, decorating it with dried and pressed white stargazers.

"We need them now," I told her, thinking not just of her illness and Jeni and John and what had happened to me but the whole planet, and she nodded. "But you are mine, my darling daughter."

A woman, maybe. An angel, not.

"How are you?" I asked. "I mean, spiritually."

That wasn't a word we usually used in my house. She paused, looking at the collage, and when she looked back at me her face was more animated than it had been since she'd arrived.

"I'd say I'm good that way. I'm not ready to leave yet but when I go I know it will be all right. And I know, without a doubt, I'll stay connected to you. I'm sure of it."

I thought of Tania and Perry and even John, wanting me to bring back the soul of their dead child with them. But this was different. I nodded and kissed her hand. "I understand," I said.

"I know you feel you need to stay." She met my eyes and there was a ferocity in hers I'd never seen before. "Just promise me you'll be careful."

I went to John's the next afternoon. He was staying in a large, slightly ramshackle house overgrown with ivy. I walked upstairs and knocked on his door. It seemed strange that it was so easy to find him. But he had been close all along; I had just been too afraid to come.

He answered right away. Unshaven, wearing a plain T-shirt and jeans with rips in the knees. He stared at me and then stepped back and motioned for me to come inside. There was so much visible tension in his arm and shoulder muscles and I remembered with a clench in my pelvis the way he strained above me just before the release. I wanted to jam myself into the crook of his arm and breathe him back into me the way he had been before—a constant presence, part of my body. Mine.

My John.

Somehow, after everything, I still thought of him as that, the way, perhaps, you might think of your mother, your child, your best friend or your husband, when you see them again in an afterlife, in whatever form they have chosen.

His room was plain, only a twin mattress, a wooden dresser, desk and chair and a lamp balanced on a stack of books. No art nouveau furniture, no roses or wine bottles. The window overlooked an old oak tree. He sat on the bed and I sat on the chair across from him.

"I've been waiting," he said.

"I needed time."

"I know."

"You left them?"

He nodded.

"Is it hard?"

"It's hard. Without you."

I had so much to tell him but I couldn't speak. My throat felt crushed from inside. Love was too big for me; it was a giant, but one that meant no harm. Still it might kill me; I'd let it if I had to. I bent my head and he came and knelt in front of me and put his arms around me and together we wept. The wet from his eyes fell onto my bare arms and my tears soaked his T-shirt.

I don't know how long we sat like that, both crying, my body fastened to his, refusing to let go of him. I only know that then we were on the bed, naked, our clothes in shreds on the floor. I was feverish, the nerve endings in my scalp tingling, but I was still holding on.

In the tale, Janet/Margaret holds onto Tam Lin as he changes from beast to beast to burning coal; she does not let him go. She saves him from the queen of fae.

We didn't wake until much later. Night was filling the spaces among the leaves outside his window.

I began to sing to him, lullabies I remembered my mother singing to me.

"By my baby's cradle in the night/Stands a goat so soft and snowy white/The goat will go to the market/While I my watch do keep/Bringing back raisins and almonds/Sleep my little one sleep."

This was only one small thing of many gifts my mother had given to me. I did not ever want to let her go. I had this—her lullaby, but without her in the world it would never be enough. Still, I sang and sang it to John, into the night, and then he sang to me and as we sang I moved farther and farther away from the real world with its pain and sorrow.

I could have stayed like this, with him, forever, if only to watch the subtle shifts in his expression as he slept, the way his belly showed when he stretched awake, revealing the line of hair beneath his navel, the pallor of his face against the sheet. We made love again, his body charging into me as I closed my eyes and shivered in the rain of his sweat.

Finally we dozed and at dawn we woke together to a loud sound.

My bag had fallen off the chair and out of it rolled the doll Jeni's mother had given to me. I had put it in at the last minute before I left for John's.

He got out of bed, naked, and picked her up. Even against the pallor of his skin his knuckles looked white. "What does it mean?" he said.

Then I told him, in as calm a voice as I could manage, what had happened since I'd seen him.

John put down the doll and looked at me with too-bright eyes. "There is something I need you to see."

He opened the drawer of his desk and took out a skeleton key.

"What's it for?"

"When I came back from seeing you the last time, before I moved out, I went into Tania's basement. I knew there were things wrong with her but I never realized how much."

"John?" My eyes were watering with fear. "What are you telling me?"

His pupils were so dilated I could hardly see the green. "There was a time when I was away from them, from Tania. Around when Jeni disappeared. Remember I told you." He looked at the doll on the bed, then quickly away. "I think I'm starting to understand. But I need to be sure."

The key lay in his open palm.

"They're probably gone now, or asleep."

34. Where the key talked to the girl

There was a fairy tale where the key talked to the girl, led her to the chamber where the bones of the dead wives were hidden. This key had no blood on it, no voice, but I shivered with fever. My head felt like there were things inside, knocking around, trying to get out or send a message, like spirits warning miners of death underground.

We went in through the kitchen door, through to the parlor. It looked dusty and dim, untouched, no flowers in the vases, no music, no more tang of garlic and onions sautéed in olive oil from the kitchen; even the almost too heavy essence of rose blooming in from the garden was gone. The house smelled cold and musty.

I remembered how we had all danced night after night, the fire blazing and the smell of wine and petals mixing with smoke and their bodies flickering.

Had I really lived here or was this only another sign of the strangeness of my mind?

I followed John downstairs as quietly as possible. He opened the room with the key and flicked on a light.

"I'm going to wait outside," he whispered. "Call if you need me."

There was nothing sinister at all except perhaps for the lack of windows; but this was a basement, so, of course. A basement with a tattered brocade chaise longue and chairs, a wine rack and a table with three ceramic bowls. The first two bowls were filled with leaves and flowers and the third had a very fine powder in it. I would have examined these further but I was more interested in the dolls.

They lined all the shelves, watching me with their big, blankly unblinking eyes and secret painted smiles. Straw, wood, porcelain, bisque and plastic ones. I went around the room touching each doll with my finger—some on the lips, some on the chest where their hearts would have been—remembering how, for a few months after Jeni's disappearance, I'd have to secretly kiss every stuffed animal in my room (I still kept them there) good night before I could fall asleep, just as I'd done as a child. I was exhausted with shame by the time I was through. Obsessive-compulsive much? as Lauren would say. But at least I'd stopped that now.

Had I? I imagined going into this locked room every night and kissing each doll's cold little lips, every single pair, before I could sleep.

I put my hand on top of a small metal box painted with a picture of a tree. When I moved my hand away the box shook and—popped. A weird little man in a red cap was leering at me. Just a jack-in-the-box but those things always creeped me out. I shuddered back at him.

What was there to be afraid of? I was only looking at harmless dolls. Why had Tania locked the room? To create an aura of mystery? Or something more? Sometimes I wondered about Tania's sanity but what made me any less crazy? If I closed my eyes I could imagine the dolls whispering to me in unison, telling me a story in voices I didn't understand. And what if Tania caught me in the secret room? John had sent me here now for a reason.

A large china baby doll with real human hair, pearly teeth between rosebud lips seemed to be watching me. Beside her hung a naked marionette with black nail polish and a small tag hanging from his delicately constructed toe.

And then I saw her.

I picked up the red-haired Blythe and pulled the string so her green eyes turned blue, pink, then amber. A doll just like Jeni's.

Suddenly all the dolls really did seem to be crowding in,

trying to tell me something. I could almost hear a faint sound of breath. Was it my own made louder as I tried to hold it? I gasped for air and pulled the string on Blythe again—her eyes turned blue. She was staring at me and my breath came in such echoing gasps I thought it was hers. I even thought I felt a pulse.

When I set her down she rocked slightly on the shelf as if she were about to fall. Steadying her, I could still feel the tremor in the plastic. *Fuck.* I had to get out of there.

It was as if I were pushing through a crowd of bodies, as if I were in that crowd at the first Halloween party, trying to find air, trying to find something.

The Hello Kitty purse was sitting on a shelf, just sitting there, like a regular thing. I picked it up.

The room was spinning slowly, like a merry-go-round. My cell phone was vibrating against my hip bone, ringing, much too loudly; I had forgotten to turn it off. The screen said *Mom.* I pressed TALK.

"Hello," she said. "Honey? I had this feeling. Are you . . . ?" Tania was at the door.

"What are you doing, Ariel?" She had rarely called me by my real name.

"I was looking around," I said. My eyes tried not to flinch from hers. The round green irises floated, unmoored, in a sea of white.

"What were you looking for, Ariel? Who let you down here?"

I moved closer to her although every nerve ending shrieked at me to back away.

"Why do you have Jeni's purse, Tania?" I said loudly, holding it up, my heart beating in my mouth like a fish.

She shook her head. Sad. "Oh, Sylph, my love." Her accent

was always stronger, I realized, when she was trying to influence me. Glamour me.

"Why do you have it? Her purse."

Tania smiled. The other element of her up-to-now infallible glamour. She reached out and ran her fingers through my hair, catching the tangled ends so it hurt. I pulled away; it hurt more.

"You ask too much of me," she said.

"I what?"

"You ask. Too. Much. I'm so sorry."

"Tell me what is going on here, Tania. Tell me now!"

Her teeth white as the whites of her eyes in her golden face. She shook her head. No.

"Tania!"

"Give me the purse, Ariel."

"No. Tell me what the fuck is going on."

"Give me the purse." She snatched at it but I wouldn't let her, I wouldn't let her have it.

"What did you do?" I think I was screaming. Was I screaming?

"It had to be done," she said. "Just as you have to be."

"What the fuck!"

Then she reached out, too quick for me, and she grasped my wrist where Jeni's bracelet had once been. Tania's grip was strong and I couldn't get away, my whole body dissolving into the weakness of fear.

"We were only loving her. We thought she was the one. Perry and Burr and I. While John was gone from me. We thought she could help us but she fought." Tania paused and her eyes looked far away. "And violence ensued."

"Jeni," I said, aloud, calling for her as if, even now, she might answer. "Mom."

"The bone. Burr. This. I'm sorry, Sylph, you know too much, you see too much with your artist's mind."

Perry was there now, too, wearing the mask. The goat mask with the clattering jaw.

"Love," Tania said to him. "We have to do it again." Her eyes jagged glass. She took a small knife from somewhere inside the large sleeve of her silk kimono.

"Ariel?" My mom was screaming.

John.

Holding a cell phone. Police sirens in the distance, coming up the hill. The Hello Kitty purse clutched in my hand. I noticed it was made of pebbly white vinyl, the cat features cut out and stuck on. The silly pink flower that I knew once graced her ear was missing.

I held on to that purse with one hand, my mom's voice inside the phone in the other. They were something. They were something real.

There were men in uniforms at the basement door.

"I will cut out your eyes," Tania said to John, softly as a lullaby, as they took her away from us.

What we learned later is that on the night Jeni disappeared, Tania and Perry went out, as she said, "looking."

"That was in the days when we still looked, before the parties and the naïve undergrad groupies brought the girls to us.

"The one was on Telegraph wandering, taking pictures with her cell phone. She was very young, too young, but I couldn't help myself. It might have been the big dark eyes, the lashes, the cute little purse like something someone much younger would carry. I knew this girl was the one.

"It was easy. Girls like that, I knew what they liked. Pretty things. Maybe with a little oddness, a little edge. Dolls with too-big heads and eyes that changed colors. Dolls with little sharp teeth and flowered dresses. Porcelain dolls with pointed elf ears that could be exchanged for normal human ones. Not just dolls but vintage gowns and shoes and jewels. And food. And music. Halloween Hotel was always a good one. Oh, and the wine, of course. Made in the basement with such slight traces of cannabis, opium and ephedra that you almost couldn't detect them, unless you were a really bright chemistry student. Luckily Ian Larsen also had a crush on me, and an addictive personality, so the promise of some free bottles helped, too."

Tania and Perry went up to Jeni at the pizza place where she was standing alone at the counter. They "chatted," Tania said. Jeni told them she was from L.A., visiting. Tania said they were having a small party at their house and would she like to come, the food was better than this. Jeni said no, but politely. She asked Tania about her hair and they talked some more. Tania said she could do something cool with Jeni's hair if she wanted. Jeni laughed and said she wasn't supposed to be out alone at all. Tania said, "You're not alone," and then told her about the dolls and the dresses at home. Jeni and Tania both had an original Blythe.

Tania and Perry took Jeni home and showed her the room of dolls, the closet of dresses. Tania dressed her and Perry did her makeup and hair. It was very late by the time they ate. They were all drunk, listening to the Halloween Hotel singer, and Burr came in.

Jeni didn't seem to mind him. She seemed mostly curious. They finished their meal and she said she should be going.

"No," Tania said, "not yet."

Tania told the cops, "I tried to explain it to her, about the baby, about my other lover, John, who had left after Camille

255

died. How he couldn't deal with things and left. How hard it was for me. I'd had a hard life to begin with.

"My stepfather was the only one who had ever seemed to understand me. I thought he knew who I really was the first time he took me into his study full of books and showed me the tiny goddess statues, some with many arms, some winged, some resembling cats wearing jewelry. He showed me the magic box with the silver stars painted on the blue background. The pieces slid apart but you couldn't tell from just looking.

" 'It's a trick,' he said. 'But it's more than a trick. The magic comes in how you speak to the audience, how you smile at them.'

"He had a very white smile and dark eyes with long eyelashes, as if he wore mascara. His hands smelled of candy.

"Day after day, among the books and small painted deities from different cultures, he taught me magics and trickery. He taught me about goddesses and elemental beings and reincarnation.

"When I turned thirteen I came into his study, excited to learn the new lesson he had promised me. It was darker in there than usual; the drapes were closed. He had lit candles and there was a bottle of wine and two glasses.

"He said, 'This is how you become a true initiate. This is how you serve the goddess.'

"Goddess? I wanted to serve the goddess, to be powerful and beautiful like she was.

" 'Take off your dress,' he said. 'You must expose your full self in order to be accepted by Her.'

"I shook my head, no. Suddenly the room was cold even though it was summer and the sun shone outside.

" 'Take off your dress. It is not even yours. It belongs to me.'

"I told him no. I couldn't imagine he would do what he did next. He had never hurt me; he had never forced me. He hadn't even looked at me with anything but fatherly kindness. I had never seen it coming. My instincts were weak. I was weak.

" 'You belong to me,' he told me as he forced his way inside and all the little goddesses on the shelves wept and shattered into shards. 'Your soul is mine.'

"No magics could save me.

"My mother didn't want to know anything. Set me up with an education and some money so I'd be quiet.

"Not until I met John and Perry did it seem as if I could go on living. Until the baby died and everything came apart again.

" 'But you can help us,' I said to the girl that night."

Jeni said she needed to go. She was scared.

"I didn't mean to hurt her, not like that," Tania told the police later. "But I couldn't let her go.

"I kept the little purse locked up because I liked it so much and it reminded me of something Camille would have liked, but other things had to be disposed of. Luckily Burr was so devoted and not quite right in the head. He did what he was told. The creek bed. I knew he'd never tell. He was implicated. He was the one who'd done it, really. Plus, after that, he stopped speaking, went mute, was put away for a while. He wasn't the one for us anyway. It was John, always John. And, eventually, he came back. He never knew what happened.

"Afterward, I vowed never to force things like that. I'd have to be patient. The girl obviously wasn't the one, either. None of them were. Certainly not the girl known as Coraline Grimm, who wanted to be more than any of us, perhaps, who would have gladly given us her blood if we had asked, though it wasn't worth the trouble. But then like a miracle the other one came along. The friend. Even wearing the same clothes and the matching bracelet with the first one's name on it. So that must have been the point of the first girl, to bring this second one looking for her, right into my arms.

"Poor Sylph. I loved her, I really did.

"It's all so complicated, though.

"This human world."

Tania went on to say, "What I want you to know is that I didn't mean to harm anyone. There is, in my opinion, only one reason to be alive. That is to love. The greatest love of all is between a mother and her child; nothing else compares. When the parent betrays the bond or begins to rot from disease, when the child dies, there is no more reason to live. That is when we must seek other worlds, made of our own alchemy, our blood and bones, our elements, our very own."

I am not fooled by any of it, by Tania's reasons or her pleas. Sometimes I dream of things that I would have once called terrible, of chiseling out her green-leaf eyes with a sharp knife and replacing them with plugs of wood, just as the queen of fae threatened Tam Lin in the tale.

Sometimes I dream of Jeni, waking me from sleep, using her lashes to kiss my cheek, running beside me as we used to, by the wash near the houses where we grew up. The air smelled of tar and chlorine there. Smog hazed the hills in the distance. That dirty trickle of water in the concrete basin—that was our river. We made believe it was lined with fruit trees and willows, huts built of mud and branches, overgrown with morning glories. At night we'd sneak out there and watch the streetlights make paths of brightness on the water. Mermaid tails. We'd crawl under the chain link, slide on our butts down the concrete bank, gather weeds and wildflowers from the cracks, go home and stir mud brews for our secret ceremonies.

We were witches, we were gypsies. The garden was our otherworld. We had the power; we were girls. We had no fear.

She was supposed to be with me, here. We were going to be roommates and take the same classes and eat every meal together and fall in love at the same time. My mom getting sick wasn't part of the plan. Neither was what happened to my best friend.

Sometimes I dream of the garden of that house in the Berkeley hills. There are circles burned into the grass by those with hollow backs. Will-o'-the-wisps wheel through the night, phosphorescent lights with no natural explanation. The undying souls of the dead.

Epilogue: nine months later

I have told you a story and perhaps you will believe some of it. Or perhaps not. Perhaps it is a real story or perhaps it is only an escape from life because sometimes, when disease and death come, making you shudder and ache with the sorrow, escape is necessary. Even though death is inevitable, in the end love can conquer it, I believe that, if only in the imagination, if only in the realm of poetry. For that morning in Berkeley, California, the summer of my twentieth year (while, in Los Angeles, my mother languished and my best friend lay buried among stone angels on a green smog-rimmed hillside), I woke in the arms of my lover, our bodies marked with shadow flowers from the lace curtains, and went downstairs into the sunny garden and opened the door of my dream.

The air sparked with the strange newness of morning and the scent in the air was like lilies. A basket woven of willow branches was on the porch and I bent down and drew back the blanket that hung over the top of it.

Inside slept a child, and her big, dark brown eyes with their tender lids and flash of lashes could not more have resembled my beloved's.

Acknowledgments

Thanks to Elizabeth Hand, Denise Hamilton, Jeni McKenna, Michael Homler, Laurie Liss, Lydia Wills, Alyssa Reuben, Karen Clark, Sergeant Reynold Verdugo, Melissa Verdugo, Yxta Maya Murray, Tracey Porter, Carmen Staton, and Patrick Harpur, author of The Philosopher's Secret Fire.